The Cottage in Sweet Meadow Park

LIZ DAVIES

Copyright © 2024 Liz Davies
Published by Lilac Tree Books

This book is licensed for your personal enjoyment only. This book may not be re-sold or given away to other people. If you would like to share this book with another person, please purchase an additional copy for each recipient. If you're reading this book and did not purchase it, or it was not purchased for your use only, then please purchase your own copy. Thank you for respecting the hard work of this author.

This story is a work of fiction. All names, characters, places and incidents are invented by the author or have been used fictitiously and are not to be construed as real. Any similarity to actual persons or events is purely coincidental.

The author asserts the moral rights under the Copyright, Design and Patents Act 1988 to be identified as the author of this work.

All rights reserved. No part of this publication may be reproduced, stored in a retrieval system or transmitted, in any form or by any means without the prior consent of the author, nor be otherwise circulated in any form of binding or cover other than that which it is published and without a similar condition being imposed on the subsequent purchaser.

Dedication

To Valerie Brown, for your generosity, support and eagle eye. Thank you x

CHAPTER 1

The gates to Sweet Meadow Park were impressive wrought iron affairs which might have once been painted green but were now peeling, revealing a dull black colour underneath. They appeared to be rusted shut, and the chain and padlock were weathered and dirty.

To the side of those tall main gates with their pointed, curling spikes, was a smaller one which Molly couldn't ever remember being locked. It was currently wedged open, the bottom having gouged a groove into the pitted tarmacked path. A plaque on the wall beside it announced that the park had been officially opened over a century ago by a long-forgotten councillor.

Beyond the gates lay what had once been a popular and well-tended space, but was now more wasteland than parkland, and as Molly slipped inside, she wondered, as she so often did, what it must have looked like in its heyday. She suspected the paths would have been clear of litter, the bandstand alive with music, the flower beds bursting with colourful blooms, and the benches a welcome place to sit for a while to escape the cares of the world.

The park had once been the pride of Sweet Meadow, a green jewel in the crown of the small rural town set in the heart of the South Wales Valleys. Now though, it was little more than a place for dog walkers, for people to use as a cut-through to get from A to B, and for youngsters to congregate and get up to mischief. It had a bit of a reputation as a no-go area after dark, but Molly was sure it wasn't as bad as people made out.

If asked (not that anyone ever did) she would claim she only visited it because it was a convenient spot to eat her sandwiches when she wanted some fresh air. The park, being only a ten-minute stroll from the estate agent's office where she worked, was close enough to get to without impacting too much on her lunch break, yet far enough away to feel as though she'd escaped the office.

But that wasn't the real reason she went there.

The real reason was that Molly Brown was in love.

***

The keys to the cottage clinked heavily as Molly retrieved them from her oversized shoulder bag and hefted their weight in the palm of her hand. There must be at least twenty of them attached to the old iron ring, and she wondered what they could all be for.

Three were large and old-fashioned – the kind that might unlock the door of an old castle in a fairy tale – and she ran her fingers across the ornate bow of one of them as she approached the front door, her heart hammering and her mouth dry with excitement.

Hesitating, she gazed up at the building. She had loved this place ever since she could remember. Hidden away in a quiet corner of the park, yet not too far from the main gates, the cottage peeped out from behind the stalwart trunks of a stand of ash trees. The ground floor was further concealed by lush undergrowth. By "lush" she meant overgrown, but that was a matter for another day.

Constructed out of hand-chiselled grey-brown stone and with a slate roof, it had a door in the middle and windows on either side, a pair of windows in the eaves, and an external brick and stone chimney which she fully intended to restore so she could snuggle up in front of a log fire in the winter. Although it looked small from the front, the property extended a fair way to the rear where a kitchen and pantry were located, and it had two bedrooms and a bathroom upstairs. The bathroom had made her shudder when she had peeped her head around the door. The spiders that had scuttled for cover were bigger than the cat she'd spotted lurking in the bushes outside!

Molly knew from her research that the cottage had been built not long after the park was officially opened, and she was pretty sure it hadn't been updated much since. The outside didn't look in too bad a condition, although the boarded-up windows didn't do much for it, but the inside was something else, and she winced when she thought of the amount of work which needed to be done to make her dream come true.

Dado rails, butler sink (she'd keep that), fireplace with bread oven (hmm), creaking floorboards… it certainly had its fair share of period features; and some – the outdoor loo for instance, and the peeling wallpaper throughout – were less of a feature and more of a catastrophe.

At least it had running water, gas, and electricity, however she didn't need an expert to tell her the whole place needed rewiring urgently. Which was why she'd arranged for an electrician to come tomorrow, to give her a quote. Her main worry, apart from the mountain of DIY that needed to be done, was that he wouldn't be able to start work for several weeks, which meant that she would be spending a fortune on takeaways –

because there was no question of her not moving in immediately, now she'd bought it.

Molly had been fascinated by the house ever since she could remember, and when she was little she used to love making up stories about it. Some days she used to imagine it to be the home of a princess who was hiding from her evil stepmother (along the lines of Snow White), other days it might belong to one of the three pigs – the one who lived in a house made of brick, obviously.

As she grew older and left fairy tales behind, she would imagine living there with her very own Prince Charming and filling it with children. That it had been inhabited by the park keeper and his family when Sweet Meadow had employed someone to take care of the park, added to its allure, and she imagined how magical it must have been to grow up in such a lovely place: to hang rope swings from the branches of the ancient oak trees, to play hide and seek in the woodland area, and to swim in the pond. And that was without the performances which she'd been told used to take place on the bandstand, the ice creams that could be bought from the little cafe, and the games of chase and football that would have been played on the field, and she'd vowed that one day she'd buy the house and live in it happily ever after.

That day was today.

The cottage in the park was *hers*. She owned it.

The thought was both exhilarating and terrifying.

'Oi! Wotcha doing?'

Molly uttered a squeak as an old man, who had managed to creep up on her and was standing far too close for comfort, startled her. She slapped a hand to her pounding heart and frowned at him.

'You nearly made me jump out of my skin,' she told him accusingly, taking a step away.

'I asked you what you're doing. That there is private property. Bloody kids. Got no respect for nothing,' he grumbled.

Molly cocked her head, amused. 'You think I'm a *kid*?'

The old man peered at her. The scruffy white and tan terrier, whose lead he was clutching, peered at her also. 'You can't be more than twelve,' he grunted.

'I'm twenty-nine.'

'You don't look it.' He narrowed his rheumy eyes and his face crumpled into folds as he scrutinised her suspiciously.

'I'll take that as a compliment,' Molly said. She didn't get many, so even one from a grumpy old man was worth having.

'You can take it how you like,' he replied. 'Why are you hanging around here? Haven't you got a job to go to? Why people can't mind their own business, I don't know.'

Molly stifled a laugh.

Oblivious to the irony of his own words, he added, 'You've got no right to be messing about here. This is private property.'

'Yes, it is,' she agreed. She held up the bunch of keys. 'It's *my* private property.'

'Are you from the council?'

'No, I've bought it from them.'

'You've bought Sweet Meadow Cottage? I didn't know it was for sale.' He sounded aggrieved, as though the council should have consulted him before they put it on the market.

Molly shrugged. Maybe they should have – she had no idea who the old man was, although she thought she might have seen his dog before. She was, after all, a regular visitor to the park and she liked dogs so she tended to notice them.

'I picked up the keys today,' she told him, jangling them again, in case he thought she was lying.

'Cost much, did it?'

Molly's eyes widened at the cheek of it. 'Enough.'

That was an understatement. It had cost her almost everything she had. The bank owned the lion's share of the property, but she had no intention of discussing her finances with a total stranger.

'Excuse me,' she said. 'I need to get on.' She had booked a whole week off from work precisely to collect the keys and move in. She didn't anticipate it taking very long though, because she didn't have much in the way of furniture. Living at home with her mum and dad meant she had a distinct lack of essentials she could bring with her to her new home, and she needed to go shopping urgently. She had also better stock up on cleaning stuff – lots and lots of cleaning stuff.

Molly aimed the key at the lock, but the old man hadn't finished with her yet.

'Got a fella?' he asked.

Blimey, was he putting himself forward for the job? She had never been propositioned by such an elderly gentleman before.

'No.' She didn't elaborate. Her love life wasn't any of his business, either.

'You wanna get yourself one,' he carried on, oblivious to her reluctance to talk to him. 'I wouldn't want to live there on my own, especially if I was a pretty little thing like you.'

Another compliment? That was two in less than five minutes. She was on a roll…

She should have thanked him for his concern, opened the door and gone inside, but she simply couldn't. She had to know. 'Why? Is the cottage haunted?'

The old man snorted. 'You wish! Ghosts would be the least of your worries. What you need to worry about is youffs.'

'*Youffs?*'

'Aye. The blighters hang around the park, getting up to no good and making trouble. I blame the parents. And the school. The police need to pull their finger out and get it sorted. In my day, they would have got a clip around the ear. And the council has a lot to answer for, letting it go to rack and ruin.' He shook his head sorrowfully. 'I don't envy you,' he finished, his tone ominous.

'I'm sure it's not that bad,' she said.

'You'll see.'

Concealing a frustrated sigh, Molly turned her attention to the door. Her parents had displayed a similar reaction when she'd told them she intended to buy the cottage, and they couldn't see the vision she had for it, either. Yes, it would take work and yes, it would take money, but when she'd finished renovating it this cottage would be the epitome of cute. It was halfway there already but luckily for her, people hadn't been able to see past the boarded-up windows, the ivy crawling up the outside, and the weeds choking the path. Because if anyone else *had* spotted its potential she would never have been able to afford to buy it, as someone would surely have trumped her offer.

Heavy breathing made her hesitate, and she glanced over her shoulder.

The old man hadn't moved and was watching her with great interest. As was his dog, who was staring at her with brown button eyes, his folded ears pricked, his head cocked to the side.

'There's not a lot to see,' she said. 'It's really dark inside.' She pointed to a window. 'Boarded up.'

'I can see that for myself. I'm not stupid.'

'I didn't say you were. I thought you might have been hoping for a gander.'

'I'm not interested and I'm not being nosy. I just want to make sure the roof doesn't fall on your head.'

'It won't.'

'An architect, are you?' he snorted.

'An estate agent, actually.'

The old man chortled. 'I'd have thought you would have known better than to buy this eyesore if you really are an estate agent.'

'I really am. Now, you must excuse me, I have lots to do.'

This time he guffawed. 'You can say that again.'

Ignoring her audience and with her heart in her mouth, she fitted the key into the lock and turned it. The door opened with considerably less protest than when she'd come to view the place a couple of months ago, and she took it as a good sign.

What wasn't such a good sign was the pigeon that flapped about her head in a frenzy of feathers. The dog let off a volley of excited barks, and Molly screamed in shock as the bird flew off after depositing a nasty wet dollop on her shoulder.

'Ew.' Molly wrinkled her nose and peered at the splodge on her T-shirt, wondering whether she had any tissues in her bag.

'That's lucky, that is,' the man said, after he'd shushed his dog. The terrier glared into the branches of a tree, and the pigeon calmly stared down at it. Molly had a feeling it was laughing.

'What's lucky? Being pooped on by a bird?' She didn't think it was lucky at all. Blimmin' annoying, that's what it was.

'Nah, it's lucky you let it out. It might have died in there and the stench would have been awful.'

Thanks for that, she thought, hoping to goodness there weren't any more birds in the cottage, dead or alive.

She rooted around in her bag for a tissue, muttering darkly to herself. There must be one in here somewhere…?

'Here, have this.' The man pulled a hanky out of his pocket. It looked clean and she was about to accept his offer, with the promise of laundering it before returning it to him, but she hastily changed her mind when he spat on it. 'That should get most of it off,' he said.

'It's OK, I'll manage. Thanks all the same.' She pressed the flashlight app on her phone and held it up, illuminating a small dingy hallway. 'Nice meeting you,' she said, expecting him to walk off and leave her in peace. But she thought he was going to follow her inside when he took a step towards her, and she hastily backed away.

'What's your name?' he demanded.

'Why do you want to know?'

He grinned at her, revealing a row of yellowing teeth. 'I want to know your name because we're going to be friends.'

'Are we?'

'Yes.' He sounded very sure of himself.

'Er, right, yeah… um… hi, I'm Molly.'

'Bill,' he announced. 'And this is Patch.' And without another word, the old man turned on his heel and was off, shuffling down the path at a rate of knots.

Bemused, Molly watched him go. Then she turned her attention back to the cottage and a smile crept over her face as she hugged herself in glee.

If she had thought she was in love before, she realised she was utterly besotted now.

CHAPTER 2

Jack Feathers pushed his chair away from the desk and shook his head in irritation.

So the rumours of job evaluations and the restructuring of departments in the council were true. That was all he needed right now – more worry. He had enough to be getting on with as it was, without this.

He wished he hadn't read the email. He didn't usually bother with missives from the council's Chief Executive, because they didn't often say a lot – thousands of words written about nothing in particular and most of them extolling the virtues of the Chief Exec herself, with the occasional crumb of praise thrown to her supporters.

He wasn't bitter about it – far from it – but it would be nice for the people on the ground to receive some recognition for all the hard work they did. And he wasn't referring to himself either, although he worked equally as hard as the next person.

Jack scooted his chair back to the desk and scanned the email again, trying to pick out the relevant points in amongst the overly officious language. He was tempted to mark it as unread. Though what difference that would make, was beyond him. Besides, the email promised to follow it up with a letter. Not only that, he suspected the topic would be the conversational subject of choice in the cafeteria for the next few days.

A glutton for punishment, he logged into his private emails, reread the latest one from Della and uttered a loud sigh. He perfectly understood why his sister wanted to sell the house they jointly owned and he was delighted she had found the love of her life, but he simply wasn't in a position to purchase anywhere else. Not right now. Maybe not ever.

Della was lucky: property prices in Alaska were so much cheaper than those in the UK for a comparably sized house, and although Sweet Meadow wasn't London, prices had still risen dramatically over the past five years or so.

Ideally, he would love to buy her out, but he simply couldn't afford it. He was already paying the full mortgage, which was only fair since he was the only one living there, and it was gobbling up a considerable portion of his wages as it was. There was no way he could increase his borrowing and still be able to eat!

He knew this had been coming for a while, but it was a shock to see her request in black and white.

Another email notification popped up on his screen, this time from reception, and Jack sighed. At least it wasn't more doom and gloom he thought, as he quickly read it, noting that they had taken a phone call to request a litter pick in Sweet Meadow Park.

Not another one! This was getting to be a daily occurrence. As usual, the caller hadn't left a name or a contact number, and Jack assumed it was the same person, although he couldn't be sure. And if it wasn't litter that was being complained about, it was the youths who hung around after dark. How was that his responsibility? Litter he could do something about – teenagers were outside his remit as the Council's Parks and Highways Officer.

He had attempted to resolve the situation in the past by locking the park gates between the hours of eight p.m. and six a.m., but the number of complaints he had received from dog walkers and people who used the park as a cut through to get from the new housing estate to the railway station, had nearly broken his inbox. Besides, he couldn't justify the expense.

'There's a tree down on Dunstone Road,' Pete, his colleague, announced as he poked his head around

Jack's door. 'It's blocking both lanes and the pavement.'

'Thanks, I'll get a team onto it.'

Jack swiftly made out a job requisition request and pinged it off to one of the supervisors to action, then he got to his feet and went in search of breakfast.

Actually, it would be brunch, because he rarely had time to eat breakfast at home and neither could he be bothered to make himself sandwiches. Instead, he ate a substantial meal at around eleven o'clock, which usually consisted of a full English that would set him up for the rest of the day and give his body enough fuel to sustain him if he decided to go for a run after work.

'What can I get you, my love?' The council's cafeteria was run by a jolly lady who clearly loved her job.

'The usual, please, Sue.'

'Toast or hash browns?'

'Er, toast today, I think. And a coffee?'

'Coming right up. Take a seat and I'll bring it over.'

He paid and wandered over to a table overlooking the atrium and slid into a seat. That was another thing that galled him: the council didn't have enough money to fund his department adequately, yet they'd had plenty of money to throw around when they'd designed and built these new council offices. The building was less than two years old, all steel and glass, with no expense spared when it came to making it look impressive, as the three-storey high atrium testified.

However, expense certainly *had* been spared when it came to the behind-the-scenes offices. Jack's office was titchy and whoever had designed his workspace had evidently never worked in an office before. The angle of the desk was wrong, and the light from the window shone directly on his screen, meaning he had to keep the blinds drawn all day.

With a sigh he puffed out his cheeks, cross with himself. He was only thirty-four, but he was beginning to sound like someone twice his age. He was turning into a right grumpy old man!

'Here you go, love; a full English and a coffee.' Sue placed the laden plate down on the table, along with some cutlery and a large mug of coffee, and leant in close. 'I've put you an extra slice of bacon and another sausage,' she whispered, giving him a wink.

Jack smiled and shook his head at her. 'Be careful you don't get into trouble,' he warned. Sue was forever giving him extra portions, and he wondered whether he looked as though he needed fattening up. He wasn't a hunk by any stretch of the imagination, leaning more towards skinny rather than buffed. It was a result of all the exercise he did. It didn't do to carry too much weight when he was running upwards of twenty kilometres several times a week. He used to run marathons, and although he no longer did (too many hamstring injuries to run that kind of mileage anymore), he liked to keep his hand in, so to speak.

Picking up his cutlery, he was about to tuck in when chattering from the floor below caught his attention and he cringed. He would recognise that voice anywhere. Placing his knife and fork on the edge of the plate, he shuffled back in his seat, and risked leaning forward to peep over the balustrade, hoping he wouldn't be spotted. The last thing he needed today was for his ex-girlfriend to see him.

He was right, it was her. Chantelle, along with some of her cronies, was walking through the concourse, but thankfully she didn't look up. Since he'd broken up with her a few weeks ago, he had changed his habits somewhat. It used to be that he'd have a proper breakfast – because she insisted they ate together – and he'd eat lunch at lunchtime, which she had also expected to have with him.

If it had been up to Chantelle, they would have spent every minute of every day together: except when she was "putting her face on". For some reason, she had never let him see her without makeup, and when she had a shower or a bath before bed (with the door securely locked) she would reapply it again before she emerged from the bathroom. He had never been able to work out why. Chantelle was a pretty woman: as far as he was concerned she didn't need to wear makeup at all. Anyway, he had loved her regardless of how curly and long her lashes were, or how flawless her skin.

Loved. Past tense, and not strictly accurate.

On looking back, Jack realised he had never truly loved her, although he had cared for her. Which was a shame, and depressing, and he did feel very sorry for her, because she had clearly loved him, possibly more than was good for either of them.

Chantelle had pursued him with a doggedness that rivalled a wolf after a deer (he liked nature programmes), persistently and without any let up. Which surprised him, as he wasn't good-looking, or popular, or sociable. Jack did not consider himself a good catch.

For some reason, Chantelle did.

At first, he was flattered – what man wouldn't have been? – and he'd fallen in with her plans and suggestions, gradually letting her into his life, deeper and deeper until she'd become so entrenched that she had assumed they would get married. When she'd discovered he had no intention of asking her, despite her many and varied hints, *she* had asked *him*.

Her reaction to his stuttered and embarrassed refusal hadn't been pretty.

Which was why he was so baffled as to her continued attempts for them to get back together. It was almost as though she refused to believe he didn't love her.

He liked her immensely (or he had done until she had become so incredibly intense) and he'd found her witty and good fun to be with. But that wasn't enough of a reason to spend the rest of his life with her. Call him old-fashioned, but he wanted what his sister had. Della was head-over-heels in love with Scott. It shone out of her like light through an uncurtained window, and she was positively radiant with happiness. Jack envied her enormously.

He waited for Chantelle to move out of sight before he picked his cutlery up once more. He'd better get his brunch inside him, otherwise he would be seriously late back from his break. Anyway, Sue wouldn't forgive him if he failed to polish it all off, and he didn't want to get on her wrong side, not when there were surreptitious extra sausages and slices of bacon in the offing.

But as he munched his way through more calories than he cared to count, his thoughts returned to the email from his sister and his heart sank. He knew he was going to have to put his home on the market and find somewhere else to live. Sharpish.

CHAPTER 3

Molly didn't want to close the front door behind her, but neither was she prepared to leave it open and risk Bill having second thoughts and following her inside. Or anyone else, for that matter. She was well aware the park was frequented by youngsters, and she had been guilty of spending some of her teenage years in this very park herself, playing hide and seek (mostly praying she'd be found by Merton Hinde in the hope he'd kiss her, although he never did). Plus other games which had involved lots of running around and screaming. Alcohol was often consumed, along with other things. Molly had drunk the alcohol, but hadn't fancied the other stuff and she certainly didn't smoke, her reluctance giving rise to the nickname "boring Brown".

Molly hadn't cared.

OK, maybe she had cared a little, but not enough to have a puff of whatever it was her friends had smoked.

She had stayed sober and had spent her time alternating between mooning after Merton and gazing longingly at the cottage. Even back then, she had a feeling that one day she would live in it, and today was the day.

She still couldn't believe it.

It was dark inside, due to the boarded-up windows, which was the first thing she would have to address. She couldn't do anything without light, and until the electricity was reconnected she was scuppered if she wanted to do any cleaning. Which she did. Actually, cleaning may well have to drop to the bottom of her To Do List, because the first thing she needed to do was to chip all the old render off the walls, before the electrician came to rewire it. Then she would have to arrange for the walls to be replastered. Only after that had been done would she be able to give the place the thorough clean she was itching to give it.

Holding her phone in front of her, she walked deeper into the cottage and began tapping on the walls. They sounded quite solid, and she guessed the interior walls were made of stone, not wood and plasterboard.

Even though she had never owned a property herself and had always lived with her mum and dad, being an estate agent meant she had picked up a lot of information about building works, renovations, and what needed to be done. Right now she was going to have to put every bit of her skill and knowledge to the test to turn this derelict run-down property into the home of her dreams.

Molly drifted into the living room and her heart lifted when she saw the old fireplace again. Another thing to add to her list was to get the chimney swept and checked, but considering it was only May that was something she could afford to leave for a few months. Next came the kitchen with its butler sink and rickety old standalone cupboards. She quite liked those, but when she put a hand on the one nearest to her, it wobbled alarmingly. It was clearly rotted throughout, so there would be no option but to throw it in the skip, which meant yet more expense. However, she knew she could pick some up from IKEA if she wanted to replicate the look without spending a fortune. And anyway, she wasn't sure a fitted kitchen would look right in the cottage.

As she made her way slowly around the ground floor and then up the stairs, tapping the walls as she went, she came to a decision. She wasn't looking forward to the hard work and mess that chipping off the old render would entail, but how about if she bought one of those gadgets that checked where the electricity cables were in a wall? When she knew where they were located, it would make more sense to chase out a channel around the old cables so the new ones could be laid inside, then she could get someone in to put a skim of plaster over everything. Not only would it save her a lot of expense, but it would also save her a lot of time.

Not that any of this work prevented her from moving in *today*, because it wouldn't. Molly had been absolutely determined from the start, that as soon as she picked up the keys she was going to spend her first night as a home-owner here. Although, if she was honest, she wasn't particularly looking forward to it. The cottage was a far cry from her parents' comfy house and her snug bedroom. She didn't have a bed for one thing, neither was there any hot water, and cooking was something she could only dream about for the time being.

Nevertheless, she had come prepared. In the boot of her car was an old camping stove complete with a gas canister, a kettle to go on the top of it, a pint of milk, some tea bags and a mug. Not only that, she had a blow-up bed, a foot pump and some bedding. Oh, and a crowbar – a necessity if she wanted to try to remove those darned boards covering the windows.

As far as Molly was concerned, she was good to go, aside from shopping for cleaning products. She had meant to do that yesterday, but she simply hadn't got round to it. She would fetch everything in from the car first, and then she'd pop to the supermarket.

She was a bit reluctant to walk through the park carrying an armful of bedding and a crowbar, but it was only when she was about to relock the front door that she wondered what those other keys could be for. Guessing one of them might be for the main gates, she walked over to them, and after furtively checking to make sure no one was watching, she tried each likely-looking key in turn.

Voila! The fourth one turned stiffly in the lock, and she fist pumped the air.

Heaving with all her might, Molly tugged and yanked at the gates, and they reluctantly opened with a creak that set her teeth on edge and had her mentally adding WD40 to her list of imminent purchases.

The gates were large and heavy, and she wondered whether it would be a good idea to park a car outside the cottage like she'd planned on doing, because it would mean having to open and close these things every time she wanted to go in and out of the park. The other alternative was where she had left the car this morning, which was in a side street a short walk away. Maybe she could have a word with the council and ask if she could leave the gates open permanently, then had second thoughts as she envisaged joyriders in stolen cars tearing around the flower beds at all hours of the night.

Ha! What flower beds? She could see the vague outlines of where they used to be, but that was about it. They were seriously overgrown, with grass and weeds choking them. It was quite difficult to tell where flower beds ended, and lawn began. Or even where flowerbeds ended and the paths began, for that matter.

She hurried over to her car and got in. Feeling like an intruder, she manoeuvred the vehicle through the gates and drove slowly over to the cottage, pulling up close to the front door. She wouldn't bother to lock the gates for the moment, because she would be back out through them as soon as she emptied the contents of her boot.

Molly was nothing if not a planner, and expecting the floor to be as dusty today as it had been on the day she'd first viewed the property, she had brought some large plastic sheeting with her. So the first thing she did was to unfold it and put it on the floor of the bedroom that she intended to be the master. Then she unpacked the blow-up bed, popped it on top of the plastic and placed the bedding beside it.

When she had unpacked the rest of her stuff, she locked the cottage once more, got back in her car, drove out through the gates, clambered out, dragged the gates shut, squealing and protesting (the gates, not her), relocked them, then drove off.

Phew! That wasn't a performance she wanted to repeat two or three times a day, thank you very much. But that was a worry for another time. For now, she would have to put up with it, because she had more important things on her mind.

***

It was safe to say that Molly had never used a crowbar before. Why would she? It wasn't the sort of thing many twenty-nine-year-old women would have a great deal of experience of. However, once she had got into the swing of it, she found prising the large woodchip boards away from the windows to be remarkably satisfying, even if it was hard work and took three times as long as she thought it would. But, oh my word, once she had got the first one off, she was filled with joy.

For the first time in at least two decades, if not longer, light flooded into the living room of the cottage in Sweet Meadow Park. Admittedly, the light was filtered by several layers of grime, both inside and out, but she didn't care. Light was light, and with the afternoon disappearing fast Molly would take any light on offer. It did make her a little nervous to think that once the boards had been removed anyone could peer in until she managed to get some curtains up at the windows, but the thought of being locked inside with the boards still in place filled her with unease.

Molly had no clue where today had gone: one minute she had been anxiously waiting for confirmation that the finances were all in order so she could collect the keys, and the next it was five-thirty in the afternoon and all she had done was jimmy one board off one window.

Wanting to get the ground floor done before she stopped for the day, Molly worked her way around the building in a clockwise direction. She had started to the left of the front door, then went around to the side of the house and prised off a much smaller board which she guessed covered the pantry window (having a pantry sounded very grown up – no one else she knew had one), and then on to the kitchen.

The door to the back of the house was also boarded up, but it took considerably more effort to free it and she was hot, thirsty and panting by the time she'd finished. Debating whether to leave the final window until tomorrow, she made her way to the front of the house once more and gazed at it critically. It did look rather odd with one of the downstairs windows on one side of the door free, and the other one not.

Molly deliberately didn't look at the upstairs windows because she needed a ladder to get to those, and she wasn't looking forward to that. She didn't like heights for a start, and she also wasn't sure whether she would have the strength to hang onto the ladder and yank the boards off.

She'd tackle this last ground floor one, then she'd call it a day. She was desperate for a shower, although that was out of the question until she'd bought one of those hoses that could be attached to the taps, and neither did she have any hot water. She was also starving, having not had any lunch. She would have to make do with boiling some water on the borrowed camping stove and try to wash as best she could. And as for food, she couldn't face trying to tackle the old range yet. The thought of cooking on such a monstrosity made her shudder. Although, unless she wanted to have it taken out, she knew she'd have to get to grips with it eventually. There was no point in having it sitting in the kitchen just for show. Besides, she knew that in the winter she'd probably be grateful for it. Saying that though, she wasn't going to go to all the effort of firing it up just to warm up a tin of soup, so another item on her long list of purchases was a new cooker. Until it arrived, she had a funny feeling she might exist on takeaways.

Her mouth watering with anticipation, her mind drifted to the fish and chip supper she had promised herself this evening. So the sooner she got on with taking this remaining board off, the sooner she could eat.

Molly was about to heft the crowbar once more, when her phone rang, startling her. With a little shriek she dropped the crowbar, narrowly missing her toes, and danced away from it while simultaneously trying to extricate her phone from her pocket.

'Dad!' she cried breathlessly. 'You almost scared me to death.'

Her father's soothing voice chuckled down the phone. 'Why? What were you doing?'

'Er, I hope you don't mind, but I borrowed your crowbar.'

'I don't mind at all,' he said, 'but what I do mind is you trying to use it on those boards.'

'How did you know—?'

'Molly, I'm your father, it's my job to know. Anyway, I guessed you wouldn't wait until your mum and I came back from holidays.'

Sheepishly, Molly pulled a face. 'I wanted to do it myself,' she said.

'You always did want to do everything yourself. You're far too independent for your own good, missy. Have you managed to get any of them off?'

'I've got one more to remove from the downstairs,' she said proudly, then she sobered. 'I've still got the upstairs to do, though.'

'I hope you're not thinking of tackling those on your own?' her father cautioned.

'I *was* thinking of it, but I'm pretty sure I wouldn't be able to manage it,' she admitted.

'Thank goodness you've seen sense. We'll be home on Saturday, so I'll help you take them off on Sunday. Do you think you can wait until then?'

'I'll have to, won't I?' Molly shot back, but she was laughing as she said it so he wouldn't take offence or think she was being stroppy.

Molly could hear her mum in the background and her dad said, 'Hang on, your mum wants a word.' There was a muffled discussion as her father handed the phone over.

'Molly? How are you? I hope you're not overdoing things? Are you eating? What are you having for dinner?'

Molly stifled a giggle. 'If you let me get a word in edgeways, I'll tell you.'

'Your dad said you've taken those boards off all by yourself. I wish you wouldn't, you'll do yourself an injury. You should wait for him to give you a hand: he's stronger than you, and he knows what he's doing.'

'I know what I'm doing too.' Molly rolled her eyes. Her mum loved her to bits and she had her best interests at heart, but sometimes she could be a bit of a fusspot. 'If it's any consolation, Dad is going to help me take the upstairs ones off on Sunday.'

'Thank God! I have visions of you falling off a ladder.'

'To put your mind at rest, I haven't got a ladder, and even if I did, I wouldn't go up it.' Actually, she was telling a bit of a porky because she *did* have a ladder, but it was only a step ladder and it wouldn't reach the upstairs windows.

'I hope you're eating properly,' her mum said, changing the subject.

'Yes, Mum, I am eating.' They'd only been gone two days! Anyone would think she wasn't able to feed herself.

Her mum carried on, 'There's a lasagne in the freezer. I meant to remind you to take it out last night, but I forgot. If you take it out of the freezer now and leave it in the fridge to defrost, you can have it tomorrow. You'll have to fend for yourself this evening, but there are some new potatoes in the cupboard, and a piece of white fish you can cook from frozen, if you fancy it. Pop a few peas onto boil and make some parsley sauce, and you're good to go.'

Molly didn't like to tell her mum that she wasn't at home, and that she had no intention of being there this evening. Or any other evening. Her mother would only worry, so Molly reasoned that what she didn't know wouldn't hurt her. Of course she would pop in to see her parents (probably more than they'd appreciate), but her parents' house was no longer her home. That had changed the minute she'd picked up the keys to her very own cottage.

'It's OK, Mum, I've already set my heart on a fish and chip supper,' Molly said.

'Oh, right, well… enjoy. And don't work too hard. I've got to go, your dad is getting some drinks in. We're having a cool down at the bar before we go back to the room for a shower and get ready for dinner.'

'Have a wonderful time, Mum; love you. Give my love to Dad.'

'Will do. Love you too.' Then her mum was gone, leaving Molly with images in her head of her parents sitting at the sun-drenched bar of the all-inclusive hotel they were staying at, and feeling envious.

However, when she looked back at her cottage again, her envy quickly dissipated: she wouldn't swap a week in Menorca for the excitement she felt today. It was a shame her parents couldn't have been with her when she'd opened the front door for the first time as the property's new owner, but then again, she knew what her mum and dad were like. Her dad would have spent half an hour wandering around tutting, shaking his head, and frowning, and her mother would have done her utmost to persuade Molly to get the professionals in to gut the place.

But that wasn't what Molly wanted at all. This was her house, and she was going to renovate it her way.

***

For the middle of May the weather was quite warm. It was certainly warm enough to tempt Jack out for an evening run. He had finished work early, which was the advantage of being on flexi-time, so he had decided to do a longer route this evening. He'd had a nightmare of a day at work, and he couldn't wait to get his trainers on and pound his frustrations into oblivion. Some people had a pint to relax: Jack ran. He would come back sweaty, tired and aching, but feeling rebalanced, and whilst his worries might not have gone away, they were usually lightened a little… and today, he needed all the lightening he could get.

In all honesty, he should start sorting the house out this evening, but he couldn't face it. He would bite the bullet tomorrow, beginning with a visit to the DIY store first thing in the morning to buy paint and brushes, and maybe a dust sheet or two because he didn't want to ruin the carpets by dripping paint on them. They could also do with a good clean, so he decided he would hire one of those machines; it would be one of the last things to be done before the estate agent came to take photos.

As he ran, Jack thought about what he needed to do and the order in which he needed to do it, and he decided to tackle one room at a time rather than try to do them all at once. He would only end up running around like a headless chicken.

He'd start with the living room because he felt that would have the most impact. It also was the room that needed the least sorting out, as it only contained two large sofas, a TV, a bookcase and a small table. Or maybe he would tackle the spare room first, as it was probably the worst. Instead of putting things up in the attic, he tended to open the door, shove something in and close the door again. It had been that way ever since Della had moved out. No doubt most of the stuff in it could go to the charity shop or could be binned. He had no idea why he'd kept most of it. And the attic was quite full too, but at least no one would be able to see up there. He hoped. Having never sold a property before, he didn't know what potential buyers were likely to get up to. Would they want to root around in the eaves? He couldn't remember doing that when he and Della had viewed this house. The two of them had been so smitten with it they hadn't even bothered to check that the roof was OK, let alone go into the attic. Luckily for them it had been sound, with no leaks or loose tiles; although saying that, the survey would have picked up anything untoward.

Running steadily, his legs and his breath in rhythm, Jack pounded along the pavement, following his regular route. Every now and again he checked his watch to make sure he wasn't any slower than usual. It had been a long time since he'd hit his personal best, and he didn't think he'd be doing so today. Still, it was nice to get out. Not only was the exercise good for him physically, but he also found it beneficial to his mental well-being. He always felt calmer and more centred after a run.

He knew he was on the home straight when his feet took him into the park, and he picked up speed. He could hear a pizza and a cold glass of fizzy pop calling to him: although he wasn't hungry right now (he never was immediately after exercise) by the time he had a shower and got changed, he would be starving. Brunch seemed an awfully long time ago.

Every time he came this way he thought it was a shame that the park wasn't in a better state. But what could he do? It'd had enough money spent on it in the past, but it hadn't been appreciated. Despite the clean-up crew having recently done a litter pick, Jack was disappointed to see more discarded fast-food wrappers and plastic bottles littering the path and the grass verges. An old bike poked out from an overgrown flower bed, which he could have sworn hadn't been there the last time he'd come this way. Didn't people have any pride in their surroundings?

He supposed any clear-up was down to him and his department, but he simply couldn't justify it. Sending a crew in every day simply wasn't cost effective. And if people couldn't be bothered to take their litter home with them, they didn't deserve to have nice flower beds and well-tended shrubs to look at.

Perhaps he was being harsh, but there were so many more deserving cases council funds could be spent on.

Good grief! Someone had even vandalised the old park keeper's cottage, he noticed as he ran past.

Woah! He skidded to a halt.

The vandals were still there!

Without thinking, he ran towards them. Or rather, towards *her*, because he could only see one person, and that was a girl. She seemed to be having trouble removing one of the boards from a downstairs window, and he wondered whether the rest of her mates had scarpered, leaving her to carry the can.

'Excuse me!' he called, sounding rather officious even to himself. 'What do you think you're doing?'

The girl turned around and he was surprised to see she wasn't as young as he'd assumed. This was no teenager: this was a grown woman, who should know better.

'What does it look like I'm doing?' she barked crossly. 'I can't get this damn thing off.'

'Want any help?' he replied sarcastically. He wished he had brought his phone with him so he could call the police.

The woman stopped tugging at the board and picked up a crowbar that had been propped against the wall.

Jack flinched. That was a blunt instrument if ever he saw one.

She thrust it towards him, and he danced back a step.

'I wouldn't normally ask for help,' she said, 'but it'll be dark soon and I'm hungry, tired and cross. So I would appreciate it if you could lend me your muscles.'

'Should you be doing that?' he asked. She didn't look like a vandal – but then again, he wasn't sure what a typical vandal was supposed to look like.

The woman rolled her eyes. 'You're not the first person to ask me that question today,' she said. 'Yes, I should be doing this. I own the place.'

A light bulb went on in Jack's head as he remembered seeing a memo about its sale, and he raised his eyebrows. Good luck, he thought. He didn't envy her moving in here, but he wasn't about to tell her that.

Wordlessly he took the crowbar from her and wedged the business end in between the top of the board and the window frame itself, and put his back into it. With a grunt he felt the board give, and with a bit of persuasion it came away in his hand.

He gave the woman her crowbar back, and eased the board to the ground, mindful of splinters, then he looked at her.

Her expression had softened and he realised she was rather pretty, despite the smudges of dirt across her face. Dark hair, caught up on the top of her head, fell in wisps around her cheeks and the back of her neck, and large blue eyes stared back at him. Her lips were curved into a smile, and his eyes were drawn to them. They looked very kissable.

'Thank you, I really do appreciate it,' she said. 'I would offer you a drink, but all I've got is tap water.'

'I'm good,' he said. 'Can you manage?' He jerked his head towards a pile of boards stacked neatly to one side of the weed-infested path.

'I'm good,' she echoed with a smirk. 'I'm stronger than I look.'

Without meaning to, Jack scanned her from head to toe. Then wished he hadn't as he realised she was staring at him, her eyebrows raised.

'I'm sure you are,' he said noncommittally. 'Right, if you can manage, I'd better get going.'

'Thanks again,' she called, as he dashed down the path.

He didn't reply; instead, he waved a hand in the air without looking around and carried on going.

Better her than me, he thought as he ran the last half a mile or so to his house. Never in a million years would he have bought that ramshackle old place, especially where it was located. She would have her work cut out to make it look decent, and she might find she'd have even more of a challenge to keep it looking that way. The old park keeper's cottage had been broken into several times in the past, and every so often he'd had to send a team out to board it back up and make it secure. Ideally the building should have been demolished years ago.

All Jack hoped was that the woman hadn't paid a lot for it.

He was interested in any progress she made though, and he was already looking forward to seeing it the next time he came out for a run – although goodness knows when that would be, because he had a whole house to decorate.

But as he sprinted along his road, his thoughts weren't on his own property and neither were they on the park keeper's cottage.

They were on the woman who had bought it.

CHAPTER 4

Jack nibbled at the pizza, delicately avoiding the crust, and chewed slowly, then he popped the uneaten crust on the plate with the others and pushed the plate away. Feeling more human after a run, a shower, and some food, he picked up his glass of cola and took his plate into the kitchen. Draining the glass, he put it on the worktop and eyed the dirty dishes. He'd see to them in the morning. Or not. Washing up had never been one of his priorities, and he already had a sink full. He should get round to it, but he couldn't summon up the enthusiasm. Or the energy.

He felt drained, emotionally rather than physically. He honestly didn't want to face having to clear the house, redecorate it, and put it on the market. And he certainly didn't want to face trying to find somewhere else to live. What if he didn't find anywhere? Having listened to colleagues and friends in the past when they'd been looking at properties, he realised finding somewhere nice and within budget probably wasn't going to be easy.

Jack went back into the living room, turned down the volume on the sports channel, and reached for a pen and paper. It was time he worked out his finances properly, and then he would be in a better position to know what he could, or couldn't, afford. He obviously wouldn't know for definite until the house sold and he received his half of the equity, but right now he could make a couple of guesstimates, although those guesstimates would be rather vague considering he wasn't totally sure of the market value of his house.

He mused for a while, then checked a couple of property sites on his phone to see what any similar houses in Sweet Meadow were going for, to give him a starting point to wrangle a few sums. Eventually he had three columns, the first being the lowest estimate, the second being a middle estimate, and the third being the highest. The lowest one made him want to cry. The highest wasn't a great deal better, but at least it gave him more wriggle room, although much would depend on what the property achieved in terms of sale value. He also needed to take into account how quickly he'd be expected to move out. From the brief foray into estate agent land, he hadn't seen anywhere he both liked and could afford. It was either one or the other.

Might it be better to rent for the time being? But he was reluctant to step off the property ladder now he had one foot on it.

The problem was, he knew properties without a chain sold faster and were less likely to have hold-ups in terms of completion, and he appreciated that Della wanted her half of the money as soon as humanly possible. Maybe he *would* look into renting. It was a pity his mum lived so far away, otherwise he could have moved back in with her for a while, although he still would have expected to pay his way.

But that was out of the question, so it was back to the drawing board.

He was still brooding about his sister and his circumstances when the phone rang. 'I was just thinking of you,' he said.

'Nothing bad, I hope?' Della asked.

'Not at all. I was about to tackle the spare room,' he lied, crossing his fingers to ward off any bad luck.

'That's why I was ringing,' Della said. 'Do you need me to come back to help with putting the house on the market?'

Jack heard the subtext – she didn't trust him to do it in a timely manner. Either that, or she was even more desperate to sell than he had originally thought.

'I can manage,' he said, and his mind flashed to a young woman who'd said exactly the same thing to him barely two hours ago. He wondered how she was getting on.

'I'm sure you can,' Della said soothingly. 'But give me a shout if you need any help, yeah? Just for you to know, there is nothing in the house I want to keep, so if you come across anything of mine, please feel free to get rid of it.'

'I will,' he promised. There were a lot of his own things he needed to get rid of, too.

They chatted for a while, Della full of her news, excitement with her new life flowing through the airwaves and cloaking him in a fog of envy. Three years younger than him, she'd always been the livelier of the two siblings, full of get up and go and joie-de-vivre. Jack was more staid, more conservative, which was probably why he had landed a job in the council and hadn't made a new life in the wilds of Alaska.

With a sigh, he heaved himself up off the sofa and decided he might as well stop fannying about and get on with it. He had a house to clear, clean, and decorate, and sitting on his backside wasn't going to get it done, so he made a pact with himself that he would ring the estate agent first thing in the morning and get them to come around on Monday, if possible. That would mean he had six whole days to strip the place and redecorate.

Jack felt better now he had a deadline. It would give him something to work towards and stop him from lazing about feeling sorry for himself. So with that, he grabbed some rubbish bags from underneath the sink and headed up the stairs. He had years of accumulated junk to sort out, and he was determined he was going to do it tonight.

***

There was one advantage of having the boards still in place on the upstairs windows, Molly conceded later that evening – no one could see in. She had several candles lit, both in the bedroom and the bathroom, and they provided a surprising amount of illumination for her to eat her supper.

As soon as she had finished heaving the final board on top of the ones she had already taken off, Molly had retreated inside, locking the door firmly after her, and had spent a good twenty minutes pumping up the airbed and arranging the bedding on top of it. Then she had braved a thorough wash in cold water whilst standing in the hastily cleaned bath. It hadn't been a particularly pleasant experience, but at least she had managed to swill the dust and grime from her skin. Dressed in clean clothes, she had ventured outside once more (this time not bothering to take the car because she couldn't face trying to open the gates again) and she had walked into town to purchase some fish and chips and a can of fizzy pop.

Being careful not to shake the pop too much, she had hurried back, darting through the little gate and scurrying along the path to the cottage, glancing this way and that to make sure there wasn't anyone taking an undue interest in what she was doing, mindful of the old man's warnings from this morning. Once inside, she'd locked the door again, and had climbed the stairs to drop in an ungainly heap onto the airbed to eat her food.

Despite the shadows and the occasional noise from outside which she didn't want to think about too much, it was quite cosy in her little bedroom. Far from feeling enclosed, she felt cocooned, as though the cottage was wrapping her in a warm hug. She had felt that way about it the minute she'd stepped inside the door when she'd come to view the property, but back then she had been imagining it light and airy and fully furnished: not dark, and bare, and empty. So it was quite nice that she still felt this way, despite the lack of amenities.

She had her phone for company (she had been very careful with the charge to make sure it didn't run out) and she listened to music for a while as she ate the succulent white fish and the fluffy aromatic chips, covered in salt and vinegar. When she finished, she wrapped up the remains of her meal and took it downstairs, not wanting to smell fish and chips for the rest of the night, then she went back to her bedroom, changed into her pyjamas and settled down for the night.

It wasn't late, barely ten o'clock, but she was exhausted. It had been an incredibly exciting day, even though she hadn't managed to achieve half of what she'd hoped. Smiling to herself, she thought of one of the property development programmes on telly she was addicted to – Kevin someone or another hosted it: she couldn't remember his name. In practically every episode, he always expressed incredulity at the homeowner's budget and timeframe, consistently advising them that everything would take twice as long and cost twice as much as they expected. He had been right as far as this cottage was concerned – removing the boards from the downstairs windows had taken three times as long as she had anticipated, and she would still be there now if it wasn't for that guy who was out running, and who had kindly offered to help.

She turned the music off and blew out two of the three candles in the bedroom, leaving one burning because she didn't want to wake in the middle of the night and discover it was pitch black. Then she snuggled down under the duvet and nuzzled her head into the pillow.

As she waited for sleep to claim her, the guy from earlier drifted into her thoughts once again. He had been slim, more a marathon runner's physique than a sprinter, and his Lycra outfit hadn't left much to the imagination. She blushed as she thought of the way she had ogled him when he'd had his back to her whilst he had been prising the board off. His bum had been all firm and muscly, as had his legs.

She wondered whether she would see him again. She wouldn't be surprised, assuming this was one of his regular running routes, and from the way he had challenged her, he clearly knew the park.

She thought back to his assumption that she had been up to no good. Several people who had been out walking their dogs or using the park as a cut-through had given her curious looks, and one or two had asked her what she was doing. She had been happy enough to explain, proud to be the owner of this lovely old cottage. Some people had wished her luck, one old lady had snorted her disbelief, and the gentleman from this morning – Bill and his little dog, Patch – had asked her whether she knew what she was letting herself in for.

Crossly, she thumped the pillow: her brain was still whirling, but she knew she had to get some rest. Tomorrow would be as busy, if not busier. First thing in the morning she would pay a visit to the DIY store and pick up all the bits she would need in order to chase out the channels where the new electrical wires were to go, and she also wanted to buy one of those thingamajigs to test where the old ones were. Whilst she was there, she would choose some light fittings, because not one room had anything other than a bare wire dangling from the ceiling.

She wondered whether she'd have to choose the sockets and the switches too, and she reminded herself to ask the electrician when he came tomorrow. She prayed to goodness he would be able to turn the electricity on for her, even if it was only on a temporary basis until she got the place rewired. She would book him for that too, as soon as he could fit her in. And whilst the place was still a mess, she might as well hire a machine to sand down all the floorboards upstairs. The downstairs was covered in lino, and she hadn't yet had the courage to lift it up and see what was underneath. She didn't think it was floorboards, and she assumed it was probably concrete. *But you never know*, she said to herself: *there might be a quarry tile floor somewhere*. She could always live in hope.

Still thinking about what she needed to do tomorrow, Molly drifted off.

She didn't know how long she had been asleep (it could have been a few minutes, it could have been an hour) but she woke with a start, hearing a noise outside, and she lay there listening to the sounds of raucous laughter and yelling, and guessed the park had some night-time visitors.

Propping herself up on her elbow, she reached for her phone, thankful she'd had the foresight to leave a candle flickering. It was eleven-fifty, so she'd probably only been asleep less than an hour. Exhausted, she lay there for a few minutes, wondering how long this din would carry on, before getting out of bed and stuffing her feet into her trainers.

Creeping downstairs, she eased into the living room, sidled up to the window and peered through it. It was dark outside, but there was some reflected light from the street near the main gate, and from her vantage point she could make out the swings and slide in the kiddies' play area and what had once been a roundabout, but now lay drunkenly on its side and didn't move. Next to the play area was a path leading to the field, and to the side of the path were overgrown flowerbeds and broken benches. On the right of the cottage was a derelict bandstand and another boarded-up building which had once been a cafe.

The noise was coming from the bandstand, and she could see several shadowy figures in the distance. As she watched, a small red dot briefly flared into life and she guessed it was a cigarette or a joint being passed around.

Molly stayed at the window for some time, wondering when those people were going to go home, but it was only when they finally made a move and began walking towards the cottage did she realise they were kids. She'd guessed they weren't particularly old from the shrieking and the squealing of female voices, but she hadn't realised how young they were. Even in the darkness she could tell they weren't much older than fifteen or sixteen, perhaps not even that. Did their parents know they were out? And didn't they have school in the morning?

Gosh, she must be getting old. Ten years ago it could have been her on the bandstand. In fact, it most certainly had been. Although not quite as late as this. If she had stayed out later than ten o'clock on a school night, her mum and dad went ballistic. And neither had they liked her hanging around the park. It wasn't so bad in the spring and summer, and even into early autumn, but it wasn't somewhere she had frequented in the cold, dark, winter months.

She continued to watch until the last teenager trailed out through the gate, a fag in one hand and the glint of what might have been a can in the other. Molly wondered what it contained: her bet was beer or cider.

It was such a shame these youngsters didn't have something else to do in the evenings, other than hang around the park smoking and drinking. She guessed they probably didn't mean any harm – she certainly hadn't and neither had her friends – but en mass she had to admit that a group of teenagers could be intimidating. It wouldn't be so bad if they took their rubbish home with them, but she knew from past experience there would be litter scattered throughout the grass come the morning. Maybe if the park had some litter bins…?

Then she remembered there had been bins in the past, but they had been kicked over and occasionally even set fire to.

Suddenly Molly sagged against the window, her forehead touching the glass. What the hell had she been thinking? This cottage might be beautiful (or rather it would be once it was renovated), but the rest of the park wasn't. She had been coming here long enough to know it wasn't one of the nicest places to visit, so what on earth had possessed her to buy a property that was located inside its gates?

Had she just made one of the biggest mistakes of her life?

Molly refused to believe it. She had known what the park was like before she'd put an offer in on the property, and the knowledge hadn't prevented her from buying it – although the reality of being here alone at night clearly wasn't something she'd thought through properly. But this was her house, and she wasn't going to let a few noisy teenagers make her regret buying it.

Molly took a deep breath and straightened up.

The park was quiet now, still and silent, with not even a breath of wind to stir the leaves on the trees, and the calm gradually seeped into her.

Ahh, that was better.

She remained standing by the window for a while longer, continuing to let the peace of the night ease her jangling nerves. If that was the worst it was going to get – a few rowdy teenagers letting off steam – she could cope.

A shrill bark made her jump, and for a second she thought the youngsters had returned and her heart sank, but when she saw the slinking figure of a fox glide along the path in front of the cottage, a feeling of wonderment stole over her – there was a *fox* in her park. Wow…

Was there any other wildlife here, she wondered?

She knew there were plenty of birds, because she saw and heard them regularly, and once or twice she had spotted a squirrel while she was eating her sandwiches on her lunch break, but never once had she considered that a fox might live here. Did that mean there were rabbits? Otherwise, what did the fox eat?

A dismaying thought occurred to her – it probably scavenged for discarded take-away food.

There still might be rabbits, though. The park didn't just consist of unkempt flowerbeds and broken swings. On the far side, and running almost the full length of it, was an area of woodland: a wide swathe of almost impenetrable trees whose upper branches swayed and sighed in the wind. It was impenetrable because banks of thorny brambles grew between the trunks, some of them higher than her head in summer, and far too prickly to push a way through. Tall clusters of magenta-flowered rosebay willowherb also grew in abundance (she knew what this plant was because her mum constantly moaned about it sprouting up in her garden) and ferns inhabited any spaces where the brambles hadn't taken hold.

At the furthest point from the big main gates and her cottage, was a pond surrounded by a meadow. The pond was a decent size, and rumour had it that it was at least twenty feet deep in the middle. By rights, it should be fenced in, but as no one went near it due to the number of supermarket trolleys and car tyres dumped in it, it had been left as it was.

The remainder of the park consisted of a large central field which had once been used for football practice but was now full of weeds that were only mown when the council remembered to do it, and the disused bandstand and the boarded-up cafe. The council certainly did like boarding things up, didn't they?

Molly was about to return to bed, the fox having failed to reappear, when she saw a solitary figure shuffle into view.

It was the dog she recognised, rather than the man, because the chap was bundled up in an overcoat and wore a trilby hat. The dog was Patch, which meant the man had to be Bill.

Although Molly was certain Bill couldn't possibly see her, he nevertheless stopped, turned his face towards the cottage and tipped his hat.

Molly, still convinced he couldn't see her, put her hand up to the grimy glass anyway.

A single nod from him showed that he could.

Instead of feeling disconcerted, Molly felt comforted. Bill might be old, but he seemed to be looking out for her, and she returned to bed with a warm glow in her chest.

CHAPTER 5

Molly slept surprisingly well, but when she awoke and checked the time, she realised it was only five forty-five. She remained there for ten minutes, hoping to get back to sleep, not ready to start her day yet, but her mind was too full of the things she needed to do, so she decided to get up.

The first thing was to grab breakfast from a cafe then go to the DIY shop, but it was too early for that, so she used the camping stove to make herself a cup of tea, setting it up outside the back door and crouching over it until the water came to the boil. Tea made and mug in hand, she decided to go for a stroll. Even though technically her property consisted of the cottage and the area immediately surrounding it (she had pored over the detailed boundary lines, so she knew exactly what she owned and what she didn't), she nevertheless felt the park was also hers by extension.

So she felt it only natural to wander around its grounds at six-thirty in the morning with a mug of tea in her hand.

She had never been in the park this early before, and the peace and solitude surprised her.

The dawn chorus was very much in evidence, filling the air with the songs of hundreds of birds, and she gravitated towards the woodland, keen to feel close to nature. The trees were vibrant with new leaves, the colours ranging from an almost pale mint to deep emerald, and although she had no idea what many of them were, she vowed to find out. She would have loved to venture further under the shaded canopy, but there was far too much undergrowth, so she contented herself with skirting around it, following the treeline and gazing over the field. The area was large and flat, and would be perfect for games of football, or even for picnics, but it currently sprouted a carpet of buttercups, daisies, dandelions and thistles, which bees and other flying insect seemed to be drawn to in large numbers.

Sipping her rapidly cooling tea, Molly made her way along the edge of the field towards the meadow surrounding the pond. Early morning dew soaked through her trainers and dampened the legs of her jeans, but she didn't mind. There was no one else in sight, and apart from the birds and buzzing insects, the only other sound was the distant rumble of a vehicle. She never would have believed the park could be so beautiful and so peaceful, and she vowed to try to get out early every morning to savour the beauty of each brand-new, unsullied day.

However, her pleasure was somewhat dampened by the sight of the choked pond. Weed grew thickly around its edges, and the water was murky and dark. She could see the handle of a shopping trolley poking through the rushes, and on the bank next to it lay a couple of car tyres. Despite that, a small black and white bird was perched on one of them, its long tail twitching up and down as it bobbed. She didn't know what species it was, so maybe a trip to the library to borrow a book on native British birds might be in order.

Molly nearly dropped her mug and let out a shriek when a large insect buzzed past her nose, and it took her a second to realise it was a dragonfly as she watched its swooping and darting flight, memorised by its iridescent beauty. And there was another one, and another. Perhaps the water wasn't as dead as it looked, if these things lived around it, and as she gazed at the surface she noticed lots of small flies hovering inches above the water.

When something rose from the depths and fell back with a splash, leaving concentric circles rippling across the surface, she realised the pond had fish in it. Wow! She'd had no idea, and she wondered whether anyone else did.

Her wonderment swiftly turned to despair though, as she approached the old bandstand and saw the amount of rubbish left behind. And not only there: as she had strolled around the park she had spotted empty packets, plastic bottles, cans and food wrappers. She didn't know whether they had been blown there by the wind or they had been carelessly thrown away, but she sadly guessed it was probably the latter.

She must have a word with the council – maybe if there were litter bins, people would use them. Personally, she couldn't see why people didn't take their rubbish home with them, but clearly it was too much of an effort for some, so perhaps bins would be the solution.

Not only that, the paths could do with serious weeding and the edges of the beds needed tidying up, so she could at least tell where they were supposed to be, plus many of the overgrown bushes would benefit from a serious trim.

She paused for a moment, eyeing the sad state of the bandstand. Several roof tiles were missing, and paint had peeled off leaving the raw wood exposed. One of the supporting posts leant at an alarming angle, and she wondered if it would eventually collapse and bring the roof down with it – which could be dangerous, so that was another thing she would have to have a word with the council about. *Overgrown* she could cope with, *dangerous* definitely not. Didn't anyone ever inspect these places?

Although Molly couldn't do anything about the state of the bandstand, she might be able to do something about all the litter: if she bought one of those grabby litter-pickers she could easily pop out each morning and gather what she could find. She knew it would be a never-ending task and a thankless one, but this was *her* park damn it, and she hated to see it so neglected.

With another deep sigh, she tore her thoughts away from the unloved park and turned her attention to the cottage, recognising that her home was her number one priority. She had to live there, and the sooner she got it ship-shape the better.

Moving more purposefully, she was striding along the path leading from the bandstand to the cottage and making a mental shopping list in her head, when she saw a familiar figure.

'Hi, Bill,' she said, giving the old man a big smile and bending down to pet Patch. 'You're out bright and early.'

'He gets three walks a day, he does,' Bill replied, 'otherwise he gets unruly.'

'Did I see you out last night, about eleven-thirty ish?'

Bill gave her a keen stare. 'I don't go out late,' he retorted grumpily. 'Too many youffs.'

'Yes, there were one or two around last night,' she agreed, and left it at that. She didn't want to moan about it and get an "I told you so" off the old man.

Patch who had been staring up at his master, his ears pricked and an intent look on his face, jumped up, his front paws bumping the old man on the leg before dropping back down to the ground and licking his lips.

'Now, now, Patch, you know this isn't for you,' Bill said.

Molly noticed he was holding a Tupperware box containing some dark brown chunks and she wondered if it was Bill's breakfast, and hoping it wasn't because it didn't look particularly appetising.

He saw the direction of her gaze. 'It's for the dog,' he said, adding, 'Not my dog,' when she glanced down at Patch. 'It's a stray. You've probably seen him.'

Molly shook her head. 'I don't think so. I did see a fox last night, though.'

'Oh aye, there are one or two of those about. They're after the rabbits.'

'So there *are* rabbits? I did wonder.'

'Aye, and you might find a hedgehog or two, although they're getting more scarce. But this isn't for them, either.' He gave the box a shake. 'This is for the dog. If you see him, don't be worried; he's a bit nervous but he's quite friendly.'

'Can you describe him?'

'He's about this high—' Bill put out a hand and patted the air between his hip and his knee '—jet black and as skinny as a whippet, but I think that's because he's not been fed for a while. He might be a cross between a greyhound and a Labrador, but I can't be certain. Whatever he is, he's a mongrel and he's hungry.'

'Where is his owner?'

'He's a stray, isn't he?' Bill retorted. 'Didn't you listen to anything I said?'

'Somebody must have owned him at one point,' she persisted.

'They might well have done, but they don't own him now. He owns himself.'

'Have you spoken to the dog warden?'

'No, I damn well haven't and I'd appreciate it if you didn't, either,' Bill snapped. 'They'll only take him away, and if nobody claims him they'll have him put down.'

Molly was horrified. 'Surely that doesn't happen?'

'They say it doesn't,' Bill replied ominously, 'but I bet it does. Leave him be; he's happy enough, and I try to feed him when I can.'

Molly wondered how the poor thing managed in bad weather, but she thought it best not to ask because she didn't want to upset herself. Even so, the image of a freezing dog hiding under a bush with the rain hammering down on a dark November night, pushed its way into her thoughts. Maybe she could have a look for a second-hand dog kennel? It wouldn't be anywhere near as nice as being inside next to a warm fire, but it would be better than bare earth and dripping leaves. She would buy some dog food this morning, and leave it out for him later. No doubt Mr Fox would get to it first, but at least she'd have tried.

'Quiet!' Bill hissed, nudging her so hard with his elbow that she staggered. 'Look.' He pointed and Molly followed the direction of his finger.

'Oh my,' she whispered. 'Is that him? The stray dog?'

'It is,' Bill confirmed. 'Don't move and don't say anything.' He passed Patch's lead to her and she grasped it, winding the leather around her hand.

Slowly, very slowly, Bill walked forward, and she could hear him crooning to the animal, the words indistinct. Whatever he was saying, it caught the dog's attention, because the pooch's folded-over ears pricked up and his tail, although hanging low between his back legs, wagged uncertainly. Bill took a few more paces until the dog started whining and looking behind him, then the old man eased the lid off the top of the Tupperware box and placed it on the ground before backing slowly away.

The dog waited until Bill had gone a safe distance, before hesitantly coming forward, one tentative paw at a time. His nose was twitching, and he kept looking from the box to Bill, and then beyond Bill to Molly, licking his lips as he did so. Whether it was because she had hold of Patch and the stray dog thought that anyone who a dog trusted must be OK, but Molly's presence didn't seem to bother him unduly, and very soon his head was down and he was gobbling up the food.

He ate it in three or four frantic gulps, then he looked at Bill, tail wagging as he licked his lips.

'I'll bring you some more tonight,' the old man promised.

'Let me,' Molly said. 'I don't mind feeding him.'

'You'll have to earn his trust,' Bill warned.

'I'm sure I can do that.' She gave Patch's lead back to Bill, and began to walk slowly toward the stray dog. 'Has he got a name?' she asked out of the corner of her mouth.

Bill murmured, 'Not as far as I know.'

'In that case, I'll call him Jet.'

'I don't think he cares what you call him as long as you feed him,' she heard Bill mutter.

Judging that she'd gone close enough because the dog was looking distinctly nervous, Molly halted, crouched down, and held out a hand. 'Here boy, come on, come to Molly,' she said. 'There's a good boy. You're a good dog, aren't you? Such a good dog.'

Jet's ears pricked again, and for one moment she honestly thought he was going to find the courage to come closer to her, but suddenly his head jerked up, he tucked his tail between his legs, whirled around and dashed off across the field.

'Damn it,' Molly muttered, straightening up and feeling disappointed. But when she turned to look at Bill, she realised it wasn't her who had sent the dog scuttling for cover: it was a middle-aged man walking briskly towards them.

'Morning,' he said cheerfully, and carried on walking.

'Morning,' Molly called. She turned to Bill. 'Do you think the dog will come back soon?'

Bill shrugged. 'Not likely – he's had his breakfast.' He tugged at Patch's lead and started walking. 'Maybe you'll see him tonight.'

'I hope so. No doubt I'll see you around later.'

Her only response was a grunt, and she watched the old man for a moment, before returning to the cottage to collect her bag and her car keys. She had places to go and things to do, and the sooner she started, the sooner they would be done.

***

Besides being able to finish early if he wanted, the other advantage to flexi-time working hours was the opportunity to start work later, and Jack wanted to pop into the DIY store before work this morning so he could go straight home and get started on the decorating this evening.

The shop had only just opened and he was one of the first through the door, and was pleased to find it quiet. He wanted to be able to go straight to the correct aisle, pick what he needed and go to the till, without having to dodge round hordes of browsing shoppers.

Clutching a list in his hand, he made for the paint section, walking purposefully and with grim determination. However, he was soon brought up short when he saw the huge variety of finishes, colours, and brands on offer. He and Della had decorated the house together when they had first bought it, but Della had been the one to go shopping for the paint they'd needed. She had picked the shades for each room, and he'd had no say in the matter. He hadn't wanted to. He had been happy enough to contribute muscle power and the reach with his longer arms, but he hadn't been interested in what colour went where, and he had to admit that the subtle shades of difference in whites hadn't registered at all. Apparently, there was a shade called Early Dawn on three of the living room walls, but as far as he was concerned they appeared to be white, so white was what he had decided to go for today. Della had chosen to paint the fourth wall a weird dingy colour, and he intended to paint that white too.

He hefted a massive tub and hoped it would be enough to do the whole house. Then he hesitated: he had picked up matt, but there was a similar tub with the word "silk" emblazoned across the front. Would there be much difference?

He caught movement out of the corner of his eye and, assuming it must be a sales assistant, he said, 'Excuse me.'

But when he looked properly, he realised the person he had spoken to was a customer. And one he recognised, to boot.

'Hello, again,' he said, when the woman who had bought the cottage in Sweet Meadow Park stopped to look at him, her gaze curious. 'I thought you were a member of staff, and I was about to ask you what the difference is between matt and silk emulsion, but I can see you aren't.'

'No, I don't work here. But I can tell you what the difference is. Matt is exactly what it says – it's a matt finish, kind of buff.' For some reason a hint of colour spread across her cheeks, and she bit her lip. Frowning slightly, she continued, 'Silk has got a slight sheen to the finish. Personally, I prefer silk because it's easier to clean. If you wipe a damp rag over a matt wall some of the paint comes off, but that doesn't happen if you use silk. It also tends to reflect light so it can make a room seem brighter and more airy.'

Jack was impressed. 'Thank you. Silk it is. And while you're here, can I pick your brains again?'

She laughed. 'You can try. What is it you want to know?'

He dearly wanted to know whether she would go for a drink with him, but he was too scared to ask, as she might think he was stalking her. Besides, tempted as he was, he was still feeling raw from Chantelle, and he had enough going on in his life without adding a new romance to the mix.

'I can't use this on woodwork, can I?' he asked, gesturing to the tin of emulsion he was holding.

'I wouldn't recommend it,' she replied. 'For things like skirting boards and door frames you should go for gloss or satinwood. And now you want to know the difference between those two, don't you?'

'If you don't mind?'

'Gloss is far, far shinier, and white gloss will yellow over time. Satinwood will also discolour slightly too, but not as much and not as quickly. If I were you, I'd go for satinwood. Do you need any help in deciding which brush to use?'

Now she was being sarcastic. 'No thanks, I can manage,' he said, smiling to himself. Those were the exact words she had used to him yesterday evening, and suddenly he felt embarrassed because he was flirting with her and she wasn't flirting back. 'Right, thanks for your help. I'll let you get on.'

'You're welcome.' She gave him another one of her lovely smiles, then she was gone, leaving him staring after her.

She was as pretty as he remembered, but if he bumped into her again he would aim for friendly yet distant, just as she had been with him this morning.

CHAPTER 6

'Good morning, Watkin and Wright, Astrid speaking, how can I help?' The woman sounded friendly, but Jack's heart was in his mouth. He *so* didn't want to do this.

'I… erm… want to put my house on the market. How do I go about it?'

'Can I take some particulars?' She asked several questions and after Jack had given her his answers, she said, 'One of our agents will come out to view the property and suggest an asking price, then they'll take some notes and photos. You'll need to sign a contract agreeing to our terms and conditions, and that's it.'

It seemed far too easy a process for all the heartache that parting with the house was causing him.

'When would it be convenient for someone to call?' the woman asked.

'Um, Monday? After four?'

'Let me check the diary.' He heard clicking, then she came back on the line. 'That's fine. I'll have to juggle a few things around, so I can't give you the name of the agent right now, but they will have ID with them.'

'That's OK. Thanks for your help.'

'You're welcome.'

The phrase reminded him of the woman who'd bought the park keeper's cottage. Her reply of "You're welcome" after he had thanked her in the DIY store earlier today, had sounded just as professional.

He pushed the thought of her away: he should be concentrating on work, not on his personal life. But even as he checked his emails, his mind was still on her, and it didn't help when he saw that reception had informed him that he'd had another one of those anonymous calls complaining yet again about the amount of litter in the park and demanding to know what was going to be done about it.

As he read it, he had to agree that the situation wasn't the best. He had been running through the park on a regular basis for a number of years, and he'd noticed the steady increase in littering, and he was also very aware of how unkempt and unloved the park was looking. Which brought him neatly back to the woman who had bought the park keeper's cottage. The cottage itself would be lovely once it was done up, and no doubt she would do something nice with the surrounding gardens. But as for living within the park itself, he wasn't sure that was such a good idea.

His tummy gave a loud rumble and he realised it was time for brunch. He had been up and out quite early this morning, and he was more than ready for something to eat.

Securing his computer, he picked up his jacket, checked to make sure he had his wallet, and made his way to the council's cafeteria. It was grandly called The Meadow, with the word "restaurant" underneath, but nobody was fooled. It was more canteen than restaurant, and the acoustics were appalling: at peak times, such as between one and two in the afternoon, you could hardly hear yourself think. He much preferred the peace of eleven-thirty: too late for the breakfast and the mid-morning crowd, and too early for the lunch people, the cafeteria was usually quiet at that time, and he wasn't disappointed today.

'Alright, Jack?' Sue grinned at him. Her round face was pink from the heat of the ovens, and her cap was askew. 'What can I get you, my lovely? A full English?'

'Maybe not today,' Jack said. If he wasn't careful, he would end up eating a full English breakfast every single morning, which wouldn't be good for either his arteries or his waistline. 'What else have you got?' What he meant was, what else was ready to serve, as lunch didn't technically begin until noon.

'The cannelloni is ready, so how about that with a nice bit of salad and some garlic bread?' she suggested

'It sounds delicious. A portion of that, please, and could I have an orange juice to go with it?'

'No coffee today?'

'Maybe I'll have one later, if I've got time.' He paid and waited with his tray, but as usual Sue waved him away.

'Get off with you! You know I always bring it over,' she said, and he beamed at her. She reminded him of his mum, and he vowed to ring her this evening in between painting. Last night he had spent four hours sorting out the spare room and giving it a good clean. So when he got home this evening, he would have a quick bite to eat and put a coat of paint on the walls, then take a break and call his mum, before sorting out Della's old room.

To be fair, there wasn't a great deal left in there because his sister had taken most of it with her or dumped anything she didn't want in the spare room. It shouldn't take long to wash down the walls and the woodwork, and by the time he'd done that maybe he would be able to put a second coat on the spare room walls if they needed it. He was praying they didn't.

He glanced up as a shadow fell across his table, a ready smile on his lips, and was about to thank Sue when he realised it wasn't the cook-in-charge who was standing next to him – it was Chantelle.

His heart sank.

'Someone is pleased to see me,' Chantelle said, her lips curving into a seductive smile.

'Er, I thought it was Sue,' Jack said.

Chantelle's expression darkened. 'Sue who?' she demanded.

'Sue, who works in the cafeteria.'

'Her? She's old enough to be your mother.'

Jack was horrified. 'You don't think…?' he spluttered. 'I can't believe you'd think such a thing! Sue is married.'

'And if she wasn't?' Chantelle snapped.

'It wouldn't make any difference – she's just a nice lady. Anyway, she isn't that old.'

'So why is she bringing your food over to you? Do you always get special treatment?'

'Not always, no.' Jack was on the defensive.

'I think she fancies you. She certainly doesn't bring *my* lunch over to *me*.'

Jack didn't blame her. If he were Sue, he wouldn't have wanted to bring Chantelle's food over to her, either.

'Excuse me.' Sue's voice came from behind him, and he leant to the side as she pushed between him and Chantelle to put his plate down on the table along with his orange juice. 'Be careful, the plate's hot,' she said, totally ignoring Chantelle. 'And if you eat all that, I might have a nice bowl of sticky toffee pudding and custard for you.'

'I shouldn't,' Jack said, but he was grateful, nevertheless.

'Hmm.' Chantelle's mouth was in a straight line and her eyes had narrowed as she watched the cook walk away, before turning her attention to Jack once more. 'I haven't seen you for a while. Where have you been hiding?'

'I haven't been hiding anywhere.' His appetite had suddenly vanished.

'You certainly haven't been coming here for lunch,' Chantelle retorted.

'I have. I come here every day,' Jack said, then wished he hadn't.

'Changed your hours, have you?'

'Kind of.' Now he was getting all defensive. Surely it was up to him what time he had his lunch? He didn't have to answer to her, even if she did work in HR.

'Wait there, I'll grab a coffee and I'll join you,' she said, and Jack wondered if he could change his mind about eating his cannelloni here and ask if he could have it to go instead.

But, darn it, he wasn't going to let his ex-girlfriend drive him away. He had already changed his habits once to avoid her, and he refused to change them again. He would just have to make it abundantly clear to her that they were over. He'd hoped she had got the message after he'd asked her to move out, but clearly she hadn't.

In a way he couldn't blame her, because he had always been a bit of a pushover where Chantelle was concerned. He'd never stood up for himself and had tended to let her walk all over him. Looking back, he couldn't understand why he had put up with her for as long as he had, but he had genuinely cared for her and at one point he'd even managed to persuade himself it was love. But her controlling ways and her insistence that he didn't have a life of his own and had to spend every non-working minute with her, had finally got to him.

The last straw had been when she had wanted to join him on his runs. He didn't want company when he ran, he wanted solitude, and peace and quiet so he could clear his head and concentrate on putting one foot in front of another. When he'd told her that, she had accused him of not loving her.

Unfortunately, in a moment of clarity, he had agreed with her, and the next few hours hadn't been pretty. He'd had a devil of a job trying to convince Chantelle he'd meant it when he'd said they were over. He had felt a total heel asking her to leave but this was *his* house, he'd bought it with Della, so there was no way *he* was going to move out. Chantelle had been the one to move in with him, not the other way around.

And for another thing, he wasn't entirely certain how it had happened. One minute she had been sharing a flat with a friend, the next she had moved her large collection of scarves and makeup into his bedroom, and was giving out her new address to all and sundry. He couldn't remember asking her whether she would like to move in. It had sort of happened. And suddenly discovering that he had a live-in girlfriend had been quite a shock. That was what he meant by allowing Chantelle to walk all over him.

He realised she was doing it again, as she sat down next to him, far too close, and placed a cup of black coffee in front of her.

'I miss you,' she told him, and Jack stared balefully at his lunch. When he didn't say anything, she said, 'I'm sorry. I know I was being silly about Sue, but I get so jealous when I see you talking to other women.'

'You *were* being silly,' Jack agreed, grateful that at least she had recognised how ridiculously she was behaving and was apologising for it. Sue didn't deserve Chantelle's animosity.

But his jaw clenched when Chantelle added, 'I should have realised there's no way you'd go for an old bat like her.'

Jack shook his head in disgust.

Unfortunately, Chantelle thought he was agreeing with her, and continued, 'Still, I suppose it comes in handy if you get free sticky toffee pudding.' She raised her eyebrows and gave him a smirk.

'It's not free,' Jack protested. 'I pay for the food I eat.'

'But I bet she gives you extra portions,' Chantelle persisted, the smirk lingering.

'I'm sorry, you'll have to excuse me.' He got to his feet and pushed his chair back. 'I've lost my appetite.'

'Don't be like that, Jack,' she pouted. 'I was only teasing.'

That was the problem with Chantelle, Jack thought: he could never be sure whether she was being nasty or whether she was teasing, and he didn't intend to linger to find out. Those days were long gone.

He picked up his plate, gulped his orange juice down and went to walk away, but stopped when he felt Chantelle's hand on his arm. Pointedly he looked down at it, then he looked at her face, and was dismayed to see her eyes brimming with tears.

'I miss you,' she said in a small voice. 'We had some good times, didn't we?'

Jack shrugged. 'Yes, we did,' he agreed, but there had been far more bad times than good, especially towards the end.

'Do you fancy going out for a drink for old time's sake?' she asked, and when he hesitated, he watched in horror as the tears spilled over and trickled slowly down her cheeks.

Oh blast, he hated it when women cried. He never knew what to do. Should he put his arm around her? No, best not, she might get the wrong idea. But he couldn't walk away and leave her in tears, could he?

Resigned, he sat back down, and she smiled sadly at him. 'Can I take that as a yes?'

'I don't think that's a good idea,' he began, but before he could say anything further, she jumped in with, 'It's just a drink, Jack, nothing more.'

He had an awful feeling it would be more, *much more*, and definitely more than he could handle.

'How about this evening, unless you're busy?' She raised her eyebrows again and gave him a questioning look. Tears still glistened on her cheeks but no longer fell, he saw with relief.

'I am busy, as a matter of fact,' he said. 'I'm in the middle of decorating.'

'Oh? Do you need some help? I'm a dab hand with a paintbrush. I could also help you pick some colours if you like – I thought some of the shades in your house were a bit grotty, to be honest.'

'Thank you, but there's no need. I'm painting it all white.'

'How boring. What you need is a nice feature wall in a bright colour to draw the eye, instead of that nasty drab shade. But it's got to be a colour that complements the room and one you can live with,' she carried on.

'I have no intention of living with it. The house is going on the market. I'm selling up.'

Chantelle blinked. 'Why? I thought you liked living there.'

'I do, but Della and Scott want to buy the guest house they're working in, as it's come up for sale, so she needs her share of the equity.'

'Where are you going to live?'

'I've no idea at the moment,' he admitted, 'but I haven't started looking yet, and I'm sure something will turn up.'

'You know I've moved back in with Mel?' Chantelle said, and Jack could feel his shoulders sag. He knew exactly where this was heading. Mel was her old flatmate and Chantelle had never been happy living with her.

He glanced at the big clock above the door and got to his feet. 'Is that the time? Gosh, I've been here longer than I thought. I've got a meeting in ten minutes. Must dash. Sorry!' And with that he picked up his plate again and made a run for it.

To his dismay, he could hear Chantelle's heels clacking behind him, and he had almost made it to the door after depositing his plate in one of the clear-up areas, when she caught up with him.

'Let me know if you find anything of mine. I'm bound to have left something.' She gave a tinkling laugh. 'I can easily call round for it.'

'Will do,' he called and barrelled out of the cafeteria, almost running down the corridor as he headed towards his office.

When he got there, he closed the door behind him and leant against it, panting. Dear God, the woman terrified him. Why, oh why, had he let slip that he was looking for somewhere else to live? Because he knew without a shadow of a doubt that the next time he saw her she would be armed with lots of details from estate agents, and would be hinting heavily that it might be a good idea if they moved in together.

Over his dead body! Chantelle was in his past, even if she didn't want to believe it, and that was where she was going to stay.

CHAPTER 7

'Blimmin kids,' Molly muttered, as she drove the car up to the park gates. There were several teenagers lingering by the park entrance, gazing at her with sullen expressions as she shooed them out of the way to open the gates.

She was about to get back in her car, when one of them shouted, 'How come you've got the keys for them gates?'

'None of your business,' she replied haughtily. Maybe if the boy had asked the question nicely, she might have given him a proper answer.

'Did you nick 'em?'

'No, I did not!' She slid into the driver's seat and slammed the door shut rather harder than she'd intended, started the engine and eased past them, feeling slightly intimidated.

She was aware of their eyes on her as she drove around the path and into the grounds of the cottage. The area was quite open, and it occurred to her it might be a good idea to fence her property in. It might be another layer of nuisance, but it would also be another layer of security. At the moment anyone could wander in through the park gate, stroll over to her cottage and peer in through the windows if they had a mind. Was fencing it in something she would be allowed to do, she wondered? Yet another question for the council.

She began unloading her purchases as the kids dawdled past. They were in school uniform, the boys wearing black trousers, white shirts and burgundy blazers, with their ties either at half-mast or not knotted at all, and one of the girls was wearing such a short skirt that it made Molly shiver as she thought of the draught.

Molly hefted a bag out of the boot with both hands and settled it on the ground between her feet, before pulling the lid of the hatchback down. She knew it was ridiculous, but she intended to lock the car while she took this lot inside, because she didn't trust those kids one little bit.

Glancing around to check whether they were still there, she was cross to see one of them fling an empty crisp packet into the grass.

'Excuse me, you need to pick that up,' she called.

'No, I don't.' The boy's expression was belligerent as though daring her to challenge him.

Molly knew it was silly but she couldn't help herself. 'Pick it up this instant,' she said. 'Littering is an offence.'

'Make me.' The rest of the teenagers, there were six in total, had come to a halt, enjoying the show.

'You know I can't,' Molly said, 'but if a small animal gets its head stuck inside and suffocates, you will be the one to blame. Does that make you feel big?'

'Ooh,' one of the girls said. 'Get her.'

Molly knew she was fighting a losing battle. She honestly didn't know why she should even step into the breach. They clearly didn't care about the environment, or their impact on it, or about other people. Selfish, that's what they were, and no amount of having a go at them would make them change their minds. All she was doing was creating animosity and making a fool of herself.

In a fit of pique, she left her bag of shopping next to the car, marched over to the group of youngsters, bent down and snatched up the crisp packet, then held out her hand. 'If anyone has got any more rubbish they'd like to fling about, you might as well give it to me,' she said.

The kids glanced at each other. One of them shrugged and muttered, 'She's a nutter.'

Molly was beginning to think the girl's assessment was right. No one who had any sense would challenge a group of kids like this. Especially considering she was on her own. You heard such stories these days…

The group began to move off, one of them pulling out a packet of cigarettes, and Molly was quickly forgotten. She hoped. So it was with a feeling of unease that she saw the one who'd said "Make me", turn round and glare at her. He stared her in the eye for long seconds before looking away, leaving Molly feeling more than a little shaken.

Which was why the first thing she did after bringing all her purchases inside, was to phone the council.

'Hello? My name is Molly Brown and I've got a complaint about Sweet Meadow Park,' she began as soon as the phone was answered. 'Who do I need to speak to, please?'

'That'll be the Parks and Highways Department,' the receptionist said. 'Would you like me to put you through?'

'Yes, please.' Molly stood tapping her foot and chewing at her bottom lip as she waited, and had worked herself up into a fine old tizzy by the time someone came on the line.

'Parks and Highways, Pete speaking, how can I help?'

'I've got a complaint about Sweet Meadow Park,' she said, 'and I want something done about it.'

'There's a complaint form on our website, if you'd care to fill it in,' the man said.

'Actually, I don't. I want to speak to someone in person.'

'You want an appointment?' the bloke sounded a little put out.

'Yes, I believe I do.' She could put her point across much better in a face-to-face meeting rather than over the phone. 'Is that possible?'

'Um, yeah, hang on a second, I'll check Jack's diary.'

'Jack who?'

'Oh, sorry, it's Jack Feathers. He's the Parks and Highways Officer and he's better equipped to deal with your complaint than I would be. Erm… here we go… will two-thirty tomorrow be okay for you?'

'Two-thirty is fine, thank you.'

When Molly came off the phone, she was pleased that she hadn't had to fight to get an appointment to meet with someone, and before she went to bed tonight she would make a list of things she needed to discuss with him. First on the agenda was the subject of litter and bins, then she might mention the stray dog (on second thoughts perhaps not, as she recalled Bill telling her what might happen to the poor thing) and whilst she was at it she also wanted to inform him of all the layabouts hanging around in the evening. Finally, she wanted to inquire whether she needed permission to fence in what was, in effect, her own land and her property. Maybe she should lead with that instead of all the complaints, she reflected, not wanting to run the risk of alienating him from the outset.

Still feeling upset, Molly peered out of the living room window to see if any of those kids were still hanging about, but she didn't see anyone. What she did see though, was a large black dog.

It was Jet, and she hurried to find the dog food she'd bought. Thinking he might be hungry and seeing that he was a decent sized animal, she had bought several large tins. Not knowing how much a dog his size would eat, she quickly prised the lid off the first one she laid her hands on, and scooped half the contents into the bowl she'd also bought, hoping he wouldn't have disappeared by the time she went outside.

He was still there, sniffing around one of the bushes on the edge of the path, and she clicked her tongue at him, catching his attention. He looked at her, and as his ears pricked up she thought what a handsome chap he was. Jet-black as his name suggested, he was quite muscular although rather on the lean side, with dark brown eyes and a black nose. She had seen greyhounds before and he was much chunkier, but he wasn't as chunky as a Labrador, and she guessed Bill was probably right in his assessment that the dog might be a cross between the two.

She walked a few paces towards him and stopped, putting the bowl down on the ground, and then she stepped back.

His nose was twitching frantically, and she could see his tail wagging ever so slightly. He was clearly interested in what was in the bowl, but if he wanted it he had to come closer. She wasn't going to back away any further.

'Come on, boy, come on,' she called softly, crouching down so she wasn't bigger than him, hoping it would make her appear less intimidating. She didn't bother holding her hand out, knowing he would be far more interested in the food than in her empty palm, and she watched him approach cautiously, one eye on her and one eye on the bowl.

Molly remained perfectly still, speaking quietly to him until he gradually edged nearer and stuck his nose in the bowl.

This meal was gone as quickly as the one earlier this morning, and he was soon licking his lips and looking for more.

Molly laughed softly. 'I think that's enough for now,' she said. 'If you're a good boy, you can have some more later. We don't want you being sick, do we?'

She wished she had thought to fill a bowl of water for him, but it hadn't occurred to her. The poor thing must be thirsty, although he could probably drink from the pond and she suspected that might be where he quenched his thirst. It was lucky he hadn't caught something nasty, and she shuddered.

The next time she was out shopping, she would buy another bowl for water. If she left it outside by the front door and filled it every day, at least he'd know where he could get a drink.

Human and dog stared at one another for a while, Molly trying to convey that she was harmless and hoping the dog would see her as a friend, but eventually she knew she had to make a move. The electrician would be here in an hour, and she wanted to make a start in marking out where in the walls the electricity cables and the water pipes lay, before he arrived.

She was almost inside the cottage before she realised she had company, and she whirled around in a panic, thinking it might be one of the teenagers. However, when she looked down, she was astonished to see Jet. The dog was only a couple of feet away, looking at her with pleading eyes, his tail wagging.

'Do you want to come in?' she asked, and his tail continued to wag so she pushed the door open and stepped to the side.

Jet didn't move, so she went into the hall, wondering what the dog would do.

He moved forward a couple of paces, keeping the same distance away from her and when she stepped further into the hall, he followed. When she went into the living room, he came with her. He didn't appear to be unduly bothered, and she wondered whether he had lived indoors before.

Molly had brought the empty food bowl in with her so, moving carefully and slowly so as not to alarm him, she went into the kitchen, rinsed it out and filled it with water before putting it on the floor

The dog walked straight over to it and started lapping greedily, flicking water all over the tiles with his tongue. Molly laughed, and the dog stopped and lifted his muzzle, droplets dripping from it. He seemed to be grinning at her.

Molly fully expected him to leave once he'd had a drink, because the front door was still wide open, but he didn't. Instead, as soon as he'd had his fill, he gave himself a shake, then lay down in front of the range with a sigh.

'Make yourself at home, why don't you?' she said to him.

Not liking to leave the front door open, Molly walked into the hall and was about to close it, when she called to the dog.

'Jet, come here, boy.' She heard a grunt and then the click of claws on lino as the dog trotted into the hall and stood at the bottom of the stairs. 'Do you want to go back out, because I'm going to close the door now,' she said to him.

The dog stared expressionlessly at her.

'Are you sure? Last chance?'

The dog continued to stare.

'OK, but I don't expect you to have an accident, do you hear me? If you want to go out, you have to tell me.' She had no idea how the dog was supposed to do that; maybe bark, or whine, or something. 'Fine,' she said. 'You can stay if you want, but I warn you I'm going to be busy.' Then she caught herself and wondered what she was doing speaking to a dog as though it was a human being.

Feeling emboldened by the calm expression on the animal's face, Molly moved nearer.

Jet stood his ground. His tail was down but it was wagging timidly, and so far he'd not shown any signs of aggression so Molly wasn't unduly worried. She didn't have a great deal of experience with dogs, but she was hopeful this one was a gentle soul.

Once again, she crouched down and held out her hand.

This time the dog sniffed it, then he gave her fingers a lick, which made her giggle.

His eyes widened and his ears pricked at the sudden noise, but he didn't seem too perturbed.

Slowly Molly stretched her hand out further until she could touch the fur on the top of his head and she gently stroked him. His coat was velvet smooth, almost silky, and he pressed his head into the palm of her hand and let out a little whine.

'Are you enjoying that?' she asked.

The dog whined again, and his eyes slowly closed.

Molly would like to stay there all day, stroking the animal, but time was ticking on and she had so much to do. She hadn't begun to check the walls for the wires behind them yet, and the electrician was now due in less than an hour, so, after giving Jet a final pat, Molly got to her feet.

She expected the dog to remain where he was, and was surprised when she found him padding behind her, and he continued to keep her company as she moved from room to room, aiming the thingamajig at the walls and drawing a line in permanent marker whenever she found a wire or a pipe. Thankfully, the job was quite easy and she didn't find anything untoward: everything was where she expected it to be, coming straight down the wall, or up it, to end in a socket or a switch. The only anomaly was the kitchen, where there seemed to be a wire going straight across. Strange. Anyway, she marked it and reminded herself to have a word with the electrician when he arrived.

She was just finishing up in the spare bedroom, when Jet stiffened and began to growl.

'What is it, boy?' she asked, wishing she could peer through the window, but the upstairs ones were still boarded up. Then she heard the sound of an engine and for a moment she had the awful thought somebody had carjacked her little Citroen, before realising it was probably the electrician. When she'd returned after her shopping trip this morning, she'd deliberately left the big main gates open so he could bring his van in. Or that was the reason she'd told herself for not getting back out of her car and closing the gates at the time, refusing to admit the youngsters had made her feel uncomfortable.

Jet continued to rumble deep in his chest as the engine noise ceased and a vehicle door slammed shut.

Molly bounded down the stairs, the dog hot on her heels, and dashed towards the front door, opening it just as the person standing on the other side raised a hand to knock.

She blinked, wondering who this woman was and what she wanted, but then she glanced at the van and noticed the writing on it. It definitely belonged to the electrician – the company's name was emblazoned on the side. The woman was also wearing overalls and was carrying a toolbox, and the penny finally dropped: *she* was the electrician and Molly cursed herself for being so stereotypical.

'I was expecting a man,' she blurted, adding hurriedly, 'The person I spoke to on the phone was a man.'

The woman nodded. 'My dad. He's out on another job. My sister is a sparky, too. We are a proper family business with proper family values. Can I come in?'

'Sorry.' Molly stepped to the side, pushing the dog back with her legs.

'Cute,' the woman said. 'What's his name?'

'Jet.' Molly was relieved to see Jet had stopped growling and was now wagging his tail. It was an uncertain wag, but at least it was one. 'Good boy,' she said, giving him a pat. 'He's a stray.' She spoke to the dog again. 'And he could do with a bath. He's stinky.' Jet shot her a nervous look and Molly laughed. 'I think he knows what the word bath means. Yes, you are having one,' she warned him. 'No arguments. If I can get the electricity turned back on, you're going to have a bath.'

'We can't have a stinky dog, can we? So, let's see what we can do,' the electrician said, and Molly crossed her fingers as Jet allowed the woman to stroke him.

She was relieved that after Jet's initial warning growl, he had accepted the electrician's presence. On the other hand though, she was impressed he'd warned her of a potential intruder. He clearly felt at home here, and she was surprised at how safe he made her feel.

'I'll show you where the fuse box is,' she said, but as she opened the door to the cupboard under the stairs, Molly had a thought which stopped her in her tracks.

Jet would make an excellent early warning system and guard dog. No one would mess with her if he was around. Now all she had to do was to persuade him to stay.

CHAPTER 8

'Yes, Dad, it needs rewiring. I've got it covered.' Molly shifted the phone to her other ear and wedged it into her shoulder. 'He's fussing,' she mouthed at Jet, who was watching her solemnly as she swished the warm water around in the bathtub.

She hoped her shampoo would do in lieu of having any proper canine stuff. It was supposed to make her hair extra shiny, although she hadn't noticed any difference, but surely it couldn't do any harm to use it on the pooch just this once. She was too tired to go shopping for canine shampoo right now, and too dirty from all the DIY she had done today. Besides, it was too late to pay a visit to the pet shop. But the takeaways would still be open though, so she'd have a quick shower after the dog had his bath, then she would nip out and fetch some supper. Jet had a tin of succulent duck and vegetables which she would feed him while she ate her sweet and sour chicken with rice.

'Are you still there?' her dad asked.

'Sorry, I was running a bath.'

'Mind you don't try to do too much in one go,' he advised. 'You can take your time. It's not as though you're in a hurry to move in.'

Too late, Molly thought guiltily. She had already moved in. She hadn't told her mum and dad yet because she knew they would be dismayed to see the condition of the house. But with the boards off the windows downstairs, she didn't want to leave the cottage unattended overnight, especially after seeing the kids hanging around the bandstand last night and her run-in with those teenagers this morning. She doubted they meant any real harm (they were just being kids) but she couldn't help feeling unsettled.

'Are you and Mum having a good time?' Molly asked, eager to change the subject.

'We're having a great time,' her dad confirmed. 'We're about to go down to dinner, so I thought I'd give you a ring while your mother is making herself beautiful. Not that she isn't already beautiful,' he added hastily, and Molly heard her mum say, 'Flatterer', and she smiled.

She was glad they were enjoying themselves. They had stressful jobs, and they deserved some time off. It would be soon enough to tell them she'd moved out and was living in squalor when they came back. There was no point in worrying them now. Anyway, they wouldn't be home until the weekend, and that was four whole days away. She could achieve a lot in that time.

The electrician was coming back on Thursday to rewire the place (she couldn't believe her luck that they were able to do it so quickly, but they'd had a cancelation apparently) so at least the electrics would be safe, and Molly had arranged for a plasterer to come on Monday to skim the ceilings and walls. She estimated it would probably take him at least a week to complete the whole house, but when it was done the improvement would be incredible. Whilst he was doing that, she planned on sanding the floorboards upstairs and preparing the skirting boards and doorframes for a new coat of paint. At some point she would need to replace the bathroom suite (it was a weird peach colour) and install a proper shower, and she still needed new kitchen cupboards, but that could wait for a while.

After wishing her parents bon appétit, Molly put her mobile carefully out of reach and called the dog to her.

Jet slunk into the bathroom, his tail between his legs, practically crawling across the floor, and he whined apprehensively as she splashed the water, trying to persuade him it wasn't as bad as it looked. His dark brown eyes gazed up at her pleadingly, and she almost relented, fleetingly wondering whether she should change her mind about his bath after all. But as he had nowhere of his own to sleep and she didn't like the idea of him flopping down on the bare floorboards upstairs, she fully intended to let him lie on the bottom of her bed. But if she was going to do that, she'd want him smelling considerably sweeter than he did now. Hopefully her coconut and vanilla shampoo should do the trick.

Tomorrow she would pay a visit to the pet shop and buy him a bed of his own, plus a collar and a leash, and some toys to play with. She would also buy him some treats, too, in the hope she could train him, although he did seem remarkably well behaved for a stray, and she couldn't help wondering what his story was and what had happened to him. She didn't know an awful lot about dogs, but from the way he behaved she didn't think he had been badly treated, although he was rather nervous of strangers.

She had been delighted when he had let her know there was someone approaching the cottage earlier, and it had been a revelation when she realised how safe and secure the dog made her feel. He would soon inform her if there was anyone untoward around, and it was that which had given her the idea of adopting him. He seemed happy enough with her and he seemed to trust her and, provided he didn't run off the first chance he got, she would assume she was now his new owner.

Jet stood placidly in the bath (she'd had to lift him into it and he was heavier than he looked), his tail tucked between his legs, ears down and head hanging as he gazed up at her with accusing eyes.

'It's for your own good,' she told him. 'You don't want to sleep on a hard floor tonight, do you? Besides, I think you like cuddles, and I'd much prefer cuddling a sweet-smelling pooch than a stinky one. I'll get you dried off, then I'll have a quick shower and go in search of supper,' she promised. Now that the electricity had been switched on, she vowed to cook herself a proper meal tomorrow, but for this evening a takeaway would have to do.

He also probably needed to go out for a wee too, unless he'd had an accident in the house, which she prayed he hadn't. She hadn't noticed any wet patches, but then she hadn't been looking. With a sigh, she realised it was going to take her a while to get used to having an animal to care for.

With Jet duly bathed and rubbed down with one of the dustsheets, he was most concerned when she stood under the shower. He sat on his haunches a few feet away, looking at her worriedly, and she kept having to reassure him that she was OK and that she didn't mind getting wet.

When she caught herself holding a full-blown conversation with him, she laughed out loud. What was she doing? Anyone would think the dog could understand her. But from the look in his eyes, she thought perhaps he might.

She quickly dried herself off, changed into clean clothes, and went downstairs. The dog followed her, and she told him to stay as she slipped out through the front door and closed it behind her. She was worried about leaving him on his own in the house, hoping he wouldn't feel abandoned, but she had no choice. She couldn't risk taking him with her if she walked into town, because without a collar and lead she wasn't convinced she would be able to keep him safe. She'd have to rely on him walking quietly by her side, and she wasn't sure he was able to do that. But neither did she want to have him loose in her car if she drove. So that was something else she needed to get – a harness to keep him secure while she was driving. She debated whether to take the car, but she decided to jog to the Chinese takeaway and jog back, rather than have the hassle of opening and closing the main gates again.

She was breathless when she got back with a bag full of aromatic goodies, but she needn't have worried. Jet was lying sphinx-like in the hall, his front paws stretched out in front of him, staring at the door with his ears pricked. She had suspected he hadn't moved, which made her feel quite guilty, but at least she hadn't been out for long. She would have to have a serious think about what she was going to do with him when she went to work next week, but at least she would be able to nip home on her lunch break to let him out and maybe even take him for a quick walk. And she could even pop in between property visits as well. Anyway, she reasoned, it had to be better than him living rough.

Before she dished up her own meal, she emptied a tin of dog food into Jet's bowl and broke it up with a fork. As expected, he wolfed it down in a matter of seconds then sat and stared at her.

'Was that nice?'

He uttered a small whuff.

'Crumbs, I think you really do understand me,' she said, but when he whuffed again she realised he wasn't woofing at what she said, he was barking because he could smell something very nice coming from the bag.

'Oh, you want some of this, do you? I'm not sure it'll be any good for you,' she said. 'Maybe you could have one of the chicken balls, but only one: I don't want you being sick.'

She wished she had a table and chairs she could sit at to eat her supper, but she didn't, so she took the bag, a plate, and a knife and fork up to the bedroom and sat on the edge of the blow-up bed. Fully expecting Jet to try his best to get his nose on her plate, she was pleasantly surprised when he obediently sat and watched her.

However, after a while the watching made her feel guilty, as his gaze latched onto her plate and followed every forkful up to her mouth, then back to her plate again, until she eventually gave in and offered him one of the chicken balls.

It was gone in a trice.

'I don't think that touched the sides,' she admonished. 'You could at least pretend to chew it and not gulp it down.' She gave him another, after making sure it wasn't covered in sauce in case it gave him a bad tummy.

Food eaten, she decided to take a stroll around the park. She thought Jet could do with stretching his legs before bed and not only that, he probably needed to attend to some business.

Feeling nervous in case he ran off, she kept a close eye on him as he dashed over to the nearest tree and lifted his leg, the expression of bliss on his face making her giggle. She must remember to let him out at regular intervals, she remonstrated with herself. The poor thing must have been bursting but hadn't known how to tell her.

Apprehensively she began walking along the path that took her onto the field, praying he wouldn't decide to take off, but apart from scampering here and there, sniffing frantically, his whiplash tail wagging from side to side, he didn't go far. Laughing as he bounded around her in big circles, Molly carried on walking, following the treeline, taking the same route as this morning, and headed towards the meadow and the pond.

But before she got there, she had a change of heart.

What if Jet decided he wanted to go for a swim? She had just got him clean and sweet-smelling – the last thing she wanted was for him to stink of dirty pond and to be covered in mud. She would wait until she had bought him a collar and lead before venturing that way again, so she swerved to the right and carried on across the field, wishing she had a ball for him to chase. She had a feeling he was a ball-chasing kind of dog.

After circumnavigating the field a couple of times it was starting to get quite dark, so she made her way home via the boarded-up cafe and the derelict bandstand. Disappointed to see there was yet more litter scattered along the path and in the grass and the bushes, she kept having to call Jet to her when he showed too much interest in the rubbish lying around. She had bought an extendable litter-picker from the DIY shop this morning, but in all the excitement of today she'd forgotten to bring it out with her, but vowed to try to remember it tomorrow. She would take a rubbish bag with her as well and collect as much as she could, not only to try to make the park look more respectable, but also to prevent Jet from eating something he shouldn't or cutting himself on a shard of glass or a sharp can.

Tonight, like last night, there was a crowd of youngsters hanging around the bandstand, but this evening Molly didn't feel anxious. Even though Jet hadn't shown the slightest hint of aggression (apart from the warning growls at the electrician's arrival), he made her feel safe and secure, as though he was protecting her, and she noticed with interest how his gait became stiffer as they grew closer to the bandstand, and he didn't move from her side until they were well clear of it.

When he bounded ahead of her as they reached the edge of her property and scampered up to the front door where he waited for her, his tongue lolling out the side of his mouth, Molly felt tears prick the back of her eyes.

'It looks like we've both got a new home, doesn't it?' she said to the dog, and the tears broke free to trickle down her cheeks at his answering lick.

CHAPTER 9

Jack sat up straighter when he noticed the meeting in his electronic diary. He could have sworn it hadn't been there yesterday, but now he was to have a meeting this afternoon with someone called Molly Brown regarding Sweet Meadow Park. Was he finally going to meet the phantom caller face-to-face? He certainly hoped so! He was getting mighty fed up with his inbox being stuffed full of messages from reception stating that an anonymous caller had rung yet again, complaining about the state of the park.

If only whoever it was had left a phone number he could have called them back and explained the limitations of council funding. Instead, they seemed to get their kicks by ringing the council and complaining anonymously. He didn't even know whether the caller was male or female.

But maybe he did now, and he was looking forward to meeting Molly Brown in person and putting her straight.

For some reason the morning went slowly, and he was glad to escape to the cafeteria for a spot of lunch before heading back to his office and dragging up a few facts and figures he could use to present to Molly Brown. He had no doubt she would be belligerent and wouldn't want to listen to his explanations, but surely even she couldn't argue with figures that were in black and white?

As the time of the meeting grew nearer, Jack looked up the dates of the various attempted clean-ups of the park and compared them to the complaints he had received. From what he could gather, it didn't take more than a few days after he'd sent a crew in for another complaint to arrive, which was disappointing. He knew littering and fly-tipping was a problem throughout the borough, but for some reason it seemed to be worse in Sweet Meadow Park, and he couldn't for the life of him think why. Every park and every public area had issues with litter, overflowing bins, and anti-social behaviour, but none were complained about as much as the one in Sweet Meadow.

He honestly didn't know what he was expected to do about it. In the past he had sent in crew after crew to clean it up and he'd also arranged for benches to be replaced, bins to be installed, for the grass to be mown regularly, and the pathways to be kept weed-free. But less than a week after such an undertaking, the complaints came rolling in again. If people were so bothered about the blasted park, perhaps they should do something about it themselves, instead of hiding behind anonymous phone calls! Didn't they realise he only had a certain amount of funding at his disposal? He couldn't keep throwing money at it. He would like nothing better than for the park to look pretty and well cared for – after all he ran through it three or four times a week himself – but if the people who frequented it didn't care about it, why should the council? It was simply throwing good money after bad.

When the receptionist told him that his two-thirty appointment had arrived, Jack lifted his jacket off the back of the chair where it had been hanging, slipped his arms into it, and straightened his tie. Then he grabbed a file containing his findings, and prepared to do battle.

Hoping he would be able to put this thing to bed once and for all, Jack strode across the concourse and walked over to reception.

'Molly Brown?' he asked Doris, who was manning the desk.

'She's over there.'

Jack turned in the direction she was pointing.

Oh look, he noticed with pleasure, fancy seeing the woman who had bought the park keeper's cottage, the one who—

He stopped in his tracks. Bloody hell, it was *her*, wasn't it? *She* was Molly Brown – the one who had been complaining and leaving messages.

His heart sank. For some reason he had been expecting a middle-aged or elderly lady, wearing a tweed skirt, a frilly blouse, and with sturdy sensible shoes: not a woman who he was quite attracted to and whom he might have asked out for a drink, if he hadn't been feeling so raw from his relationship with Chantelle.

He caught her eye and Molly smiled when she saw him.

As he walked over to her, she said, 'Hello again, fancy seeing you here. How are you getting on with your decorating?'

Jack was flustered. 'Um, yes, fine, great, thank you. Are you Molly Brown?' He was hoping he'd made a mistake and that this wasn't Molly Brown at all. But there were only three other people waiting in the reception area and they were all male.

Confusion spread over her face. 'Yes, that's me. How do you know my name?'

'I'm Jack Feathers, Parks and Highways? We've got a meeting.'

'*You're Jack Feathers?*'

'Yes, is that a problem?'

'Not at all. I just had no idea it would be you.'

'I had no idea Molly Brown was you, either,' he said, sharper than he'd meant to.

She blinked and her eyebrows rose a notch.

'Shall we go in here?' He indicated a side room.

'Fine,' she said, the friendliness of a few seconds ago melting away.

His heart sank even further. She'd be even less friendly when she heard what he had to say.

He opened the door for her, and she went in ahead of him. Gesturing for her to take a seat, he sat in the chair opposite and opened his folder. He could see her looking at it warily.

'I must say, it's nice to finally put a face to all those phone calls,' he said. 'I think it's been one or two a week for the past year or so.' He wasn't entirely sure how long he had been getting them – it might be less than that, but it felt considerably longer.

'Excuse me?' She was staring at him quizzically.

'The phone calls about the litter and the anti-social behaviour from a certain sector of society?'

Now she was frowning. Clearly she didn't like being challenged about it.

'What phone calls?' she asked.

'Come along Miss, or is it *Mrs* Brown? We both know it's you who's been making the phone calls. Now, I have no problem with that,' he continued, 'but I wish you had left your name and number so I could have rung you back and explained the situation.'

'It's *Ms* Brown, and the only phone call I made was the one I made yesterday when I booked an appointment to see you.' Her tone was frosty and a spot of colour had appeared on each cheek.

Jack was flummoxed. Was she telling the truth? He didn't see any reason for her to lie, especially not when she was sitting there in front of him. 'It wasn't you?'

'It most certainly was not! Do I look like the sort of person who would make anonymous phone calls? If I've got something to say, I'll say it to your face. Which is why I'm here today. Can we move on?'

'Yes, of course, sorry. I must have got the wrong end of the stick.' Oh dear, this wasn't going well, was it?

She shrugged and looked pointedly down at the papers in front of him.

Jack took the hint and got on with it. 'Can you tell me why you wanted to see me?' he began, wondering if it *was* to do with the littering and the anti-social behaviour, or whether she had something else on her mind. He had already got the person behind the anonymous phone calls wrong, so he might have got the reason for Molly wanting a meeting with him wrong too.

'As you're aware, I've recently purchased the old park keeper's cottage,' she began, her words and her tone rather formal, and he guessed she was still quite annoyed. 'I want to know if I'm allowed to fence off my garden area. The land behind the cottage isn't a problem because its boundary is the actual perimeter fence of the park itself, but I'm referring to the front of the cottage. At the moment any Tom, Dick or Harry could wander up to my front door and peer in through my windows. I'd like to know whether I can fence it in.'

Jack blinked. He hadn't been expecting that. Relieved that she wasn't going to have a go at him about the state of the park, he shuffled the papers, stalling for time as he tried to think of any reason why she couldn't put a boundary fence around the cottage.

'Let me see,' he said. He tapped his pen against his chin as he thought, hurriedly going through numerous bylaws in his mind before coming to a decision. 'There's no reason why you can't, but I'm not sure a six-foot high brick wall would go down too well. We would probably want to make sure the fencing was in keeping with that around the rest of the park.'

'Do you mean derelict, rusting and with paint peeling off?' she shot back.

He deserved that. 'What I meant is, you either use metal railings similar to those around the perimeter of the park, or possibly some kind of a picket fence would be acceptable.'

'Can I go with a picket fence?' she asked. 'I quite like the sound of that. And I wouldn't want a six-foot-high brick wall either,' she added.

'Good, good, that's settled then.' He began to gather his papers up, before realising Molly was staring at him pointedly.

'Is that all?' he asked.

'No, it's not. I'm in agreement with your phantom phone caller in that the amount of litter in the park is unacceptable. It's everywhere, and it doesn't help that there aren't any bins. What are you going to do about it?'

Jack felt on safer ground. 'I'm afraid there's not a lot we *can* do about it,' he said, and hurried on as she opened her mouth to argue. 'You see, the park has already had a considerable amount of man-hours and money spent on it, all to no avail. Here, take a look at this.' He shoved a summary in front of her, hoping that would do, but if it didn't, he had reams of paperwork behind it to back it up.

He watched her face as she read it quickly. The way her lashes curled and the arch of her eyebrows proved to be particularly interesting. As did the curve of her cheek and the faint smattering of freckles across her nose. She was biting at her bottom lip, and he caught a flash of white teeth as she nibbled. Once again Jack wondered what it would be like to kiss her, but even as the unnerving thought entered his head, he swiftly shoved it away.

He cleared his throat. 'Do you see what I mean?'

'I do, but that doesn't mean the park should be left to rot,' she argued. 'If anything, it's a danger to the public and to wildlife.'

'I'm aware there are issues,' Jack interrupted. 'We do have plans to remove the bandstand and the old cafe, and to fill in the pond.'

'Oh.' For some reason the woman sitting in front of him didn't look too pleased with his answer.

'Is there a problem?' He would have thought she would be delighted with the news.

'You do realise that the pond is a haven for wildlife?'

'It's a haven for shopping trolleys,' he muttered.

'Precisely, which is why it needs dredging.'

'*Dredging?* I don't think so.' Jack was horrified. There was no way the council would stretch to dredging the pond in Sweet Meadow Park. However, he could probably make a case for knocking down the bandstand and the old cafe, and then use the debris from those buildings to fill in the pond. Pop some gravel on top, followed by a bit of earth… job done! No more danger to the general public.

'I was hoping the bandstand could be repaired,' she said, trying a different tack.

'That would cost too much, I'm afraid,' Jack replied, without hesitation.

'Have you looked into it? Or are you just saying no for the sake of it?'

Jack didn't appreciate the insinuation. 'I don't say no for the sake of it,' he retorted. 'I'm saying no because the council has limited funds and far more deserving causes on which to spend them.'

'So you're refusing to help?'

'I'm not exactly refusing, I'm just not in a position to.'

'Is there anyone who is?'

'No. I run the Parks and Highways Department,' he said. 'I'm the one responsible for its budget.'

He thought he heard her mutter 'Jobsworth' under her breath, but when he said, 'Sorry, I didn't catch that?' she narrowed her eyes at him.

Her full lips were set in a straight line, and her gaze was flinty. 'You're telling me that nothing can be done to clean up Sweet Meadow Park and restore it to its former glory?'

'Hang on a sec, I thought you were asking me to sort out the litter? Not to give it a complete makeover.'

'Litter bins would be a start,' she said.

'Litter bins have proved ineffective in the past in reducing littering in the park,' he countered. 'I see no reason why installing new ones would solve the problem. The residents of Sweet Meadow appear not to value the park, and I don't believe putting a couple of bins here and there would alter the general public's attitude.'

Molly said nothing, she just looked at him, her gaze steady.

Jack felt like squirming.

Eventually she said, 'That's it? That's your final word on the matter?'

'I'm afraid it is.' Jack gathered his papers together once more.

Abruptly Molly got to her feet, shoving her chair back. 'We'll see about that.' And with that, she flung the door open and marched out.

Jack watched her stride across the concourse, heading for the revolving doors, and even as he was glad to see the back of her, he thought the back of her was rather nice. Her hips were swinging in her well-fitting jeans, her waist was small, her head was held high, and her hair bounced in its ponytail.

He watched until she was out of sight, thinking it was a pity that they'd got off on such a bad foot, because she really was extremely pretty. Despite not wanting another relationship, he could still admire a beautiful woman and he could still feel attracted to her, even if he didn't have any intention of doing anything about it.

Jack smiled ruefully. If he ever intended to immerse himself in the dating game again, she would be exactly the sort of woman he'd ask out.

Then he swiftly wiped the smile off his face when he spotted Chantelle glaring at him. She was standing near the exit and he guessed she must have seen him staring at Molly.

Lowering his head, he picked up his folder and shot out of the meeting room, hurrying to his office. If Chantelle felt threatened by Sue from the canteen, then goodness knows how she would react if she realised that he fancied the socks off the new owner of the cottage in Sweet Meadow Park.

***

Molly stormed out of the council offices, angrily shoving at the automatic revolving doors because they didn't move fast enough, and strode into the car park. She was furious, even though she had already guessed that the council wouldn't be prepared to do anything about the park, because if they had been, they would have done so already. Obviously she wasn't the only one to have complained, because that Jack guy had thought she was someone else, someone who clearly made a habit of it. Perhaps she should start complaining on a weekly basis, too? Although, she didn't think it would get her anywhere. Maybe if she got a petition together? If she drummed up some interest in the park, persuaded people to write in, or phone, or e-mail, or anything really, the council would have to sit up and take notice.

As she unlocked her car and sank into the driver's seat, she tapped her fingers crossly on the steering wheel, recognising that most people wouldn't want to get involved or were just plain lazy, and if something didn't affect them directly, they weren't interested. She knew she would have scant luck in persuading people to put pen to paper, so to speak. She could always go around knocking on doors and collecting signatures but, if she was honest, she didn't have the time. Not at the moment, not with trying to get her house habitable. She would have to see to that first before she turned her sights on the park.

At least Jack had agreed that there was no reason why she couldn't fence in her property, and she was glad she had tackled him about that before she'd spoken of anything else, guessing maybe he wouldn't have been so helpful if he'd realised he was going to be questioned about the council's responsibility to keep the park in a decent condition.

Jack Feathers was nothing more than a jobsworth. He might be good-looking and she might think he was hot – she cringed when she recalled how embarrassed she had been when she'd met him in the DIY store yesterday and how she'd blushed when she'd uttered the word "buff", thinking it described him perfectly – but today he was nothing like she'd imagined him to be. When he had come to her rescue as she was trying to get the final board off the downstairs windows, she'd thought he was kind and thoughtful, and muscular. Scratch the muscular bit. It didn't do to dwell on his physical attributes, because his looks certainly didn't match his insides. In fact, she thought he had been quite dismissive, and she'd had the feeling she was nothing more than a nuisance and an annoyance, and he couldn't wait to get rid of her.

She'd show him; as soon as she had managed to break the back of the work she needed to do on the house, she would tackle the garden, and then she would expand into the park itself. She'd start with the flower beds nearest to the main gate. An hour here and an hour there should see them tidied up and dug over. She didn't have the money to plant anything, but she was pretty sure once she'd got rid of all the weeds there might be some decent shrubs and perennials lurking in them.

There *was* something she could do immediately however, and that was to litter pick, and she had done precisely that when she had taken Jet for his morning walk.

She smiled as she thought of the dog. Last night she'd felt considerably safer having him by her side, and although she'd planned for him to sleep near her feet, she had woken up with her nose buried in his neck and her arm around his chest. He'd snored a bit, but she hadn't minded: it had been quite comforting. She hadn't appreciated being woken at five-thirty though, but once she was awake and on her feet, and with her hands around a cup of tea, she forgave him.

Once again he'd stuck close by her as she strolled around the park with a rubbish bag in one hand and her litter picker in the other, and once in a while he had even picked up a plastic bottle and had brought it to her, dropping it at her feet, and she began to appreciate some of those stickers she'd seen which stated "I prefer my dog to people". Jet had more of a social conscience than many of the people who used the park, she concluded.

She supposed she could also include Jack Feathers in that statement. She certainly preferred Jet to *him*. He couldn't care less about Sweet Meadow Park, which was a surprise considering he'd jogged through it the other evening. He clearly didn't give two hoots about it. Fancy wanting to tear down the old bandstand! She admitted it needed some repairs, but it was a piece of history and it would be sacrilegious to destroy it.

Giving the council offices a baleful glare, Molly started the engine and made her way towards the builders' merchant, where she purchased a pair of wooden gates, a smaller side gate, several sturdy posts, a spade, a couple of bags of quick-drying cement, a wheelbarrow and forty metres of picket fencing, all to be delivered tomorrow. Goodness knows when she would have time to build the fence, but at least if the materials were on hand, she could make a start. For now though, she had to pop to the pet shop and buy some necessary items for Jet, and then go to the supermarket to find something for tea. Oh, and she needed to buy a fridge.

At the rate she was spending money, her bank balance was emptying faster than the dog's food bowl!

CHAPTER 10

Molly had never used a range in her life and she was sceptical about using one now. But it was either that or go hungry, because she fully intended to make herself spaghetti bolognese for tea, but she couldn't do that without something to cook it on.

As well as purchasing a fridge, she had also bought a new oven, but the items weren't coming until Friday and she didn't think her bank balance could carry on being able to afford takeaways every evening, and neither could her waistline. So she'd bought a bag of salad leaves, half a cucumber and a couple of tomatoes, which she intended to eat with her spaghetti bolognese this evening. But first, she had to cook it, and until the oven arrived the only option was to light the range. It sat in an alcove at the far end of the kitchen, black and menacing, and she eyed it with caution.

She was right to. Even though she had looked up instructions on how to light the fire on the internet, thirty-five minutes later all she had to show for her efforts was a kitchen full of smoke and a pile of pathetic ashes. Not only that, she guessed it was probably a good thing she hadn't lit it, because no doubt the chimney would need sweeping. Even though she'd assumed the chimney in the sitting room would need to be swept, it hadn't occurred to her until now that there would be a chimney attached to the range in the kitchen.

Good grief, adulting wasn't easy, was it? And neither was home ownership.

There was nothing for it but to use the old camping stove, so she took the ingredients for her meal outside and cooked her supper al fresco. It would have been fun if she hadn't *had* to do it; if she had been camping properly with friends and had a couple of glasses of something fizzy and alcoholic, she might have enjoyed the experience, but as it was, using the camping stove was simply a means to an end. However, once she had loaded up her plate with spaghetti and salad, she felt quite pleased with herself, so she continued with the al fresco theme and sat on the back step to eat it, with her plate on her knees and Jet by her side.

'Stop dribbling,' she told him as he gazed mournfully at her food. 'It's not your best look.'

She'd already fed him, but the dog was a dustbin on legs. He seemed to be perpetually hungry, and he hoovered up the little bit of spaghetti she gave him and looked for more.

Meal eaten, she picked up the dog's lead and attached it to his newly purchased collar, then she grabbed a ball and popped it in her pocket.

'Shall we go for a walk?' she asked, and the dog bounced excitedly around her legs, nearly tripping her up.

Molly had hardly got out of the door, when she spotted Bill and Patch in the distance. Jet saw them at the same time, and his tail began to wag furiously, clearly recognising the old man and his canine companion.

As she approached, Molly was aware that Bill was studying the dog.

'Well, I never,' he said, when she grew close enough to hear him. 'Have you taken him in?'

'I certainly have. I couldn't have a stray dog wandering around the park, not when I'm living here.' She nodded at the cottage. 'He seems to have settled in, but it's early days yet.'

'He's looking better already,' Bill said, and she fell into step with him as they dawdled along the path.

Seeing that there was no one else around, Molly let Jet off the lead, and the two dogs sniffed each other and began to play.

'You haven't taken those boards off them upstairs windows,' Bill pointed out.

'Not yet. My parents are away on holiday at the moment, but they'll be back on Saturday, and my dad said he'd help me remove them on Sunday. I haven't got a ladder – well, not one that reaches up to the first floor, and even if I did, I wouldn't trust myself on it.' She was about to say that she'd also had help with the last of the downstairs ones, but it brought Jack Feathers firmly into the forefront of her mind and she didn't want to think about him right now. In fact, she didn't want to think about him at all. He had been such a disappointment.

But even as she was busy trying to divert her thoughts away from his face, her eyes were scanning the park, hoping to catch a glimpse of him in his Lycra and his trainers.

'I see you had an electrician in,' Bill said.

Crikey, the old man didn't miss much, she thought. 'I did. The cottage needs rewiring.'

'It needs a lot more than that,' he grumbled.

'Actually, it's not too bad. Surprisingly the building itself is sound. I wouldn't have bought it otherwise.

The inside needs updating, but most of it is cosmetic, although I intend to leave some of the period features.'

'The rats, you mean?'

'There aren't any rats,' she objected. 'And if there were, I'm sure Jet would see them off. I'll probably have to get new windows at some point and new exterior doors, but the interior doors are lovely. They are old fashioned, with oval panes of glass in them, and they're made from real wood – none of this woodchip rubbish. And you ought to see the bannister. They don't make them like that these days.'

'Seen a lot of bannisters in your time, have you?'

'Actually, I have. You forget I'm an estate agent. I get to see a lot of properties.'

'Oh, yes, so you are. In that case, I'd have thought you'd have more sense than to buy that old place.'

Molly smiled. If she was honest, she had to admit she had let her heart rule her head. Although the park keeper's cottage hadn't been terribly expensive, neither had it been dirt cheap, and with the cost of the renovations...

Telling herself it would be gorgeous when it was finished, even if that did take a while due to lack of funds and her being only one person, she lifted her chin. 'I like it,' she replied firmly.

'That's OK, then,' Bill said. 'I still wouldn't have bought it,' he added.

'So you keep telling me.' She took a breath. 'I went to the council offices today.'

'Oh, aye?'

'I met with the Parks and Highways Officer to complain about the state of the park.'

'Bet you didn't get anywhere.'

'No, I didn't,' she admitted. 'I told him the park needed litter bins, and there might be some issues with health and safety. He came back with the news that the council is going to demolish the bandstand and the old cafe, and they're going to fill in the pond. That's not what I wanted them to do at all.'

'Got any better ideas?'

'Yes, I do. Do you go walking around the pond?'

'Not often these days.'

'It's got a shopping trolley in it, maybe more than one. And discarded tyres. I suggested that they dredge it, but this Jack chap was having none of it. Doesn't he realise it's a magnet for wildlife? And I would love to see the bandstand restored and the cafeteria opened again.'

Bill was looking at her strangely. 'Who do you suggest is going to pay for all this?' he asked.

'The council, of course.'

'They've got other things they need to spend their money on. All those ruddy great big potholes in the roads for a start.'

'But aren't parks important, too?'

'Only if people appreciate them and use them,' Bill shot back.

'That's more or less what he told me. He also said they've tried to make it nice in the past, but people around here don't appreciate it.'

'They don't. You've seen for yourself the youngsters hanging about till all hours of the night, smoking and drinking and dropping their fast-food wrappers everywhere.' He gave her a meaningful look and she knew he'd definitely seen her peering through the window the other night. 'I have noticed something, though,' he said. 'There ain't so much litter this past day or so.'

'That's because I picked it up this morning,' she admitted.

'I thought the council had been out.'

Molly snorted. 'Fat chance. I'm going to try to litter pick every morning. There's no point in me whingeing about it if I'm not prepared to do something about it myself.'

'Good for you.'

'And not only that, I've also decided I'm going to try to spruce the park up a bit.'

It was Bill's turn to snort. 'Haven't you got enough on your plate?'

'I have,' she agreed, 'but it won't hurt to tidy up a flower bed or two.'

'You'll be lucky if you manage even that. The park is a big place. You'll need an army of people to knock it into shape.'

'I was only thinking about a couple of flower beds,' she replied, chastened.

'If I was younger, I'd give you a hand.' Bill looked cross, as though he was annoyed with himself for his advanced age.

'That's OK, I can manage,' Molly assured him, but deep down she wondered whether she could manage at all. It was one thing to say she was going to tidy up the park, it was another thing to do it. Still, she would try her best, and she would also keep on at the council.

First, though, she had a cottage to renovate.

***

Jack didn't appreciate feeling a heel, but that was exactly what he felt like today. After his meeting with Molly Brown, he returned to his office feeling rather discontented. He wished he had the funds available to help clean up the park, but he simply didn't have them. It wasn't his money to spend, and he was accountable for every penny of it. If there was an immediate health and safety issue he could do something about it and he would, but as for making the park a more pleasant place to be, his hands were tied. His budget was set for the rest of the financial year and nearly all of it was already accounted for, and he knew exactly where the peaks and troughs would be in terms of expenditure. There was money set aside for emergencies such as when trees needed to be felled or cleared, but that didn't mean to say he could spend it willy-nilly.

He'd gone home in a right grump, and totally out of sorts. He felt as though he'd let Molly down personally, even though it was a professional matter, and he felt he was to blame for her obvious disappointment. He could tell she thought so too, by the look in her eyes.

He had intended to go for a run this evening to let off some steam before he returned to his decorating, but unless he varied his route he would end up going through the park, and he didn't think he could face it.

Instead, he dinged a ready meal in the microwave and gulped it down, burning the roof of his mouth in the process, before hastily changing into some old clothes. Picking up the paintbrush once again, he went upstairs and examined the walls in the spare room critically before deciding they would do. He couldn't see any obvious bits he'd missed, so he re-hung the curtains after giving them a quick once over with the iron, and then he closed the door. One room down, six more to go: seven if he included the hall, stairs and landing.

Feeling daunted, he walked into his sister's old room. Before he'd downed tools last night, he had given it a good sort out and a thorough clean, and had draped everything remaining in the room with old sheets so he would be ready to start work as soon as he got home today.

He had painted one and a half walls and was on a roll, when he heard a knock on the door. Jack thought about ignoring it, as he wasn't expecting any visitors and neither was he expecting a parcel. It was probably someone out canvassing; local elections were coming up shortly, which, he suspected, was one of the reasons there was a job evaluation exercise taking place at work, and rumours that every department was going to be restructured and some of them amalgamated. He tried not to think about it because it made him feel sick. He didn't know what he would do if he was made redundant. His living arrangements were precarious enough as it was, without adding losing his job to his worries.

He cursed himself for not questioning Chantelle yesterday when she'd cornered him in the cafeteria, but he had been too eager to get away. She might know what was going on, what with working in HR, so the next time he saw her he vowed to pick her brains.

On second thoughts though, maybe he wouldn't. For one thing, she shouldn't tell him anything, and for another it didn't seem right cosying up to her just to get information. He didn't want to give her any hope they might get back together.

Chantelle was still very much on his mind when he went downstairs to answer the door, and for a moment he thought he must have conjured her up when he saw her standing on his step, smiling brightly and holding a bottle of wine.

'What are you doing here?' he blurted.

'That's charming,' she said pushing past him and walking into the hall.

Jack blinked, hesitating before closing the door and going into the living room after her.

'Did you want something?' he asked, thinking she had a cheek to barge in.

'A couple of things, actually,' she said. 'I wondered if you'd found anything of mine?' She simpered and fluttered her eyelashes at him. 'Anything *personal*. The sort of thing you couldn't bring to work.'

Jack was flummoxed. 'Like what?'

'You know, underwear...?'

'Sorry, no. Have you lost something?'

'Not that I'm aware of, but you never know,' she said. 'Would you like me to help you look?'

'If you haven't lost anything, there's no point in you looking for it, is there, because you don't know what you're looking for,' Jack pointed out reasonably.

'Never mind,' she said. 'The second thing is, I thought I'd give you a hand with the decorating.'

He realised she was wearing brand-new white overalls and her long blond hair was tied up with a length of fabric in a messy bun on the top of her head. Knowing Chantelle as he did, it had probably taken her ages. Her makeup was also immaculate, as usual. He wondered how she would cope if she got paint on her nails, and he realised that along with the bottle of wine, she also had a pair of bright yellow gloves in her hand.

'I don't need any help,' he began, but before he could say anything else, she said, 'Nonsense. Of course you need help. It's unreasonable of Della to expect you to decorate the whole house by yourself.'

'But she can't help,' Jack reminded her. 'She's in Alaska.'

'Lucky for some.'

'Yes, I suppose it is.' He didn't envy Della being in Alaska as such, but what he did envy was the fact that his sister had found love. She was blissfully, deeply, madly in love.

'I still think she could have made an effort to come back and help,' Chantelle was saying. 'It's not fair to leave it all to you. But you don't *have* to do it all on your own, do you? I'm here now.'

'It's fine, honestly.'

Chantelle ignored him. 'Shall we tackle this room first?' She was gazing around the living room, her nose wrinkling.

'I'm doing upstairs and working my way down.'

'Oh, *upstairs*.' Chantelle shot him a look from underneath lowered lashes. It was meant to be seductive, but all Jack felt was nervous. 'I see you've started without me.' She pointed to his clothes

He glanced down at his old T-shirt and faded joggers. There were smears of paint over both of them. 'Look Chantelle, I don't mean to be rude, but I don't need your help. I'm sure you've got other things to do.'

'I've kept this evening free especially for you,' she said, and he shook his head in despair.

There was nothing for it, he was going to have to be extremely blunt and tell her to leave.

He opened his mouth to tell her precisely that, when she said, 'There is something else. I mentioned yesterday that I'm back at my old place, living with Mel. It's not ideal. She wants her boyfriend to move in, so she wants me to move out. I thought that considering both you and I will soon be homeless – unless you've managed to find somewhere else already?' She looked at him questioningly and he shook his head. 'Then might it be a good idea for us to find somewhere together? It would make total financial sense,' she added.

It wouldn't make *emotional* sense, Jack thought. It would be the most disastrous thing he could think of doing. He had managed to get rid of her once, and he couldn't imagine how difficult it would be if both their names were on the rental agreement. He shuddered at the thought.

'I don't think so,' he said. 'Chantelle, you know I think the world of you, but me and you don't work.'

'I can see that,' she said, but the look in her eyes told him she didn't see that at all. 'This would be as friends,' she insisted.

'No, sorry.' He said it as gently as he could, but he could see the disappointment in her face, which quickly turned to anger. Chantelle had never liked being thwarted.

'Don't come running to me when you haven't got anywhere to live,' she snapped. 'I was only trying to be friendly. I was doing this for you, not me, because I've already got something lined up.'

Despite himself he said, 'You have? Good for you.'

'And I didn't mean we would be anything other than housemates, because I wouldn't get back with you if you begged me. I'm seeing someone else.'

'I'm pleased for you,' he said mildly, wondering if it was true. Only yesterday she had come on to him, suggesting they got back together, and this evening she had openly flirted with him.

'He's ten times the man you are,' she said. 'He knows how to treat a woman.'

'That's good.' Jack was nodding inanely, wishing she would leave. He knew she was trying to save face and his rejection must hurt, but she was taking things to the extreme.

'Don't bother seeing me out,' she said, thrusting the bottle of wine at him. 'Consider this a moving present.'

Jack took it automatically and as he was dithering, wondering whether he should hand it back to her, she strode past him and into the hall. He hurried after her and was just in time to see her waltz through the door and slam it. The frame rattled as the whole house shook, and he winced.

If it was at all possible, Jack felt even more of a heel now than he had done after meeting Molly Brown. It wasn't as though he'd treated Chantelle shabbily, but she had made him feel as though he had. They simply weren't compatible, but she didn't seem to understand that, or accept it.

However, his overwhelming feeling was one of relief that she'd gone. Which made him feel even worse.

How can you live with someone for nearly a year and feel nothing for them? Did that make him a bad person?

He hoped not, but even as he was thinking it, Molly's face popped into his mind. She clearly thought he was, and in some ways he couldn't blame her. For the umpteenth time that day he wished he could do something to help. Maybe he could litter pick? It was a thought.

Sighing despondently, he dismissed the idea. He had far too much going on in his life at the moment to think about adding anything else to it. His immediate concern was getting the house ready before the estate agent arrived on Monday to take photos, and when that was done, he simply must turn his attention to finding somewhere else to live. After he'd gone to bed last night, he had been unable to sleep and had scrolled through various property sites for ages. He would bet his last pound he'd probably end up doing the same thing again tonight.

The problem with painting, Jack mused as he rollered his way across another wall, was that it didn't occupy the brain, and yet again he found his thoughts turning to the woman living in the park keeper's cottage.

He didn't know why she kept popping into his mind, but he couldn't seem to get rid of her, which annoyed him considerably – because even if he was interested in her (he wasn't: he didn't have the time nor the energy) he had a feeling he had well and truly burnt his bridges as far as she was concerned.

CHAPTER 11

Although Molly's week off had been extremely hard work and she was so exhausted she could do with another – this time lying on a beach and being served cocktails by a hunky waiter – it had been incredibly fruitful.

She could hardly believe the difference between last Monday and this. This time last week, she had been looking forward to collecting the keys to her brand new home. And now, within the space of seven days, she had moved in, the cottage had been rewired, she'd sanded the floorboards upstairs, had removed the grotty lino from downstairs to reveal the most gorgeous tiled floor (it had been criminal to cover it up), and yesterday her dad had helped her take the boards off the upstairs windows.

Her mum had come with him and she had been absolutely shocked and horrified at the conditions under which her only daughter was living, and had tried her utmost to persuade Molly to come home to live until the plastering was done, at the very least.

Her dad hadn't been quite so concerned: he had been more interested in poking a screwdriver into the wooden window frames to check whether they were rotten. Thankfully they weren't. They'd probably do her another couple of years, but for that to happen she needed to sand them down, taking them back to the bare wood and revarnishing them; yet another job to add to her ever-growing list. Plus, one of the upstairs panes was cracked, so she would need to get it replaced.

Her mother's face when she had seen the interestingly coloured bathroom suite had made Molly giggle, though. She had insisted on donning a pair of rubber gloves and liberally splashing bleach everywhere, as though she could remove the colour.

'It's not too bad,' Molly had said. 'Actually, it's growing on me. It's quite retro.'

'Retro isn't a word I would have used,' her mother had said. 'Try old-fashioned. Past it. Horrid.'

However, her parents had managed to persuade her to come to their house for Sunday lunch: Molly certainly wasn't going to turn that down. And neither was Jet. To Molly's surprise, her parents had accepted the dog without question, probably too shocked about everything else for the animal's presence to register. Molly had driven over with Jet strapped into the passenger seat. He had sat there, trying to stick his nose out of the window, his ears flapping in the breeze, and when she got to her mum's he'd behaved impeccably. In fact, he'd positioned himself in the kitchen and had spent most of the time staring longingly at the oven door with the delicious smells emanating from it.

'I'm still not sure about you living in the middle of the park,' Teresa had said. 'Even with your new guardian.'

'He's a softy,' Molly said, playing with Jet's silky ears.

'That's what I'm worried about,' her mother retorted. 'He's not exactly a guard dog, is he?'

'Oh, I don't know,' Molly had replied. 'He certainly tells me if there's anyone around. Thankfully he doesn't bother if they're walking along the path, but as soon as somebody steps onto my property, he has a good shout about it.'

Her dad had questioned her about the neatly stacked fencing and wooden posts down the side of the house, and when she'd told him she intended to fence in her land, he'd nodded his head in agreement. 'I think that's an excellent idea,' he had said. 'You don't want the general public wandering into your garden.'

After work this evening, Molly fully intended to make a start on putting up the posts. She had watched numerous YouTube videos on how to erect a fence, and she was fairly confident she should be able to do it. The hardest part would be digging the hole, but she had a nice sharp shovel with a pointed end, and lots of determination and enthusiasm. She had also bought a spirit level and some cheap plastic buckets, and she intended to use one of the boards taken off the windows to mix the cement on. She had it all worked out, and she was feeling very pleased with herself. The only fly in the ointment, was her having to go to work today, because she would love nothing better than to crack on with the fence building.

The other reason Molly was reluctant to go to work was because she didn't want to leave Jet. She had left him on his own a couple of times over the course of last week because she'd had no choice – she hadn't been able to take him to the shops, or to her appointment at the council offices – and neither did she have any choice today. She had to go to work.

After making sure Jet's water bowl was full and he had been out for a wee, she gave him a chew to gnaw on to keep him occupied while she was gone.

'I won't be long,' she told him. 'Be good and I'll be back in a couple of hours.'

She had no real idea when she would be able to take her lunch break, because it would depend on whether she had any viewings, but she was certain she could pop back at least once, if not twice, throughout the course of the day to check on him.

'How was your week off?' Astrid asked, after they'd made a cup of tea.

Molly had missed chatting to her friend and colleague, even though she hadn't missed being at work. Astrid was a few years older than her and was divorced, with two young sons, but despite their personal lives being so different, she and Molly got on like a house on fire.

'Really good thanks.' And she preceded to fill Astrid in on what she'd been getting up to, ending with, 'I've even managed to get myself a dog.'

Astrid raised perfectly arched eyebrows. 'A puppy?'

'No, he's an adult dog. I'm not quite sure how old he is – maybe three or four? It's a guess really, because he's a stray. He was living wild in the park, and for some reason he decided he liked me and followed me into the house. I didn't have the heart to shoo him back out again.'

Astrid said, 'I had a boyfriend like that once. He used to follow me everywhere. I couldn't get rid of him. If truth be told, I think I would have preferred a dog.'

'I certainly do!' Molly cried.

She'd not had a boyfriend for at least eighteen months, not a proper one. She had been on several dates during that time, but none of them had led to anything. There was only one man she would have liked to have seen again, but he hadn't seemed too interested in her, so she hadn't pursued the matter. There were plenty more fish in the sea, and she was only twenty-nine, so had loads of time to find someone she wanted to settle down with. And that certainly wasn't going to be anytime soon, because she didn't have time to date right now, and probably wouldn't for some months to come. Besides, there wasn't anyone she wanted to date.

Unbidden, Jack's face swam into her mind and she gave a huff of exasperation.

'What's wrong?' Astrid asked.

'It's nothing. I was thinking about some guy at the council offices.'

'What guy?'

'I had a meeting with him to try to persuade him to do something about the park, but he was having none of it.'

Astrid was giving her a strange look. 'You're blushing.'

'I am not. It's warm in here.'

'Not that warm,' Astrid argued. 'What's he like, this guy?'

'A jobsworth,' Molly said, her tone implying that she didn't want to talk about it anymore.

Astrid didn't take the hint. 'How old is he?'

Molly typed her password into the computer and stared pointedly at the screen, refusing to answer.

'What does he look like?' Astrid persisted. 'You're still blushing.'

'I'm not blushing,' Molly declared. 'I'm annoyed with him, that's all. What have I got on today?' she asked, changing the subject.

Astrid pulled a face. 'I'll get it out of you eventually,' she warned, before switching to work mode. 'I thought I'd break you in gently this morning so you can get on with some paperwork, but this afternoon I've arranged some viewings. One of them is showing a couple around the house on Digby Avenue – the vendors have dropped the price, and it's starting to get some interest – and the second is a new instruction. It's not far from you, so I thought you could do that on your way home.'

Molly smiled at Astrid's thoughtfulness. Although Molly might not have wanted to be here today, she did love her job, and she loved the people she worked with. There were four of them in the office: Astrid who made all the appointments, balanced the books, and dealt with the solicitors, Mike who owned the agency, and Ricky, who was Molly's counterpart.

She was soon in the swing of it again, concentrating on her job and only thinking about her lovely cottage and her gorgeous dog now and again. But in amongst those thoughts, the Parks and Highways Officer's handsome face persisted in putting in an appearance, much to her annoyance.

She blamed Astrid – it was her fault for teasing her about him.

***

Jack finished work as soon as he could, and hurried home. Although he had been up since the crack of dawn to make sure the house looked as perfect as possible, he was still paranoid about it being in a mess.

It had been one hell of a rush to complete all the decorating, and he'd only finished yesterday afternoon. After spending the rest of the evening cleaning (he had even taken everything out of the kitchen cupboards and wiped the shelves down in case any potential purchasers had a mind to look inside), he'd been exhausted. It didn't help his frame of mind that he'd have to keep the house as pristine as it was now for several weeks, or even months, to come – depending on how long it took to sell. Jack didn't regard himself as a particularly messy person and he cleaned the house on a regular basis, but he'd not had to face having strangers traipse through his home before, and the thought made him anxious.

By the time four o'clock arrived, Jack found himself pacing around the living room, into the kitchen and back again, and with each circuit he peered out the window to see if there was a strange car parked outside.

It was just his luck that he was on the furthest reach of his circuit (ie. in the kitchen) when the doorbell rang, making him jump.

Clearing his throat and plastering a smile on his face, he hurried to answer it. He was about to say, 'Hello, thank you for coming,' when he froze. Because the person standing in front of him was none other than Molly Brown.

Jack panicked, wondering how on earth she had got his address, concerned she was stalking him.

But to his surprise, she seemed equally as shocked.

For a moment the two of them stared at each other, then both began talking at once.

'You go first,' he said, hoping that the sooner she explained why she was here, the sooner he could get rid of her. He didn't want the estate agent turning up when there was a mad woman on his doorstep.

'I'm from Watkin and Wright, Estate Agents,' she said, then stepped back to check the house number attached to the wall next to the front door. 'This *is* number four, isn't it?'

Jack nodded, his mouth dry.

'And this *is* Oakland Road?' she asked.

He nodded again.

'And you *do* want to put the house on the market?'

Jack cleared his throat again. 'Yes, I do. You had better come in.'

Molly gave him a professional smile that didn't quite reach her eyes, and stepped into his hall. She had a briefcase with her and she was wearing a navy skirt suit, and looked incredibly smart. She was also as pretty as he remembered. More so, because she had a sexy secretary thing going on; but even as the thought crossed his mind, he felt disgusted with himself. He shouldn't be thinking of her in that way. Not when he was about to do business with her.

'Where do you want to start?' he asked. 'I've not done this kind of thing before.'

Her smile widened. 'Don't worry, I have,' she said. 'Quite a few times, actually. I'll take some details, then you can show me around. After that, we'll discuss what price to put it on the market for.'

'OK.' He led her into the living room and indicated for her to take a seat.

She sank gracefully into one of the armchairs, tucking her skirt around her knees and crossing her legs at the ankles, then she reached into her briefcase and pulled out a tablet.

'Can I check that your name is Feathers? Jack Feathers?' she asked.

'That's correct. I gave my name to the woman when I rang up to make the appointment.'

'I'm sorry,' Molly said. 'I've got it down here as Betters. I'll amend it now. Have you got an e-mail address?'

He gave her that, and she asked several more questions about the property itself, which he answered to the best of his ability.

'I think that's it for the time being,' she said eventually. 'Can I take a look around?'

'Yes, of course. Would you like to begin with the kitchen?'

'Why not.'

He showed her the way, then stood back as she got a little machine out of her bag and aimed it at the walls.

'What's that for?' he asked.

'It's an electronic tape measure,' she said, jotting down the room's dimensions. 'This is a nice size,' she added, gazing around. 'There's space for a table, which is always a bonus for a family house. Although it could probably do with new units, but don't worry, the asking price should reflect that.'

'And what price should I ask?'

'We'll come to that later, shall we? I'd like to see the rest of the house first.'

Jack felt extremely odd taking her upstairs, and very self-conscious when she poked her head into the bathroom, and then into his bedroom. There was nothing personal on show, not even photographs, because he had read online it was best to declutter and depersonalise any property before it went on the market. But still he felt as though she was invading his inner sanctum and he was acutely aware this was his private space that few people got to see.

Still, he reasoned, it was probably much like visiting the doctor. He might be embarrassed at having a boil on his bottom (not that he'd ever had) but the doctor would have seen hundreds of bottoms and no end of boils, so it wasn't something he should feel embarrassed about. The same applied to estate agents, he figured. Molly would have been inside hundreds of homes, so this was probably just another house to her, and he was just another vendor.

Yet he still couldn't shake the feeling of being deeply uncomfortable.

He was about to close his bedroom door, when he had a sudden image of Molly's head on his pillow, and he blinked rapidly to dispel it.

Good grief, what on earth was the matter with him?

Deciding the stress of the past week must be getting to him, he took a deep breath and followed her downstairs.

Seated once more in the living room, she got down to the brass tacks of talking about money, and his brain was soon buzzing with words like 'asking price' and 'offer', until he wasn't sure whether he was coming or going.

'Does that sound acceptable to you?' Molly asked.

She had suggested a figure and although he wasn't entirely happy with it, he knew he should bow to her expertise. She sold houses for a living, so she must know what she was talking about. Besides, it wasn't particularly unreasonable when compared to other properties of similar size and condition in the local area, so he was fairly certain she wasn't pitching it low just to get a quick sale. Ultimately though, it was his decision, and he decided to go with her estimate.

At least now he knew where he stood, assuming he achieved that figure. His financial situation wouldn't be brilliant, so his best course of action would probably be to find the cheapest place he could to rent, and then live as frugally as a monk for the next few years until he'd saved up more money for a bigger deposit.

'If you don't mind me asking, what is your situation with regards an onward chain?' Molly asked.

'There isn't one.' He would just have to find somewhere a bit sharpish as soon as he and Della accepted an offer.

'Good, that will help with its saleability. If you move out sooner rather than later, I'm even more confident of a swift sale.'

'You are?'

She nodded. 'This is a nice sized house in a good location, not too far from a good primary school and the station. It will be a nice starter or second home for a family. Three bed houses in the price range you're thinking of putting yours on the market for usually do quite well.'

Jack was crestfallen. Even though he knew it was inevitable the house would be sold at some point, now that the reality of his situation was sitting there staring him in the face, he felt rather sad. This house was only supposed to have been a stopgap for him and his sister, and so it had proved for Della; but for him it had been home for the last nine years. It was going to be very strange moving out, and even stranger living somewhere else.

'Is there a problem?' Molly asked.

'No, of course not,' Jack said, but he knew he didn't sound convincing.

'Is there an issue you're not telling me about? Problems with the neighbours? You do have to declare these things you know,' she added sternly.

'Nothing like that, believe me.' She continued to look sceptical, so he explained, 'It's just I've no idea where I'll be moving to.'

She appeared relieved. 'Have you not seen anything you like?'

'It's complicated.'

'I see,' she said.

He seriously doubted she did. Then he realised she must think he was referring to a breakdown of a relationship or a marriage. Feeling the need to explain but not wanting to go into detail, he said, 'I can't afford this house on my own, so I'm being forced to sell, but the problem is, I can't afford to buy anything else either, because I'll only realise half the equity.' Crumbs, *he* was beginning to sound like an estate agent now.

Molly continued to stare at him, but didn't say anything, so he went on, 'I don't suppose you've got any cheap houses to rent on your books?' It wouldn't hurt to start looking now. If he timed it right, he might be able to move seamlessly from one to the other. He wasn't going to hold his breath, though – he never had that kind of luck. He would probably end up paying over the odds for something, or kipping on someone's sofa until he got himself sorted.

'I'll have to have a think,' she said.

'A flat will do, or even a shared house if I'm desperate. I might have to move fast if this sells as quickly as you think it might.'

'I'm sorry, we don't deal with shared housing. You should look on Gumtree or in the local paper for something like that.' Her expression was sympathetic, with a hint of pity underlying it, and he wished he hadn't said anything.

He didn't feel like enlightening her. It was none of her business. He'd said too much as it was.

She was continuing to stare at him, but her expression was no longer one of sympathy. It was puzzled, and he could see a dawning realisation on her face but he wasn't sure what it meant.

'How do you feel about DIY?' she asked.

'It's OK…' What did that have to do with anything?

'What I mean is, are you any good at it?'

'I can put a shelf up, if that's what you're referring to.'

'How about fence posts?'

'I put the fencing panels up at the back.'

'Good,' she said. 'In that case, I think I might know of somewhere.'

'Oh?'

'It's a room in a house, so you *would* be sharing with someone, and it's not in the best condition. In fact, helping with the renovations, especially the garden, would be part of the terms.'

'Where is it?'

'About half a mile from here.'

'How much is it? I assume I'd be renting a bedroom and sharing the facilities, and would I have my own bathroom?'

'Sorry, it would be just the room, with use of shared areas, including the bathroom. For the right person there would be no rental charge, as long as they agree to help with the renovations. And the er… grounds.'

'Who would I be sharing with?'

'The owner of the property.'

'It's a thought,' Jack said, excitement rising in his chest. To live rent-free somewhere for several months would certainly help when it came to increasing his savings. From his research, he knew that rent could be as much, if not more, than paying a mortgage. It sounded ideal, and he wondered what the catch was.

'I think I'd like to take a look at the property first,' he said. 'And meet the owner.'

Molly seemed to hesitate, and she gazed at him for so long that he wondered what was wrong, and he began to think she might be toying with him.

Then she took a deep breath and seemed to come to a decision. 'You've already seen the property,' she said, 'and you've met the landlord.'

Jack had no idea who she could possibly mean. 'Who is it?' he asked, baffled. As far as he knew, he didn't have any acquaintances in common with Molly.

When she said, 'It's me, I'm the landlord,' she could have knocked him down with a feather.

***

What the hell had possessed her to do such a thing, Molly asked herself. What *had* she been thinking? She didn't know this guy from Adam – as far as she was concerned, he could be a serial killer, or a conman, and she had just invited him to live with her.

But when the idea had come to her that he could move into her spare room, it had seemed the solution to all her problems. Not only would she have another person in the house to make her feel more secure (Jet was doing a sterling job, but he was only a dog, after all), she would also have the benefit of Jack's muscles. With him helping, she could build the fence around the garden in a matter of days, not the weeks she had been anticipating, and once that was completed, he could make a start on sorting the garden out.

She had another plan for him too, but that could wait until he'd moved in. When she had told him she needed help with the grounds, she hadn't just been referring to her garden…

Jack's mouth was hanging open. 'Excuse me? Did you say…? Are you the…? You want me to…?'

'Move into my spare room and help me renovate my cottage?' she supplied. 'Yes, that's right.'

'And you're not going to charge me any rent?'

'Not if you make yourself useful.' If only he was aware of what she meant by that, he might run a mile, she thought.

Jack was wearing such a comical expression that, despite her misgivings, she had to laugh. He looked like a cartoon character who had just been hit over the head with a rubber mallet.

'Shall I leave you to think about it?' she suggested, stuffing her tablet back into the briefcase. 'In the meantime, do you want to go ahead with the instructions for the sale of your property?'

'Um, I suppose.' He seemed to gather himself. 'I mean, yes, please do.'

'I'll get the contract drawn up and email it to you tomorrow,' she said. 'And here's a copy of our fees and terms and conditions. If there's anything you don't understand, or anything you're not happy with, give me a call.' She handed him a business card.

He took it without looking, his attention on her as he stared into her eyes.

Molly's heart gave a sudden lurch, and she swallowed nervously. He was staring at her as though he wanted to gobble her all up, bones and all.

'Yes,' he said. 'I'd love to move in with you.'

'Great. Er, when?' Flipping heck, this was escalating fast!

'How about Friday?' he suggested.

'Fine. Good. I'm um, looking forward to it.' That wasn't what she'd meant to say at all. What she had wanted to say was that she'd changed her mind, that it was a silly idea and he was to forget she'd mentioned it. But he was gazing at her with those blue eyes, and she felt as though her brain had turned to mush and she was finding it hard to breathe.

'Do I have to sign anything?' he asked.

'Er, I suppose you'd better had,' she said, struggling to focus. 'I'm sure I can cobble— um, prepare a contract. I'll email that to you tomorrow, as well.' Suddenly practicalities began to rear their heads and her brain fog cleared enough for her to ask, 'Will you be bringing your furniture with you?'

'I'd like to, if you've got room for a few things.'

Didn't she just! And it would solve her immediate problem of not having any furniture of her own. 'You can bring it all, if you like; I've got plenty of room,' she said. 'Don't you want to see the inside of the house before you decide? I've got to warn you, it's not the Ritz.'

'I'm sure it'll be fine. Is it OK if I book Friday off and move in sometime during the day? If I can get a removal van, that is.'

Gosh, he seemed keen. *Too* keen, and she wondered if he had another motive besides the obvious one of needing a cheap (*free*) roof over his head.

She decided she was being silly. Of course he didn't. How could he have known she was going to ask him to move into her cottage when she hadn't known herself until a few seconds before she'd opened her mouth?

He was just being frugal, and knew a good deal when he saw one.

She wondered whether he would still think it a good deal when she told him what he had to do in exchange for rent?

'There is one more thing,' she said, and part of her hoped he would change his mind when she told him what it was. 'Do you like dogs?'

CHAPTER 12

Jack closed the door softly and leant against it, wondering what he had just agreed to. Only last week he had refused Chantelle's suggestion they move in together, and now he had agreed to live with a woman he barely knew and whom he suspected didn't think very highly of him.

But – and this had been the deciding factor – he didn't have to pay any rent. He would be able to save most of what he earned, and he wasn't going to be living with Molly forever – just until he was in a more secure financial position. It would only be for a few months, six hopefully, twelve at the most, and as soon as the renovations were completed and the garden had been sorted out, there wouldn't be an awful lot to be done. He would be able to kick back and take it easy.

The thought did occur to him that when it got to that stage Molly might well want to renegotiate his terms and conditions, but he would face that issue if, or when, it arrived. For now, it was a perfect solution.

Or it would be if he wasn't seriously attracted to his new landlord.

Giving himself a mental shake, he decided to go for a run. Running usually cleared his head, allowing him to see more clearly. Anyway, he could do with the exercise, having done very little for the past week, too busy cleaning and decorating.

At least it was done now, and within a few days his house would be on the market.

He still wasn't keen on strangers poking around his house, but it had to be done, and not having to be there to witness it was a bonus. It was almost worth taking Molly up on her offer for that alone.

Feeling angsty, he laced up his trainers and jogged on the spot for a few minutes, then followed it up with some stretches. Satisfied that nothing hurt and that he had warmed up sufficiently, he set off, determined to only think about putting one foot in front of the other for the next hour.

***

'I think I've done something stupid,' Molly said. As soon as she'd arrived home, she had immediately phoned Astrid in a panic.

'Oh dear – you've not long left the office. What could you possibly have done in such a short amount of time?' Astrid's voice was tinny and distant, and Molly guessed her friend was probably driving home.

She cradled the phone between her ear and her shoulder as she petted Jet, who was mighty pleased to see her. 'I've taken in a lodger.'

'*Another* stray?'

'I suppose he could be called that.'

'Let's hope there aren't any more dogs living wild in your park, otherwise I can see you taking them all in.'

'He's not a dog. He's a man.'

'A real man? A *human* man?'

'Uh huh,' Molly murmured.

'Bloody hell! Who? When? I mean, you didn't mention anything about this earlier.'

'That's because it's only just happened.' She took a deep breath. 'You know the new instruction I went to on my way home?'

'Mr Betters? Oakland Road?'

'That's the one – but his name is Feathers, not Betters. I've offered him to move into my spare room. Rent-free.'

'*You've done what?!*'

Molly held the phone away from her ear. Astrid's shriek was almost so high that only dogs could hear it.

'In exchange for his help in getting the cottage and the garden sorted,' she added. 'So, it's payment in kind.'

'Are you mad? You don't know anything about him.'

'I know where he works.'

'Where he *claims* to work,' Astrid growled. 'He could be lying. In fact, he probably is. He sounds like a right con man to me.'

'He definitely works where he says he does. I know. I met him there last week.'

'Where?'

'The council offices.'

There was silence for a moment, then Astrid said, 'I'm pulling over. Hang on.'

Molly waited, and as she did so she scrolled on her phone, but she couldn't find him on social media at all, although she did find him on the council's website.

Astrid came back on the line. 'He works for the council, you say? And you met him last week?' There was a pause, then she cried, 'Now I get it! You sly thing! Fancy him being the same guy.'

'It's not like that,' Molly protested. 'It's a business arrangement.'

'Yeah, right…' Astrid's disbelief was very much in evidence.

'I've got a plan,' Molly said. 'Remember I told you I tried to persuade him to do something about the park, but he refused?'

'You called him a jobsworth.'

'That's right, I did. Well, my plan is that he lives in the cottage rent-free in exchange for helping me renovate it, but what I didn't tell him is I also expect him to help me sort out the flower beds in the park. And that's only for starters. He'll help me get the park ship-shape, one way or another,' she warned.

'Do you think he'll go for it?'

Molly wasn't sure. 'Probably not, but I can try.'

'Keep me posted,' Astrid said. 'Oh, and I want a photo. I've got to see what this guy looks like!'

'You'll have to wait,' Molly said. 'He's moving in on Friday. Please tell me this isn't a stupid idea.'

'It's not a stupid idea. Much.' Astrid chortled. 'Look him up on the internet and send me the link.'

Molly winced. 'I don't think he's on social media – I've looked. There's a photo of him on the council website, but it's not a very good one. I'll send it to you now.' Molly studied it for a second, before sending it to Astrid.

There was a moment of silence, then her friend said, 'Phwoar, he's not bad, is he? He can sort out my flower beds any day!'

'Behave yourself. He's not that good-looking.'

'Are you kidding? He's lush. I like my men a bit nerdy. You've got to be able to have a conversation with them afterwards – if you know what I mean.' Astrid's laugh was positively bawdy.

'I don't know what you're talking about.' Molly sniffed and stuck her nose in the air.

'I don't believe you do,' her friend agreed. 'It's been so long since you've slept with anyone, you've forgotten what goes where.'

'I wish I hadn't phoned you,' Molly grumbled.

'I'm not. This is priceless!'

'Glad I amuse you. I'll see you tomorrow.'

'You definitely will! I want to know *everything*.'

Molly blew out her cheeks. She valued Astrid's opinion, but right now she didn't think she had been much help – Molly still wasn't certain whether having a lodger was a good idea.

With a sigh, she changed out of her work clothes and took Jet out for his evening constitutional. Fresh air would do her good and Jet could certainly do with burning off some energy.

'Do you think I've been silly?' she asked him as the pair of them wandered across the field.

Jet ignored her. He was far too busy darting around and sniffing, his tail wagging uncontrollably.

Molly had brought a pair of secateurs with her, with the intention of snipping away at some of the undergrowth in the woodland. She knew there was a path right through it from top to bottom, and she had a vague idea of where it started, and had every intention of clearing it over the course of the next few months. She would only do a little bit at a time, because she had a feeling it would take a while, and the house and her own garden were more important, but considering she had to take Jet for a walk every day, she thought she might as well do something useful. Litter picking in the morning when it was quiet and after the yobs had emptied their pockets all over the park the evening before; and path-clearing through the woods in the evening, to avoid those same teenagers who hung around the bandstand.

She had also brought a pair of heavy-duty gardening gloves with her because those brambles looked seriously fierce. She remembered watching a programme once, (it might have been a David Attenborough one) where the growth of individual stems of brambles was speeded up, and she shuddered. It had been like watching an alien, blindly pushing other plants out of the way with deadly determination.

As she snipped, picking up each disconnected strand and flinging it aside, she thought back to her conversation with Jack earlier. No one had been more surprised than she to discover he was the man who wanted to put his house on the market. To be fair, he had seemed quite surprised to see her too, but she felt they'd both been very grown-up about it, and very professional, and after the initial awkwardness, she had managed to convince herself it was just another job.

It had been fascinating to see the inside of his house though.

Ow! A thorn managed to pierce her skin through her gardening gloves, and she stamped on the nasty stem irritably, before taking her glove off and sucking at the offending finger. That would teach her to daydream and not concentrate on what she was doing.

After about half an hour, she decided she had done enough for one day: she had cleared a path approximately a metre deep, and about a metre wide. She'd give it another go tomorrow night, if she had the time.

Even though she'd been physically busy, her mind hadn't been, and she had once again found herself thinking of Jack and his house. He had hinted that he hadn't had any choice in selling it, and he was only going to achieve half the equity, which made her think he was in the middle of a failed relationship.

Of course, there might be other reasons for him having to sell the house. He might have overextended himself financially and run up a huge debt, or maybe he was a gambler? If so, he probably wasn't a very good one. *Were* there any good ones? Molly had no idea.

She recognised she was probably being silly, and she might never discover the reason. Maybe after he'd moved in, he would tell her. She wouldn't ask though, because it wasn't any of her business.

After circumnavigating the field and throwing the ball for Jet to chase, Molly took him home. The walk had done her good and she was feeling refreshed, and Jet was more than likely ready for his tea. He was panting hard, his bright pink tongue lolling out of the side of his mouth as he plodded next to her. The bounce had gone, and she was pleased to see she'd worn him out for five minutes.

She fed the dog first, then set about making her own supper, and once it had been eaten and she felt suitably refuelled, she had a good look at the newly plastered walls and ceiling in the living room. The plasterer had done a good job. He had taken the old skirting boards off as promised, explaining he wouldn't put them back on until the walls had dried out. Molly planned on removing the old paint and sanding them down, but that would be a job for later this evening, when it was too dark to work outside.

Calling the dog to her, she retrieved her shovel and the spirit level and went to check on the post she had put in yesterday. She gave it a tentative tap and when it didn't move, she gave it a shake. It seemed firm enough, and she was happy that the quick-drying cement had done what it promised. Hesitantly she checked the post with the spirit level and was relieved to see it was straight. She'd had visions of it keeling over in the middle of the night; or worse, being pushed over deliberately.

Using the tape measure, she measured the distance between this post and where she planned to put the next, and began to dig.

It didn't take long before she was puffing and panting, and sweat trickled down her back. Jet lay on the grass, watching her, his intelligent gaze never leaving her face, and she returned to her earlier conversation.

'Do you think I've been stupid?' she asked him again, but all he did was stare adoringly back at her. 'What if you don't like him? I haven't thought this through, have I? I was blinded by having another pair of hands to help, and male ones at that. I know I said I wanted to do this myself, but really, there are limits. I think it's more important I get everything finished quickly, than be precious about it.'

Jet continued to stare at her, his tail wagging gently.

'I think I'd better introduce you to him,' she continued. 'If you don't like him, I'll have to tell him the deal is off. You come first,' she said, and Jet's tail wagged faster as though he understood what she was saying.

She had Jack's details with her in her briefcase, so she would give him a ring and invite him around. It was also a good idea for him to make sure he was happy with his room, and not solely to check that Jet didn't see him as a threat or an intruder. She wouldn't call him now though; she would wait until she had put this new post in. By then it would probably be getting dark anyway, so she would have to go inside.

Whilst she had been measuring, digging and cement mixing, she had been aware of people walking up and down the path, and if she hadn't noticed them herself, Jet had. Each time he would let out a little whine, and she would look up, expecting to see Bill at some point.

She didn't see the old man, but she did see a number of other dog walkers, two women who were out jogging, an old lady with a carrier bag who scowled at her, several groups of youngsters, and a man with a young boy on a bike.

To her shock, she also saw Jack.

Molly didn't know why she was so surprised: he probably ran through the park on a regular basis.

They locked eyes, and he stuttered to a stop.

Molly tried to keep her eyes above his neck, but her gaze dropped to his broad chest and slim hips. He was wearing shorts, and she admired his legs. Then she realised what she was doing and hastily dragged her eyes back to his face, only to catch him checking her out too.

Molly could feel herself blushing, and she wondered whether the faint hint of colour on his face was because of the exercise, or because he knew she had caught him staring.

'Hi, again,' he said, and she saw him swallow and wondered whether he was as nervous as she.

'Hi. I've been thinking,' she began.

His expression became wary. 'What about?'

'You being my lodger,' she said. 'I might have been a bit hasty.'

Disappointment replaced the wariness. 'I see,' he said woodenly.

'I thought perhaps you'd better have a look inside the cottage before you made your decision,' she explained. 'And you'd also better meet Jet.'

'Jet?' Now he was looking puzzled.

'My dog.' When she pointed to the animal, Jack did a double take.

'Sorry, I didn't notice him.' The colour on his face grew more pronounced. 'Is he friendly?'

'He is with me,' Molly said, 'and with my parents. And with Bill, an old guy who walks his little terrier through the park. Jet was a stray and Bill had been feeding him. I didn't like the thought of the poor thing living on his own in the park in all weathers, so he moved in with me.'

Jack chuckled. 'Sounds a bit like me, doesn't it? Very soon I could be a stray, although I do draw the line at living in the park.'

'You do realise that's precisely what you will be doing when you move into my cottage?' Molly pointed out.

'That's different,' Jack said.

It was different in that he would have a roof over his head, but that was about it, Molly thought. Jack most definitely *would* be living in the park, with everything that entailed, and her thoughts flitted to the past three evenings. Friday and Saturday had been particularly noisy, and she wished she'd had a telly so she could have turned the volume up full, to drown out the noise the kids were making. On the following mornings, there had been treble the amount of litter than there had been previously. She'd assumed things might have quietened down on Sunday night, what with there being school the following day, but it had been just as bad.

Jack and the dog were eyeing one another. Jet looked impassive; Jack looked apprehensive.

'Come closer,' Molly urged.

Hesitantly Jack stepped forward a couple of paces.

The dog didn't move.

Molly was relieved when Jet didn't growl, and she guessed it was because he didn't feel the need to warn her.

'I haven't had much to do with dogs,' Jack said out of the corner of his mouth. He hadn't taken his eyes off the dog.

'Don't worry, neither have I. I'm learning as I go along.'

'That's not very reassuring. Are you certain he doesn't bite?'

'Not to my knowledge. Put it this way, he hasn't bitten *me*.'

'He wouldn't dare,' Molly thought she heard Jack mutter, and she suppressed a smile. Suddenly she found herself hoping very much indeed that Jack and Jet got on.

Jack crouched down and held out his hand. 'Come here, boy,' he said, and Molly smiled again. For someone who professed to know nothing about dogs, he was acting just the way she hoped he would: getting down to the dog's level, speaking softly and holding out his hand for the animal to sniff.

Jet got to his feet and padded closer to Jack. His tail was twitching, but Molly wouldn't call it a full wag. When he was about a metre away, Jet stopped, stretched out his neck and sniffed Jack's hand.

Jack froze. Then to Molly's delight the dog's tongue shot out and he licked Jack's fingers. Jack snatched his hand back with an expression of disgust on his face.

'Ew! He slobbered all over me.'

'Don't be a baby. All he did was lick your hand. I think you've got the seal of approval. He likes you.'

Jet's tail was now wagging, and he leant against Jack's legs.

'Is he supposed to do that?' Jack asked.

Molly said, 'I'm not sure what dogs are supposed to do. Perhaps it means he likes you or trusts you, or maybe he's feeling tired and wants to lean on you. Would you like to come in? I think you ought to see where you'll be living. That is, if you still want to move in.'

'I can't.'

Molly felt acutely disappointed. Now that her fears that Jet wouldn't like him were unfounded, she hoped Jack wasn't going to pull out. 'Oh, OK.'

'You don't understand. I can't move. If I do, he'll fall over.'

Molly giggled. 'No, he won't. Jet, come here, there's a good boy.' Jet trotted over to her and she put a hand on his head. 'Is that better?' she asked Jack.

'Much.'

Relieved, Molly showed him inside. 'It still needs an awful lot of work, which is why I want some help,' she explained.

She watched Jack's expression as he took in the bare walls of the hall and the stairs, and then saw his face brighten when he walked into the sitting room.

'It was plastered today,' she said. 'It's going to take about a week to do the whole house.'

'Crumbs, this makes a difference,' Jack said. 'I love the fireplace.'

'It is nice, isn't it? It needs re-blacking, and the chimney definitely needs to be swept, and I'm pretty sure I can do something with these floor tiles. I'm not sure what: I'll have to look it up.'

'Are you planning on doing all this yourself?'

Molly bit back a smile. 'Not anymore,' she said. 'I was hoping you would do some of it.'

'Me? I don't know the first thing about sweeping chimneys.'

'I'll get a professional in to do that,' Molly assured him. 'Although, if I could do it myself, I would, but I don't want to get it wrong and risk a chimney fire.'

'Is there such a thing?'

'Most definitely. If you don't sweep a chimney properly there's a risk that any soot or deposits in the chimney could catch fire, and I wouldn't want that to happen.' Molly debated whether to tell him about her episode with the range in the kitchen, but she decided not to. It was better he thought her competent and capable, rather than worry she was about to burn the place down. 'But I did think you could give me a hand with the tiles,' she added.

'If you tell me what to do, I'm sure I'll be able to do it,' Jack said, but he didn't look convinced.

Molly was confident that if she could do it, then so could he. Whatever it was that needed doing, because she wasn't kidding when she said she'd have to look up how to go about making the tiles look like new.

She took a deep breath: now for the worst bit. 'Here's the kitchen,' she said.

'Riiight…' Jack dragged the word out.

'I know what you're thinking – those cabinets aren't the best. Goodness knows how old they are, but I'd take an educated guess as to them being relics from the 1950s or 60s.'

'You're not keeping them, are you?'

'Gracious, no. They're far too rickety. I think they're mostly rotted, but they'll do for the time being until I can afford new ones.'

'You're not going for a fitted kitchen?'

Molly shook her head. 'I don't think it would be in keeping. As much as I would like a fitted kitchen with shiny stainless steel and marble worktops, I don't think it would be right.'

To her surprise, Jack agreed. 'You could always see if you can find some second-hand ones to replace these, or I think you can buy free-standing units from IKEA.'

'That's what I was thinking,' Molly said, glad they were on the same wavelength. Not that it made any difference – this was her house and she would furnish and decorate it as she pleased, but it was nice to get a second opinion which agreed with her own.

'I'll show you your bedroom,' she said. 'There are only two, with the bathroom in the middle, so there's no ensuite I'm afraid.'

'That's fine. I'm sure we can dodge around each other.'

Molly had a vision of meeting on the landing in the middle of the night, and she hastily pushed it away.

'Both bedrooms are the same size,' she explained, as she climbed the stairs. She opened the door to the room that would be his, and stepped back to let him go inside. 'This will be replastered too,' she said, 'and there will be new coving and a new ceiling rose, and I'm replacing the dado rails and—'

'It's perfect!' he cried.

'It is?' Molly happened to think it was, but she was surprised that he did.

'If you still want me, I'll be happy to move in,' he said, turning to look at her. His eyes were shining and he had a smile on his face.

Molly's heart lost a beat. I*f you want me…* the words echoed in her mind, and with a sudden surge of desire, she realised she did want him, very much indeed.

But that would never do, would it?

Instead, she nodded politely and said, 'Good. I'll get a contract drawn up. Make sure you look at it carefully, and if you want to discuss anything please let me know. It's to protect you as much as to protect me,' she said, 'and I want to be fair to both of us.'

'I'm sure you will be.'

'Actually,' she said, 'you might change your mind when you see the bathroom. I can't afford to replace it yet, so you'll have to live with it, I'm afraid.'

'It can't be that bad?'

'Don't be so sure. Take a look for yourself.' Then she burst out laughing at the horror on his face when he saw what was inside.

'Dear God, you could have warned me that I needed sunglasses. What colour do you call that?'

'Peach, I think. It could be worse – it could be green.'

He started laughing and shook his head. 'You really do need help, don't you?'

Molly nodded. She needed a lot of help, but she wasn't just referring to the cottage…

CHAPTER 13

Jack took a final look around the house he had lived in for the past nine years, feeling incredibly sad. He had spent most of his adult life here and it was going to be a wrench to leave. The removal men were loading up the last of his possessions to take to Molly's cottage, and were about to shut the door on the van.

He gave the front door an affectionate pat as he locked it, then straightened his shoulders and lifted his chin. He had to look on this as a new beginning, and not as an ending. He was thinking of this move to the park keeper's cottage as a steppingstone on the way to somewhere else. Unfortunately, he had no idea where.

Jack almost felt like a student again as he followed the van the short distance to Sweet Meadow Park. Except this time he had a couple of smart suits, a houseful of furniture, and a job: rather than a carful of ripped T-shirts, a homebrewing kit, and a student loan.

And neither was he moving into student accommodation to live in a small cramped single room and fight over the contents of the communal fridge.

He was pleased he was able to bring all his furniture with him, everything that wasn't inbuilt or screwed down, that is, rather than have to put it into storage. He had been dismayed to find that Molly had been sleeping on a blow-up bed, and didn't even have a chair to her name. She had argued that there would be time enough to buy furniture when the cottage was completed, but Jack didn't agree, especially since some of the rooms were habitable already.

Take the living room for instance – it had been rewired and replastered, and the tiles looked OK. With a bit of paint on the walls and a rug on the floor it would be good to go. The same applied to the bedrooms. Both of them had now been replastered, and Molly had sanded the floors down. A fine layer of dust still hung in the air, he'd noticed yesterday evening, when he had popped around after work to finalise things, but it was nothing that a good hoovering couldn't sort out. The problem was that Molly didn't have a vacuum cleaner, but that was OK: he had the solution. He had one of those super-duper rechargeable things, and he suspected over the course of the next few weeks he was going to make very good use of it.

Jack was surprised to see Molly waiting for him on the doorstep as his car pulled up to the cottage and tucked in behind the van, and he caught his breath at the sight of her.

She was wearing faded jeans and a plain white T-shirt, and her hair was pulled back into a plait. She looked fresh and wholesome, and incredibly lovely.

'Shouldn't you be at work?' he asked, feeling extremely pleased that she wasn't.

'I wrangled a couple of hours off. I thought you could do with a hand.'

He suspected the real reason was that she wanted to supervise him moving in. He didn't have a problem with that: he was very aware this was her house, and he was a paying guest. Or rather, a *non*-paying guest, which made this situation even more precarious, despite the contract she had emailed to him, which he had scrutinised carefully and deemed to be very fair.

Over the following few hours the two of them worked extremely hard, arranging the various rooms to their satisfaction. And although he thought he might feel awkward, he didn't. He was beginning to feel quite at home. He guessed it was probably because all the furniture in the house was his, so it was almost like being at home. The only sticky issue had come when she'd realised he had brought two beds with him, not one.

'But I've only got two bedrooms,' Molly had protested. 'Where are we going to put the other one?'

'I thought you could have it,' Jack said. 'It's in good condition, honest.'

She stared at it doubtfully. 'It doesn't feel right, taking your things,' she said.

Jack laughed. 'You're not taking it: I'm offering. If it's any consolation, I promise to take it with me when I leave.' Molly shot him a look, and he added hastily, 'Not that I'm planning on leaving anytime soon, so don't worry. What I mean is, you won't be stuck with it. I've brought a wardrobe, a chest of drawers, and a bedside cabinet for you to use, as well,' he said. 'But if you want to sleep on the floor on a blow-up bed and live out of a suitcase, be my guest. I'll arrange to put them into storage.'

Molly narrowed her eyes at him. 'That won't be necessary.' Then her expression softened. 'Thank you, you're very kind.' She blushed and he guessed she was embarrassed because she didn't have a stick of furniture to call her own.

'Actually, you're doing me a favour,' he said. 'As I told you, I would only have had to put them into storage, or try to beg some garage space off someone. Shall I put the kettle on? We can have a quick cuppa, then I'll do some hoovering.' Ideally, he would have liked to have vacuumed *before* the removal man had carried the furniture into the room, but he hadn't wanted to hold them up.

'Do you dust as well?' she asked, twinkling at him.

'I do,' he replied, giving her a *so what* look.

'That's good, because I'm hopeless at it.'

'Don't tell me you're one of those people who dust around things? I bet you hoover around the furniture, too.'

'Guilty as charged,' she said, lifting a box onto the mattress.

'Here, let me do that,' he offered.

'It's OK, I can manage. I'm stronger than I look.'

Jack thought back to the first time he'd seen her, trying to yank a large piece of chipboard off a window frame. 'I know you are,' he said. 'Did you put in all those fence posts by yourself?'

She nodded proudly. 'I did, but there are a few more to go.'

'I'll do them,' he offered.

'We can do them together,' she said, and his heart skipped a beat again.

This was very weird: it was almost as though they were a couple.

Chantelle's face popped into his mind, and he couldn't for one moment imagine doing this kind of thing with her. She would probably break a nail, for a start.

That was unfair, he chided. When Chantelle had wormed her way into his life and his house, there hadn't been any setting up home to be done. He had already done it. She'd added a few bits and pieces, such as cushions, throws, and candles – lots of candles – but that was about it. Maybe if his house had needed some work doing, she would have happily joined in. In fact, hadn't she come over to help him paint last week?

As he filled the kettle with fresh water and plugged it in and Molly popped a tea bag into a couple of mugs, Jack was still thinking about his ex. She may well have offered to help him paint, but he had a feeling her heart hadn't been in it. And he couldn't help comparing her to Molly. Molly wasn't in the least bit scared of getting her hands dirty, and he admired that. He wasn't scared either, despite not having done much DIY or gardening in the past: he found he was looking forward to it.

But as he poured boiling water into the mugs, he had to ask himself whether he was looking forward to working with his *hands*, or looking forward to working with *Molly*? He strongly suspected the latter, and he had to remind himself this was a business arrangement. Nothing more.

***

Apart from her mum, Molly hadn't cooked alongside anyone else before. She had cooked *for* them, but not *with* them. OK, she had, but she didn't think the food technology lessons she'd had at school counted. She meant just her and one other person in the kitchen, cooking a meal together, for them to eat together.

It felt strangely intimate, and she kept glancing at Jack out of the corner of her eye, noting his strong forearms and his sure hands. Abruptly an image of those hands on her body flashed into her mind, and she had to have a drink of water to steady herself. Was this really going to work if she was having such thoughts about him when he'd only just moved in?

Maybe it would take a while to get into the swing of things, she reasoned hopefully, and she prayed that was the case, because if she couldn't control her wayward thoughts she was going to be in a fine mess.

Now and again he would look up and catch her eye, and she would glance away quickly. She knew she was blushing, but she blamed it on the heat in the kitchen.

They were making curry from scratch, and he was busy chopping onions whilst she was cubing a couple of chicken breasts, Jet lying at her feet and staring up at her hopefully.

It was very cosy, and Molly wondered if this was what being married felt like – working companionably together to prepare a meal at the end of a long day.

She stifled a sigh: this was the closest she would get to feeling married for a very long time indeed. There had to be a man on the horizon for that to happen, but she hadn't had a boyfriend for close to eighteen months. Not really. The odd night out with a guy didn't count, especially when she normally ended up being in a hurry to get away, having realised she was making a big mistake.

It was also strange to have Jack in her kitchen, because he knew where everything was better than she did. Considering most of the cooking equipment and utensils belonged to him, and he had put them away, it was no surprise. Molly felt as though she was the guest, not him. Almost everything in the cottage was his, including the very bed she was going to sleep in tonight, and it gave her a very funny feeling. He'd told her it had been in the spare room, and as he had a bed of his own, he'd probably not spent even one night on the mattress she was about to sleep on. It didn't stop her from feeling odd about it, though.

It made sense for Jack to have brought his furniture with him, rather than put it into storage, considering she didn't have any. That was one of the things her mum had been aghast about when she and Dad had popped over on Sunday – Dad to help her remove the panels, Mum to have a good nose around. Her mum had practically begged her to at least sleep in her own room at home, if nothing else, but Molly had been adamant, and she had fully expected her mother to turn up with a complete set of furniture, so she'd warned her dad to keep Mum under control. Molly wouldn't have been ungrateful – far from it – but she wanted to choose her own furniture.

So it was rather ironic that she'd not had a say in anything that was in her house now, not even a cushion.

Things have a funny way of turning out, don't they, she said to herself. And it did make for an easier life. She no longer had to sit cross-legged on the blow-up mattress in the bedroom to eat her meal as she tried to balance it on her knees. She had a proper table to sit at, and chairs to park her bottom on. The cottage felt like a home now, and she had Jack to thank for that.

Finally the meal was ready, and Molly tucked in with enthusiasm. She was starving, and the food was delicious. For a few minutes nothing could be heard but the sound of cutlery on plates, but as soon as her immediate hunger was satisfied, Molly thought she would try to get to know Jack a little better.

'So,' she began brightly. 'Here we are living together in the same house, and I don't know a thing about you.'

Jack speared a chunk of chicken. 'What do you want to know?'

'Are you from round here?'

'Sweet Meadow? I've lived here all my life. We probably went to the same school. How old are you? I don't remember you.'

'Twenty-nine.'

'That explains it. I'm five years older than you. You might know my sister, though. She's thirty-one. Della Coles?'

Molly wrinkled her nose as she thought. 'The name's familiar, but I can't place her. What about your parents? Do they live nearby?'

'I never knew my dad, or rather I knew *of* him, but he was killed in a motorbike accident not long after I was born. My mum remarried, to Della's dad, but she got divorced a couple of years ago. She lives in York now. She had a kind of a midlife crisis, and she and her sister decided to open a sweet shop there.'

'Ooh, I like the sound of that,' Molly said.

'I don't think either of them realised quite how much hard work it would be,' Jack said. 'The shop is open seven days a week, and she hardly ever gets time off, so if I want to see her I have to go visit. I'll bring you some sweets back next time, shall I? What sort do you like?'

'The old-fashioned ones in jars,' Molly said, and there followed a lively discussion about what kind of sweets they liked, and which ones they could remember from their childhoods.

By the time they had finished eating, they'd exhausted the subject and had moved on to puddings, the general consensus being that cheesecake was king and sticky toffee pudding came a close second.

Molly said, 'I'm sorry, but I've only got strawberry yoghurt or an orange Kit Kat in the fridge.'

'Orange Kit Kat?' Jack looked disgusted. 'That's really wrong. It's got to be a normal Kit Kat or nothing. Why do they do that? Take something that works perfectly well and then mess with it?'

Molly said, 'I quite like them.'

They rose simultaneously and picked up their plates, and she gave him a self-conscious smile.

Jack said, 'Shall I wash and you dry?'

'Whichever suits you best,' Molly said. She didn't mind doing either.

'I'll wash,' he said, and the matter was settled.

She was putting the last plate away while Jack was wiping down the countertops, when she announced, 'I'm going to take Jet for his evening walk, if you'd like to come.' Then she added hurriedly, 'No pressure. I don't expect you to come out with us. I wondered if you fancied stretching your legs. Unless you've done enough stretching for one day?'

They had been on their feet most of the day, but a walk was a walk, and Molly always felt invigorated afterwards. She was so glad she had Jet, otherwise she might not have realised how much she enjoyed strolling around her park.

'I'll come,' he said. 'It'll do me good to get some fresh air.'

Molly took her usual route, turning left out of the cottage, walking past the huge main gates, which she glanced at to make sure were locked, then she carried on towards the children's play area.

Jack said, 'I haven't come this way before. Is that supposed to be a roundabout?'

'I think so, but it doesn't go round anymore. And the swings aren't much cop, either.'

One of them was wrapped around the top bar by its chains, another was hanging brokenly by one chain, and there was an empty space where a third swing should have been. The only thing which could possibly be used was the slide, but even that was rickety, and the climbing frame looked positively lethal.

Molly risked a quick look at Jake to try to gauge what he was thinking, but his face was blank. She was rather disappointed, because he clearly didn't seem bothered about the state of the children's play area. No wonder nobody came here. Not only was it unsightly and the equipment didn't work, but it was positively dangerous, and the ground underneath sparkled in the late evening sun from fragments of broken glass. Thankfully the play area was fenced off, so Jet couldn't dash through it and cut his paws.

At the end of the play area was another small gate leading to the road beyond, but Molly turned right, taking Jack towards the woodland. This particular path eventually turned in a big circle leading to the disused cafe and the bandstand, but she soon left it and cut up towards the meadow.

Jack didn't say a word, but she noticed he was taking it all in, and when they reached the pond, she heard his sharp intake of breath.

'It's beautiful, isn't it?' she said. 'Or it would be if it wasn't for all the rubbish lying around.'

'I see what you mean about the pond needing to be dredged,' he said, his eyes fixed on the shopping trolley. It appeared to have been joined by another, and Molly wondered when it had been dumped there. Unfortunately, the park had four more entrances besides the main one, and even if it didn't, it would make no difference because she was out most of the day. She could hardly monitor the comings and goings of the whole park when she was at work.

'Ugh!' Jack exclaimed, ducking and making Molly jump, but then she giggled when she realised why.

'It's only a dragonfly,' she said, as it flew past his head for a second time.

'It's the size of a pterodactyl!' he cried, tracking its swooping flight. 'Oh, there are more of them.'

'It's an indication that the water is quite healthy, despite the way it looks. I saw a fox the other day, and Bill says there are rabbits here. I haven't seen any myself, but I have noticed their droppings.'

'Who's Bill? Is that your dad?'

'Bill is an old guy who walks his dog around the park. He often stops for a chat.'

Jack was looking thoughtful. 'So there *is* wildlife here?'

'Did you think I was making it up?'

He had the grace to look sheepish. 'I did wonder,' he said.

'Does that mean you've had second thoughts about doing something about the park?'

'No, sorry.'

He looked uncomfortable, and Molly winced. The last thing she wanted was for there to be an atmosphere between them. 'I shouldn't have said anything. I promise I won't mention it again.'

'That's OK.' His eyes came to rest on her, and she felt a curious tingle.

She definitely was being ridiculous. She had to knock this on the head right away. It wouldn't do for her to have a crush on her lodger!

Walking more briskly now, she led him away from the meadow and the pond, and through the grass until they reached the path once more.

'I'm surprised you're not more familiar with the park,' Molly said. 'Didn't you used to hang out here when you were a teenager?'

'I can't say I did. Mind you, I was heavily into sport, so I spent most of my time training.'

'For what?'

'The 5000 metres and the 10,000 metres.'

'Running?'

'Yeah, I was quite fast when I was younger, but not fast enough.' His expression was rueful.

'Would you have liked to take it further?'

'I thought I would at one point,' he said, 'but I didn't have the talent.'

'You still enjoy running,' she stated.

'It's in my blood. I run to unwind. I can't think of anything better than going on a 20k run after a hard day's work.'

Molly grimaced. 'I can. I prefer to go for a walk, thank you. I can't run for toffee.'

'I bet *he* can.' Jack was looking at the dog, who was still bouncing around, as full of energy now as when they had first set out.

'No doubt,' Molly said. 'Bill, that's the old man, thinks he's part greyhound.'

'I wonder if I could take him with me? Not for the whole 20k to start, because that might be too much, but maybe for a 5k run. What do you think?'

'I don't see why not. You'd have to keep him on the lead though.'

'Oh, I definitely would,' Jack said. 'Maybe after we finish our chores tomorrow, I'll go out for a short one and take him with me?'

'I'm sure he'd like that.'

Even though Molly didn't fancy running herself, she felt a little envious that Jack had offered to take Jet and not her, and for the umpteenth time she told herself not to be so silly. If he had offered, she would have had to say no. She could barely run to the nearest shop and back. Five kilometres would kill her.

There was another awkward moment when they returned to the cottage, as Molly wondered what to do with herself for the rest of the evening. It was far too early to go to bed, but she didn't think Jack would appreciate it if she started shoving furniture out of the way so she could tackle the tile floor. Just because she was driven to finish the cottage in as short an amount of time as humanly possible, it didn't mean he was. And she didn't want him to feel obliged. She might have asked him to help renovate the cottage and the grounds in exchange for rent, but she didn't expect him to work as hard or for as long as she.

It was at this point she lamented the lack of TV. Or, put it another way, Jack had brought a television with him, but there was no aerial and no broadband.

'I'm sorry,' she said, when she found him on the sofa, trying to get a signal. 'I haven't had a chance to set up broadband yet, so there's no Wi-Fi. I promise I'll sort it out first thing in the morning.'

'That's OK. I'll give them a call if you like, considering I'm living here too. I expect to pay my way.'

Molly was shaking her head. 'Oh, no, you don't,' she said. 'I'll set up the broadband and I'll pay for it.'

'But—'

'No buts; this is my house and I don't expect you to pay for things like that.'

'But what about electricity and such?

'I still have to turn the lights on whether you are here or not,' Molly pointed out. 'And I don't think you cooking a meal for yourself each evening is going to make much of a difference to my energy bill. Buy your own food, that's all I ask. Unless of course…' She hesitated. 'We could always put a certain amount each into a kitty, and buy common items like tea, coffee, and bread out of it.'

'Why don't we take it a step further?' Jack suggested. 'It seems silly cooking two separate meals, so maybe now and again whoever is home first can cook supper for both of us?'

Molly wondered whether that was what he used to do with his ex-wife or girlfriend, but she didn't like to pry. It seemed a bit forward considering they were only just getting to know one another.

'How about if we plan the meals for the week?' she suggested.

'I'm happy to do that if you are, and if there's something I want to eat that you don't like, or vice versa, we can eat separately on that evening. What do you think?'

'I think that's a brilliant idea, if you're sure. I don't want you to think you've been railroaded into anything you're not happy with.'

'I'm sure,' he said. 'But I do wish you would let me pay for the broadband.'

'Definitely not.' Molly was adamant. This was her house, and she would take care of the bills. Besides, she didn't want the hassle of having to set it up again when he left. Because he invariably *would* leave at some point. Both of them were well aware that this was not a long-term arrangement.

'But—' he began, and Molly rounded on him with a 'Shush!'

He blinked. 'Did you just shush me?'

'Yes, I did.' She lifted her chin, prepared to do battle, then she saw the twinkle in his eye. 'I think we're having our first argument,' she said, chuckling.

'No, we're not,' Jack countered.

'Yes, we are…' Molly stopped and rolled her eyes. 'I hope this isn't a sign of things to come,' she said dryly.

'I promise I'll be on my best behaviour from now on,' Jack said. 'Starting with getting the TV working.'

'I thought we'd already discussed that,' Molly began to object.

Jack held up his phone. 'We can get around it this evening by using my phone as a mobile hotspot,' he said. 'But I've got to warn you – my data, my choice of programme.'

Molly narrowed her eyes, then she shot across the room and snatched up the remote control from the floor and danced out of reach. 'Not if I've got the zapper,' she teased.

'Zapper? Is that what you call it?'

'Why, what do you call it?'

'The doofer, or the whatchamacallit. I'm going to need you to give it back,' he said, 'because I can't connect my mobile and the TV without it, so there.' He stuck his tongue out at her.

Molly stared at his mouth, feeling a sudden urge to kiss him. Dear God, and this was only day one.

'While you do that, I'll make us a cup of tea,' she said, hurrying out to the kitchen, desperate to put some distance between them, because she had a horrible feeling that inviting Jack into her home was one of the worst decisions of her life.

How could it not be, when she was already starting to fall for him?

CHAPTER 14

Jack shuffled into the kitchen, rubbing his bleary eyes and yawning. Thank God it was Saturday. He honestly didn't think he could face going into work today. He'd had one of the worst night's sleeps ever, and was feeling absolutely exhausted.

To make matters worse, Molly was already up and dressed, and was as chirpy as the birds he could hear singing through the open window.

'Sleep well?' she asked, and without waiting for an answer she continued, 'I slept like a baby. That mattress is so comfortable. Thank you ever so much for lending it to me.'

'I've had better nights,' Jack admitted, dropping heavily into a chair.

'I've boiled the kettle. Would you like coffee or tea?'

'I think it had better be coffee,' Jack said, knowing he would need all the caffeine he could get to keep himself awake today.

'You can't blame your poor night's sleep on your bed,' Molly pointed out, as she popped a spoonful of instant granules into a mug.

Jack had brought an ancient coffee machine with him, but he couldn't remember whether he had any pods for it. He'd have to buy some later. 'It wasn't that. It was all the screaming. I thought somebody was being murdered.'

'What screaming?' Molly looked puzzled. 'I didn't hear anything and neither did Jet. I'm sure he would have let me know if something was going on outside.'

'I'm not sure what it was. It didn't sound human.' Jack ran a hand through his hair, guessing it was probably standing up in spikes. 'I was about to call the police at one point.'

Molly looked worried. 'Are you sure you heard screaming? Do you think we'd better take a look?'

'Can I have some coffee first? Please?' he begged.

'Milk, sugar?'

'Just milk, please.'

He gratefully took the mug she handed to him, before adding, 'I don't expect you to treat me as a guest, you know.'

'I'm not going to,' Molly retorted. 'If you were standing right next to the kettle and making yourself a cup of tea, I would expect you to make me one, too.'

'Fair enough.' He took a gulp of the hot liquid, wincing as he burned his mouth, but it didn't take long for the caffeine to hit his system and perk him up, and he soon started to feel more awake.

'Back to the screaming you thought you heard.' Molly was tapping a finger against her chin. 'Did it sound a bit like this?'

Jack almost jumped out of his skin as Molly let out a weird shriek. 'Good grief, are you alright?' he cried.

'I'm fine.' Molly was smirking. 'Well, did it?'

'A little, yes. But not quite as shrill.'

'Are you saying I'm shrill?'

'You're not normally, but that noise was awful.'

'I think what you heard was our resident fox,' she explained. 'Remember I told you when we were out on our walk last night that there are foxes? That's the sort of noise they make.'

'It sounded as though they were killing each other.'

'I think it was a mating call,' Molly said. 'I looked it up. It scared me half to death when I first heard it.'

'Will it do that every night?'

'Probably not, but anyway you soon get used to it. *I* didn't hear a thing.'

'Bully for you,' Jack muttered under his breath, but he didn't mean it. Reassured that there was nothing sinister going on, he drank the rest of his coffee and in a louder voice said, 'What's on the agenda for today?'

'I need to give a broadband company a call, and then I have to go to work for a couple of hours. Viewings,' she added, by way of an explanation. 'When I come home, I was planning on trying to finish the fence. I would like to be able to let Jet out in the garden without worrying he'll wander off. First, though, I need to take him for a walk.'

'Would you like some company?'

'Didn't you have enough of the park last night?'

'I want to see if I can catch a glimpse of this fox.'

'You just want to check that there isn't a body out there,' Molly teased. 'This isn't Midsomer Murders, you know. You're not going to find a corpse sprawled across the bandstand.'

'I wouldn't want to,' he said. 'I've got enough drama going on in my life as it is.'

'Oh?'

Molly was gazing at him curiously, but Jack didn't feel like explaining. He certainly didn't want to talk about work, guessing that might lead to the thorny subject of council funds being diverted to Sweet Meadow Park, and he certainly didn't want to talk about Chantelle. Neither did he want to mention his housing issue in case she took it the wrong way and thought he wanted to move out. He was perfectly happy living in the park keeper's cottage for the time being, even though he knew it wasn't a long-term solution.

***

'Hang on a second, Mum,' Molly said as she walked towards her car. Jack was using an electric screwdriver to attach the fence panels to the post and it didn't half make a noise. She mouthed 'See you later,' to him as she got in and started the engine.

'What was that noise?' her mum asked.

'Jack is putting up the fence.'

'I hope you're not doing too much.'

'I'm not doing anything – I've got to go to work today.'

'Do you trust him in the cottage on his own?'

'Of course I do! He lives here.' Molly rolled her eyes, waving to Jack as he hurried to open the main gates for her. She wound the window down and called, 'Thank you.'

'Who are you talking to?'

'Jack. He opened the gates for me. He's proving to be quite handy.'

'I bet he is,' her mother said dryly.

'That's not what I meant. He is only a lodger. Nothing more.'

'Don't you think it's odd that a grown man with his own house wants to move in with you?'

'Thanks!'

'I mean,' her mum carried on, 'the cottage is hardly habitable.'

'It is now. For your information, it's looking rather cosy.'

'How can it be cosy when you haven't even got a sofa?'

'That's where you're wrong. Jack has brought all his furniture with him so I don't have to buy any for the time being.' She didn't add that she was also sleeping in his spare bed.

'I still think there's something fishy going on.'

'Anyone can fall on hard times, Mum,' Molly argued.

'Are you sure he's not a con man?'

'I told you, he works for the council.'

'It could be a front.'

Crumbs, between Jack thinking he was in an episode of Midsomer Murders and her mum hinting that Jack was part of the cast of Hustle, Molly wondered who was the most deluded.

'It's not a front.' Molly tried not to sigh.

'I want to meet him.'

'You will. He lives in my house – you're bound to bump into him at some point.'

'I want to meet him *today*.'

'I don't know what time I'll be home, and I don't know what Jack's plans are for the rest of the day.' Not only that, the last thing Molly wanted was for her mum to arrive all guns blazing, and act like she was in the FBI and Jack was a suspect to be questioned.

'I don't have to stay long,' her mum persisted.

This time Molly did sigh. Her mum wasn't going to be thwarted, was she? 'How about if you call round tomorrow?' she suggested. At least it would give her time to prepare Jack for what was about to go down.

'I've got your granny coming for lunch tomorrow, so I can't. She was hoping to see you,' her mum added pointedly.

Molly knew that tone. Her mother was guilt tripping her. 'Are you saying you want me to come for lunch?'

'I think you should,' her mum said. 'Come to think of it, why don't you bring this Jack of yours? At least I'll get to meet him.'

'He's not *my* Jack,' Molly argued, then briefly wondered what it would be like if he *was* hers, but she quickly shoved the thought away. 'I'll ask him,' she said. 'He might have something on.' She hoped for his sake he did! 'I'll let you know in the morning. I've got to go, or I'll be late for work. Love you, Mum.'

'Love you, too – and don't forget to ask.'

Molly shook her head. It was lovely that her mum was so protective, but it could also be a little stifling. She had no doubt her mother had her best interests at heart and was only looking out for her, but Molly was as certain as she could be that Jack was just a guy who worked for the council and wanted a place to stay for a while. And it wasn't as though he'd asked if he could move in with her – she had offered.

She still wondered what his reasons were for selling, but she wasn't about to ask. Not yet. She would have to get to know him better first.

***

'What's it like, living with a guy, but *not living* with him? It must be like being in student accommodation.' Astrid waggled her eyebrows.

'I wouldn't know,' Molly said. She'd sat her A-levels and had got what she had assumed was a temporary job in Watkins and Wright, Estate Agents. But the temporary job had become a permanent one and any thoughts about going to university had been swept away by the joy of earning her own money and the thought of not having a massive student debt hanging over her head.

'Me, neither,' Astrid said. 'I can guess, though. Is it awkward?'

'Give it a chance – he only moved in yesterday. Of course it's going to be awkward.'

'I mean, is it awkward because you fancy him?'

'I do not fancy him.'

'Go tell it to the pixies at the bottom of the garden. Maybe they'll believe you.'

'Shut up.' Molly sniffed and stared at her computer screen.

'Ooh, I think I hit a nerve!'

'I'm ignoring you.'

'Have you walked in on him having a shower yet?'

'No.'

'Are you going to?'

'*No!* Will you stop it?'

'I'm a single mother with two kids and no love life. How else am I supposed to get some excitement?'

'There's no excitement to be had,' Molly said.

'I bet there could be, if you tried. Does he snore? I'm not keen on a man who snores. My ex could snore for Britain. He'd win a gold if they were giving out medals.'

Molly laughed. 'I have no idea whether Jack snores or not, and I've no intention of finding out.'

'I bet you will,' Astrid said.

'Haven't you got any work to do?'

'Loads, but winding you up is much more fun.'

Molly didn't mind being teased. Astrid was a good friend and they often shared banter. But what she did mind was the sneaking suspicion that she hoped Astrid was right, and that she *would* get to find out whether Jack snored!

CHAPTER 15

'What are you up to?'

The voice came from behind and Jack looked over his shoulder to see an elderly guy standing right behind him.

'I'm putting a fence up for the owner,' he said, then he noticed the dog, a small white and tan terrier, and he wondered whether this guy could be Bill.

'Glad to see she's brought someone in. She's been trying to do it all herself. I would offer, but my arthritis is too bad. Can't risk buggering myself up for weeks.' The old gent glanced up and down the path. 'Where's your van? Do you work for a company or for yourself?'

Jack was taken aback by the directness of the man's questions. 'I… um… actually live here.'

'You do not. A young lady called Molly lives here – you don't. Who are you?'

'I'm Jack,' Jack said, 'and I *do* live here. I moved in yesterday.'

'I didn't know she had a fella. She never said.' The old man looked quite put out, then he stuck out his hand. 'I'm Bill and this is Patch.'

Jack took the hand and shook it. 'Jack, and I'm not her fella; I'm her lodger.'

Bill squinted at him, the crinkles deepening. 'There's not many lodgers who would put up a fence for their landladies.'

'I doubt there are,' Jack replied mildly. He wasn't prepared to discuss his rental arrangement with Bill, or anyone else for that matter. If Molly wanted to confide in the old guy, that was up to her.

'You're not doing too bad a job,' Bill said, examining the length of picket fence attached to the post. He walked around the other side to view it from the back. 'Nope, not too bad at all.'

'Glad you think so,' Jack said.

'You've got a fair few to do.'

'Tell me about it. I don't think I'll get it all done today. A couple more posts need to go in first. But I can get this section done.' By 'this section', Jack was referring to the area leading up to a giant slab of cracked concrete that served as a driveway. Molly had bought a pair of wide wooden gates and a smaller one to go next to them, but Jack guessed it would take two people to hang the gates properly. So he would do what he could, and then see if she wanted to give him a hand when she came home.

'How come you moved in with Molly?' Bill asked. His dog must have assumed he was here for the duration, because he was lying down with his nose on his paws and appeared to be asleep.

Jack shrugged. 'She had a room free, and I needed somewhere to stay.'

'Good. I didn't like the thought of her being on her own in this place at night.'

'It's not that bad, surely?'

'You moved in yesterday, you say? You'll see. One night isn't long enough.'

Jack thought back to the screeching he had heard in the middle of the night. 'It was a bit noisy,' he conceded. 'Foxes, apparently.'

'Aye, and the rest. When I took Patch out for a walk at about nine o'clock last night, there was a gang of youths hanging around the bandstand. Making one hell of a racket, they were. There was cans and fag ends everywhere. Molly, bless her, has taken it upon herself to clear up their mess in the mornings.'

'I know.'

'It's a disgrace, that's what it is,' Bill grumbled. 'The bloody council should do something about it.'

Jack thought it best to keep his mouth shut. 'Hmm,' was all he said. The last thing he needed was some old bloke getting on his case, as well as Molly.

'I remember when this was a lovely place to be,' Bill continued. 'There was music on in the bandstand – the Sally Army used to play there a lot – and that little tea room was open and you could get a cup of tea and a scone, or an ice cream for the kiddies. Talking about kiddies, have you seen the state of that play area? It's downright dangerous. Somebody should do something about it. A slip of a girl can't do it all herself.'

'What do you mean?'

'Molly hasn't said anything,' Bill said, 'but I know the type. She's not going to stop at picking up litter. She's going to want to sort this place out. She told me she's already been to see some chap at the council, but he was as much use as a chocolate fireguard. Waste of space, she said he was. A real jobsworth.'

'I see.' So that's what she'd thought of him. He hoped her opinion had mellowed since their fateful meeting at the council offices.

'You look like a good sort,' Bill added. 'You can help out a bit.'

'That's what I'm doing.' Jack jerked his head towards the fence.

'I mean, you can look out for her. Give her a bit of support.'

Bemused Jack said, 'I'll do what I can.' He meant it, too.

'I'd best get on. Remember what I said – keep an eye out for her. She doesn't realise what she's let herself in for.'

'I will,' Jack promised. He didn't think things were that bad, though. The only noises he'd heard last night had come from the wildlife. If there had been any youngsters hanging about, the TV had drowned them out, and they must have gone home by the time Jack had gone to bed.

Jack watched the old gent trundle away, and wondered if he was the phantom phone caller. He might very well be. Most people would have filled in the online complaints form, or would have emailed the department, but Bill struck him as the type to prefer to use a phone. In his experience, older people tended to call. But why hadn't the old chap left his name and number? It would have made life so much easier.

Jack waited until Bill was out of sight before returning to his task. He would only be able to do so much without help, because he needed someone to hold the gate into position while he put the screws in, so he did what he could, and then let Jet out. He would have liked to have had the dog outside with him this morning while he worked, but he was worried that if he was concentrating, he wouldn't be able to keep an eye on him and Jet might wander off. If that happened, he had a feeling Molly would never forgive him. Although she had told him she hadn't had the dog for long, she seemed to have developed a very strong bond with the animal. Jet slept in her bedroom, and Jack suspected the hound also slept on her bed. He wasn't sure he would like to share his bed with a dog, but what Molly did was up to her.

Jack hadn't had much of a chance to explore the area to the back of the cottage. He'd noticed from the kitchen window that it was overgrown, even more so than the front. It was like a jungle out there, and he wasn't looking forward to knocking it into shape. He had never been much of a gardener and neither had Della: one of the things that had attracted them to their house was that the garden wasn't too big, and it mainly consisted of lawn. He didn't find mowing too onerous, but he wasn't keen on pruning or weeding. He tended to hack at plants, and pull up bulbs instead of weeds.

He eyed the garden warily, whilst Jet scurried about in the undergrowth. There seemed to be an awful lot of sniffing and tail wagging going on, and now and again the dog disappeared behind a bush or a tree.

Whilst he waited for Jet to finish checking over his property, Jack decided to explore. Because the garden was so overgrown it wasn't easy to tell how big it was, so he began to fight his way through the low-hanging branches and bushes that wanted to snag his T-shirt and hold him back.

He came to a halt when he discovered what seemed to be a concrete bunker, but on closer inspection turned out to be a shed and an outside loo. He didn't mind the shed so much – it didn't have a lot in it except for a few shelves and some dusty and rusted tins of paint, but the outside toilet was a different ball game. He took one look inside and hastily slammed the door shut.

Shuddering, he risked another peep and cracked open the door a couple of centimetres

Yep, it was as he thought – that spider was *huge*.

Jack was no shrinking violet, and he didn't usually mind spiders, but he didn't think he'd ever seen one this big before outside of a zoo, and he wondered whether it had escaped. It was one of those arachnids with a fat round body and thick, hairy legs. He could have sworn it was glaring at him with venomous dislike.

Jack shut the door, a little more softly this time because he didn't want to antagonise the beast, and wondered whether Molly knew what was living in her outside toilet. He thought about telling her, but he didn't want to run the risk of her asking him to catch it, because he had an awful feeling that he would end up being the hunted and not the hunter.

Leaving the ginormous spider to lurk in peace, Jack called the dog to him and went inside the house. It was lunchtime, so he made a quick sandwich, the dog eating half of it, then got back to work.

This afternoon he was going to sand and prep all the woodwork in the lounge, ready for painting. The skirting boards were easy enough to do because Molly had already done the hard work by removing the old paint, so all that was needed was a light sanding and a quick rinse to get rid of the dust. However, the windows were an altogether different proposition. He wondered when they'd last been replaced, because they looked very old, although they didn't seem to be in a bad condition despite having at least six coats of paint on them. It was going to be quite a task to strip it all back, but he set to with enthusiasm, listening to an upbeat playlist on his phone as he worked.

If someone had asked him a month ago if he liked DIY, his response would have been "not really". He had always regarded it as a necessary evil, but now he found he was enjoying it. There was something quite satisfying in removing old paint to reveal the natural wood underneath, and he hoped Molly wouldn't paint over it.

He had also enjoyed erecting the fence, the bit of it he had managed to do. Once again, he realised there was a certain gratification to be found in working with his hands. He felt quite proud of what he'd achieved, and he prayed Molly would think he had done a good job.

As the afternoon ticked on, Jack's thoughts turned to what to cook for tea. He didn't know when she would be home, but perhaps if he made a casserole he could pop it in the oven where it could simmer gently until it was needed. And if he prepared some vegetables and new potatoes now, all he would need to do was to put them on to boil as soon as she arrived.

He was surprised to discover how much he was looking forward to seeing her. Although he'd kept himself busy, he had missed her. He'd tried telling himself it was because this was her house, but that wasn't the reason at all.

He'd missed *Molly*, God damn it. And when she walked in through the door, dropping her bag at the foot of the stairs and shouting 'Anyone home?' Jack felt like greeting her as enthusiastically as her dog, but possibly without trying to lick her face or clamber onto her lap as she crouched on the floor. He would prefer to kiss her instead.

Oh, dear me, that would never do. She would be horrified if she knew what he was thinking, so Jack darted into the kitchen to check on the casserole and hoped that the heat from the oven would hide the colour he could feel creeping into his face.

***

'The fence looks great,' Molly said, following Jack out to the kitchen, Jet at her heels.

The dog had clearly missed her and couldn't get close enough. It was a pity Jack wasn't as pleased to see her. He had sort of grunted, leaving her to wonder what was wrong.

Jack was peering into the oven, gingerly lifting the lid of a casserole dish and stirring the contents with a wooden spoon.

Ah, she thought, he's cooking. It was a well-known fact that men couldn't concentrate on two things at once, so she would wait for him to finish stirring whatever it was – which smelled absolutely delicious, by the way – and then she'd try again to tell him how impressed she was with the fence. Now that a good third or more of the picket fence was in place, she could envisage what the rest of it would look like, and she grinned.

In a remarkably short space of time, the cottage was turning into the home of her dreams.

A friend of her mother's was into embroidery, and Molly had once seen her working on a very intricate cross stitch pattern of Anne Hathaway's cottage in Stratford, and Molly had carried the image in her head as an ideal picture of what she wanted her own garden to look like. English country garden was what she was aiming for. She wanted roses climbing around the front door, she wanted purple and pink hydrangeas with their huge flowers, she wanted foxgloves and hollyhocks, and a lilac tree, and lavender growing along the edges of the path. She wanted a small pond, and a bird bath, a summer house and a hammock.

The picket fence was only the first step. Even if she couldn't do anything with the rest of the park, she could do something with her garden. She knew it was going to be a big job and that she would be lucky to break the back of it this summer, but at least she could plant wildflowers, and her mum would show her how to take cuttings from the hydrangea and other suitable plants.

Jack finished stirring and straightened up, looking very flushed. Molly noticed he'd caught the sun, or was his pink face because he'd had his head stuck in the oven?

'I was saying that the fence looks great,' Molly repeated.

'Do you think so?'

'It's exactly how I envisaged it.'

'That's good.'

Jack's answers were short and he couldn't seem to look her in the eye. There was a bit of an atmosphere too, and Molly couldn't work out why. She wondered if something had happened while she had been out, and prayed to God her mother hadn't dropped by.

'Is everything OK?' she asked.

'Yes, why? Shouldn't it be?' He looked worried.

'My mother hasn't popped in, has she?'

'No sorry, she hasn't. Were you expecting her?'

'Thank goodness for that!' Molly sighed and flopped down into one of the kitchen chairs. 'I did ask her not to, but my mum can be a law unto herself. By the way, I'm going to my parents' house for lunch tomorrow and they've invited you. My mum does a mean Sunday roast.'

'Oh, I, er…' Jack was floundering.

'Please don't feel obliged to come if you don't want to. I won't be offended.'

'It's not that I don't want to…,' he began, then ground to a halt.

'It's OK, you don't have to explain. I don't expect us to live in each other's pockets. It's just that she wanted to meet you and I'm going for lunch anyway, so I thought it would save you cooking. But if you've got other plans, that's fine.'

'I've not got any other plans, but are you sure you want me tagging along?'

'It's not a question of you tagging along, it's a question of my mother insisting on meeting you.'

Molly wondered how much she should tell him and decided she should give him a watered-down version of the truth. 'She wants to meet the guy I'm shacked up with.'

Jack's horrified expression made her giggle

'You should see your face,' she teased. 'I'm having you on. My mother doesn't think we're shacked up at all, not in that sense.' Molly could feel a blush creeping into her cheeks, and she hastily added, 'She would want to meet anyone who I was living with, regardless of gender or age. She's being nosey.'

'She's probably looking out for you,' Jack said. There was a smile playing about his mouth, and Molly hoped he hadn't guessed her mum was distrustful of him.

'I suppose she is,' she agreed.

'If that's OK with you, I'd love to come. I haven't had a proper roast dinner in ages. Gravy making isn't one of my strengths.'

'What are you cooking this evening?' she asked, hungrily. Her mouth was already watering at the delicious aroma coming from the oven.

'It's very basic, I'm afraid. It's just a chicken casserole with a white wine and tomato sauce. I threw in a couple of mushrooms as well, because they looked as though they needed to be used up.'

'Whatever it is, it smells yummy.' At that moment her tummy rumbled loudly and she bit her lip, hoping he hadn't heard.

He had and he smiled. 'I take it you're hungry.'

'Starving.'

'It'll be about thirty minutes, if you want to have a shower, or get changed.'

'That's a good idea,' she said, and she was about to go upstairs when she noticed he had also been busy in the living room.

'The window looks fabulous,' she gushed, seriously impressed. 'I can't believe you've done so much!' She felt a little guilty. She didn't expect him to spend his every spare moment doing her house up. 'You shouldn't have. You've already done enough today with the fence.'

'I don't mind,' he said. 'Honestly. I didn't have anything else to do. Do you think you'll paint it?'

'Oh definitely. I was thinking of pale blue.'

'Really?'

'Or do you think green would be better? A forest green, so it won't stand out?'

'Whatever you think.' Jack had a pained look on his face.

'What colour would you suggest?' He clearly didn't fancy either of the colours she'd mentioned.

'If you want my honest opinion, I think you'll spoil it if you paint it.'

'I can't leave it bare. It needs some form of protection. I'm scared it will rot, out there in all weathers. I know the wood is treated but—'

'Hang on, I don't think we're talking about the same thing. I thought you meant the window,' Jack said.

Molly giggled. 'And I thought you meant the fence! Start again. Window first – I don't think I will paint it. Maybe some varnish or wood stain to bring out the grain of the wood. What do you think?'

'Perfect! And as for the fence, blue is pretty, if you want people to notice it. If you don't, paint it green and it will blend in with the shrubs and the bushes.'

'Now that's sorted, I'm going to have a shower. See you in a bit.'

Molly trotted up the stairs, Jet hot on her heels, and she caught herself asking the dog whether he'd been a good boy for Jack. She had missed this daft pooch today and she gave him a hug as he leapt onto her bed. She had missed Jack too, but that was probably because she was envious that he was at home (the lucky thing!), and she'd had to go to work.

But even as she tried to convince herself that was the reason, she knew she was lying. She had been looking forward to coming home to see Jack just as much as she'd been looking forward to seeing her dog.

CHAPTER 16

Blimey, it's warm, Jack thought as he grabbed the hem of his T-shirt and dragged it over his head. It might only be May, but the temperature was more like high summer, and he could feel a trickle of sweat running down his back between his shoulder blades. Thank goodness this was the last hole. The ground he was trying to excavate for the final fence post was riddled with tree roots which he didn't want to damage. He knew from experience that damaged roots could weaken a tree, and the last thing he wanted was for the nearby sweet chestnut to topple.

He dug the spade in again, putting his back into it, his foot grinding the blade deeper into the soil. He did this a few more times until he'd loosened the earth, then he scooped it out. When he deemed the hole was big enough, he turned his attention to the last remaining bag of quick-drying cement. He would mix it up, drop the fence post in, make sure it was level, then he'd take a break.

At least he was working up an appetite for lunch. He hadn't been lying when he'd told Molly he hadn't had a proper Sunday lunch in ages, and he was looking forward to this one. He hoped Molly's mum and dad liked him. Reading between the lines and seeing Molly's expression when she'd thought that her mum had popped in yesterday, he guessed Molly's mother was concerned that a strange man was living with her daughter. He didn't blame her. If he had a daughter, he would feel exactly the same way. After all, it wasn't as though he and Molly had known each other for ages. They had only met a couple of weeks ago. He could be anyone.

Jack was offering up the spirit level to the post, making sure it was dead straight and didn't have a list, when he heard the sound of heavy paws running up to him and felt a boop on his leg. Stepping away from the post carefully so as not to nudge it, he turned around to see Jet wagging his tail so hard that his whole behind waggled from side to side.

'Where's your mistress?' he asked, then spotted Molly coming around the corner. She was carrying a black plastic bag in one hand and a litter picker in the other.

He walked forward to take the bag from her, wondering whether he should offer to go with her the next time.

'It's alright, I can manage,' she said, as he held out his hand for the bag. 'It's not heavy: it's mainly food wrappers, plastic bottles, and a couple of cans. Not much of a haul today.'

She looked uncomfortable, and he wondered whether it was because he had refused to help in his capacity as Parks and Highways Officer. But that didn't prevent him from helping personally, did it? The question was, did he want to get involved? It was one thing lending a hand with the cottage and its grounds, because that was the agreement for him to live here rent-free, but should he extend that helping hand to the park itself? Would she see it as a step towards him diverting council funds into the park, and if so, would that lead to conflict between them?

On the other hand, cleaning up the park clearly meant a great deal to her, and he could see the effort she was making and the positive impact her daily litter pick was having. Would it hurt him to go with her now and again?

The more time he spent here, the more the park was growing on him. He could appreciate what Molly saw in it, and he was finally able to look beyond the tatty benches, the boarded-up cafe, the overgrown field and the impenetrable woodland, to imagine how it must have looked when there had been an actual park keeper living in the cottage. It must have been a grand place to spend an afternoon. Nowadays, though, the only people who wanted to hang around in it were youngsters with nothing better to do and nowhere else to go. It was such a shame – for both the park and for the kids.

Molly put the bag of rubbish in the wheelie bin, then went inside the house.

Jack watched her go. He had been doing that a lot since he'd moved in – watching her. If he'd thought he was attracted to her when he'd first seen her, he was doubly so now that he was getting to know her. Despite her initial prickliness, he'd come to realise she was funny, thoughtful, and sweet. Combined with a wicked sense of humour and a quick wit, she was a delight to be around. She was also easy on the eye. Very easy. In fact, he thought she was gorgeous.

No sooner had she gone into the cottage, she was back outside again, this time carrying a couple of glasses of water. He noticed that she had also changed into her scruffs and had tied her hair up. She looked incredibly cute.

Glancing away, he uttered a gruff thanks when she handed him his water, and he downed the drink in one.

'Gosh, you were thirsty,' she said.

'It's warmer than I was expecting,' he replied, and saw her eyes flicker over his chest.

Feeling a little self-conscious, he turned away, well aware that he wasn't as ripped as he would like to be.

Who was he kidding! He wasn't ripped at all. Weedy was the word that came to mind. It was all that running he did. A sprinter needed power and muscle. A marathon runner needed to carry as little weight as possible. It wasn't fun hauling around a couple of extra kilos when you were trying to run forty-two kilometres.

By the time he glanced back at her, Molly's attention was on the last fence post.

'Good job,' she said. 'It looks brill, doesn't it?'

'It'll do,' Jack muttered. He was still feeling a little disconcerted that his top half was bare, and she had been staring at him. 'Do you think we'll have time to hang the small gate before we go to your parents' house?'

Molly checked the time on her phone. 'I don't see why not. I'll fetch the hinges and the screwdriver.'

He deliberately tried not to watch her walk away this time, for fear he was becoming fixated on her. But he couldn't seem to help himself. The way her hips swung was fascinating.

By the time she came back into the garden, he had slipped his T-shirt back on, telling himself he had cooled down sufficiently, and it had nothing to do with him being self-conscious.

Jack lifted the gate from where it was tucked down the side of the house, and offered it up to the opening between the posts. It fitted perfectly, so he marked out on the wood where the hinges were to go on the gate, and screwed them into place. When that was done, he lifted the gate again and held it in position.

'If I take the weight, can you screw this part of the hinge?' he asked.

Molly nodded and got to work. She was so close he could smell her perfume. It was light and fresh, and he inhaled deeply, the scent of her intoxicating. He breathed in again and felt a little lightheaded… Gosh, the sun must be stronger than he thought.

'There, all done.' She straightened up and stepped back, admiring their handiwork.

Jack gingerly released his hold on the gate and was pleased to see it was level.

'We make a good team,' he declared, holding his palm up for her to slap, but when she did, he yelped as a tingle shot through him. 'You don't half pack a punch,' he lied.

'Wuss,' she teased. 'Stay there, I've got a latch to put on.' She fished in her pocket and brought out a black wrought iron catch.

'Where do you want it?' he asked, holding it up against the opposite post to the hinges. 'There?' When she didn't reply, he moved it a couple of centimetres. 'Or there?'

'That's perfect,' she declared. 'Don't move.'

Once again she was so close he could smell her. Her head was bent as she fastened the latch into position and his eyes were drawn to the nape of her neck. Her skin looked very soft and extremely kissable.

Clearing his throat, Jack dragged his gaze away and stared into the distance, focusing on a tree, the shape of its trunk, the movement of its leaves in the gentle breeze... anything other than how she made him feel.

As soon as she was done, he moved smartly out of the way, giving her space to open and close the gate and make sure the latch was working.

'I'm pleased with that,' she said. 'It's coming along, isn't it? Thank you so much for helping.'

Gruffly he said, 'I didn't think I had any choice,' then he realised how that had sounded when she gave him a sharp look. Smiling to show he was teasing, he added, 'I thought that was the whole point of me being here? Room in exchange for rent?'

'Are you sure you don't mind?'

'Why should I mind? I agreed to this. You didn't railroad me into it. You're doing me a favour.'

'And you're doing me a favour, too,' Molly replied.

Then they stared at each other before bursting out laughing, and Jack realised he was enjoying helping Molly with her house and garden more than he would have believed possible.

'I'd better jump in the shower,' Molly said, sobering.

'Me, too,' Jack said, then winced. 'I mean, I'll have a shower after you,' he explained.

'I knew what you meant,' she chuckled, and she continued to laugh as she went inside.

Jack followed slowly, images of Molly in the shower plaguing him, and he shook his head to clear them away.

Unfortunately, those images quickly returned when he went upstairs and bumped into a rather damp Molly coming out of the bathroom. She had her hair wrapped up in a towel, and another secured under her armpits. The skin on her shoulders glistened with droplets of water, and her cheeks were flushed. The sight of her nearly took his breath away.

'Oh, er, sorry,' he stuttered. 'I thought you had finished.'

'I have,' she said. 'The bathroom is all yours.'

But it wasn't all his, because when he stepped under the hot spray, he couldn't help imagining Molly in there with him.

***

Molly thought she should have had a cold shower, because she was still all hot and bothered after seeing Jack stripped down to the waist and with streaks of dirt across his chest from putting the last fence post in. She'd been unable to take her eyes off the trickle of sweat working its way from the dip at his throat, between his pectoral muscles, heading south.

But when it had reached the waistband of his jeans, she had suddenly realised she was staring and had hurried inside. Hastily she'd changed into old clothes and poured them both a glass of water. Her mouth had gone dry, but it hadn't been from the warmth of the morning. Jack, on the other hand, could probably do with a drink because he'd been grafting hard, and once again her treacherous thoughts had returned to his chest.

He'd looked good enough to eat and she'd had to make a supreme effort to appear normal.

Thankfully he hadn't seemed to have noticed, but she had still been very much aware of him while they were hanging the gate. He had been standing so close that she'd been able to smell the heady aroma of man at work combined with the aftershave he wore. It had taken all her willpower not to throw herself at him.

Goodness, what was wrong with her? She hadn't felt this way about a man for a very long time. If ever.

She was almost drooling over him! Thank God he didn't know what she was thinking. If he had the slightest hint of how she felt, she'd be mortified. To make matters worse, she had almost dropped her towel when she'd emerged from the bathroom to find him standing on the landing. Talk about offering it to him on a plate!

And then, to add to her embarrassment, when she heard the shower running, she could far too easily imagine him standing there with water cascading over his body, sluicing the sweat from his chest. She could do with another shower herself – to wash such mucky thoughts from her mind.

She was still blushing as she drove to her parents' house, Jack sitting in the passenger seat. Throughout the short journey she was terribly conscious of his long legs folded into the footwell, of his knee almost touching the gear stick, and there was the smell of him again, clean and male, and totally delectable. His hair was damp from his shower, and it curled on the top of his head, one lock falling artfully over his forehead. He kept running his hand through it, pushing it off his brow, but it would inevitably flop back.

Neither of them said much on the journey, Molly because she was scared of what she might inadvertently say, and Jack was probably silent because he was tired from his exertions this morning. He was doing a good job on the fence, and she meant it when she'd told him she was grateful. She honestly didn't expect him to work so hard, but she was glad he had, especially if it meant he got hot and sweaty and took his T-shirt off.

'Stop that.'

'Pardon?' Jack was staring at her curiously.

Oh dear, she'd said that out loud.

'What did you say?' he repeated.

'Nothing.'

'I could have sworn you said something.'

'Did I? I don't think so. I might have coughed: is that what you heard?'

'That must have been it,' he said.

Thankfully Molly was able to change the subject as she pulled up in front of her mum and dad's house.

'We're here,' she announced unnecessarily, feeling surprisingly nervous. She hoped her parents liked Jack, and that he liked them. It was ridiculous, because it shouldn't matter whether her parents liked her lodger or not. This was a business arrangement, nothing more. It wasn't as though she was introducing them to her boyfriend; and she was only bringing Jack with her today because her mum had insisted on meeting him.

Her mother was in the kitchen when Molly led Jack into the house.

'Hi, Mum. Hi, Granny.' Molly bent to kiss her grandmother who was sitting at the tiny kitchen table, slicing green beans.

Her granny dropped the knife and the runner bean she was holding, and tilted her cheek to be kissed. 'Molly, my darling girl. How are you? You're looking well. And who is this young man? Your boyfriend?'

'No, Mum,' Molly's mother said. 'He's her lodger. I told you, remember?'

'I was expecting somebody older,' her grandmother said. 'Are you sure he's her lodger?'

Molly's mum sighed. 'I'm sure.'

'He's too handsome to be a lodger.' Her granny resumed slicing beans, and Molly bit her lip to hold back a giggle.

She caught Jack's eye, and bit harder.

'I'm Evelyn,' her grandma said. 'What's your name?'

'Jack.' Jack held out his hand. 'Pleased to meet you.'

Evelyn dropped the knife once more. 'Ooh, hasn't he got lovely manners.' She turned to Molly's mum. 'Teresa, are you sure he's not her boyfriend?'

'I'm sure.' This was said through gritted teeth, and Molly guessed that her mother was finding Granny difficult. Granny was hard of hearing, and she could be a bit forgetful too. Combined with a stubborn streak and only hearing what she wanted to hear, sometimes Granny could be hard work. But Molly adored her.

'Aren't you going to introduce us?' her mother asked Molly. She was scrutinising Jack from head to toe.

Molly hoped she liked what she saw. Jack was wearing a white button-down shirt with the sleeves rolled up, exposing his forearms, a pair of smart jeans, and trainers. *Molly* certainly liked what she saw.

'Jack, this is my mum, Teresa. Mum this is Jack.'

Her mum said, 'Excuse me if I don't shake hands, I want to get these potatoes peeled.'

'Pleased to meet you,' Jack said.

'I hope you like roast pork,' Teresa said, 'because that's what we're having.'

Molly thought she sounded a bit belligerent, as though she was spoiling for a fight.

Jack said mildly, 'Pork is my favourite.'

Evelyn piped up, 'She makes lovely crackling. Of course, I can't eat it nowadays, not with my dentures, but a young chap like you with good strong teeth should be able to.'

'Is there anything I can do to help, Mum?' Molly asked, trying not to laugh.

'It's all in hand. Why don't you go and find your father? He's in the shed. Hiding.'

'Good idea,' Molly said. She had been wondering where her dad had got to. 'Come on, Jack.'

She checked that Jack was following and that her mother hadn't waylaid him, and when she saw that he was, she led him down the garden path to the shed at the end.

She stuck her head around the door and saw her dad sitting at his workbench, tying flies. 'Hi, Dad. Mum said you were hiding.'

'It's best to keep out of her way when she's in one of her moods,' her dad said. 'Hello, you must be Jack. How are you settling in?'

'Good, thanks. The cottage is lovely.'

'Molly's mum and I thought she was mad to buy it, but I must admit she's already worked wonders. It looks like a different place.'

'It does, doesn't it,' Jack agreed. 'I often run through the park, and I used to think how sad it looked, boarded up and unlived in.'

'I hear she's roped you in to help.'

'She drives a hard bargain, does your daughter,' Jack said.

'She's stubborn, like her mother. I'm Duncan, by the way.'

'Pleased to meet you.' Jack held out his hand.

'Likewise.'

The two men shook, then Jack stooped down to see what her father was doing. 'I take it you're a fisherman?'

'Oh, yes, I'm an extremely keen angler,' her dad said.

'Do you catch much?'

'I don't do too bad. Of course, it's all catch and release around here, but I have got some photos if you'd like to see them?'

'I'd love to.'

'I'll show you after lunch. Do you do any fishing?'

Molly let out a slow sigh of relief. One down, one to go, she thought. Her dad seemed to approve of Jack and was happily chatting about fishing with him. She didn't know whether Jack knew anything about the subject, but he was listening avidly and asking questions, therefore her dad was in his element.

Now all Jack had to do was to win her mother around. Unfortunately, her mum was a tougher nut to crack, and Molly had seen the suspicion in her eyes.

The Spanish Inquisition began the moment Jack took a seat at the table.

'Help yourself to veg,' Teresa said.

'This looks lovely.' Jack didn't move a muscle, so Molly spooned some carrots onto his plate and he smiled gratefully at her.

She could tell he was feeling somewhat out of his depth, and she felt sorry for him, wondering how she would feel if their roles were reversed and she was sitting opposite *his* mother.

'I haven't had a roast dinner in ages,' he said.

'Don't you cook for yourself?' Teresa asked.

'I do, but I'm hopeless at making gravy.'

'What about your mum? Does she cook?'

'She does, but she lives near York, so I don't get to see her more than a few times a year.'

'Wife?'

Molly cringed.

'I don't have one.' Jack's expression was guarded.

'Girlfriend?'

'I haven't got one of those, either.'

'*Mum*,' Molly hissed.

'It's OK,' Jack said. 'She's got a right to ask.'

'Molly tells me you work for the council. What exactly is it you do?' Her mum moved the gravy boat closer to him, and Jack picked it up and poured a trickle onto his plate.

He gave Molly an apologetic look before answering. 'I'm the Parks and Highways Officer.'

'I see,' Teresa said.

Molly leapt in. 'Before you ask, he can't do anything about the state of the park.'

Her mother pursed her lips. 'Why ever not?'

'The council can't afford it,' Molly explained.

'Nonsense!' This was from Granny. 'They had plenty of money to spend on those new council offices, so I'm sure they can find some to tart up the park.'

'I wish it was that simple,' Jack began.

'How difficult can it be?' Granny demanded.

Molly speared a roast potato, wishing the ground would open up and swallow her. She shouldn't have brought him. It wasn't fair. He might be a bit of a jobsworth, but he didn't deserve this grilling.

'I'm accountable for the budget,' Jack said. 'I've got to justify where I spend the money.'

'And you don't think Sweet Meadow Park is worth it?' Molly's mum snapped.

'No, I don't. There has been quite a bit of money spent on it in the past, all to no avail. People don't seem to value the park very much.'

Granny waved her fork in the air. 'People got no respect these days. That park has got a terrible reputation. I nearly turned in my grave when I found out our Molly had bought the old park keeper's cottage.'

'You've got to be dead to turn in your grave, Granny,' Molly pointed out.

'You know what I mean. I do wish you'd bought a nice little flat somewhere.'

Molly rolled her eyes.

'I saw that,' Granny said. 'That's what I mean about no respect.'

'I do respect you, Granny,' Molly said. See, she said to herself, this was why she hadn't told anyone she was planning to buy it when she saw the cottage come up for sale. She knew her parents and her granny would object. She also suspected she wouldn't hear the end of it. 'It'll be lovely when it's done, Granny. You'll have to come and visit.'

Molly's dad said, 'She's doing a grand job. Won't accept any help from me, the stubborn little madam. She wants to do it all herself. Except for Jack.'

Thankful that the topic of conversation had moved away from Jack's personal life and on to the cottage, Molly filled her family in on its progress, ending with, 'Now that the plastering has been done, we should be able to put the skirting boards back on and the dado rails, and all the other decorative pieces, and then it's simply a question of decorating.'

Her dad raised his eyebrows. 'You make it sound very easy.'

'It hasn't been as bad as I thought,' Molly admitted. 'I assumed I would have to take all the old rendering off the inside, but I didn't, so that saved loads of time. I did have to take about twenty layers of wallpaper off though. But to be fair, it came off without too much bother. I've still got the floors to do downstairs, and of course I need new kitchen units, and the bathroom needs a complete overhaul, but I can manage as it is for now.' She glanced at Jack and caught his eye. '*We* can manage for now,' she amended.

'I still wish you would live at home until all the renovations are done,' her mother grumbled. She turned to Evelyn. 'You ought to see the mess she was living in. I wouldn't have let a dog live in it.'

'It wasn't for long,' Molly objected. 'And it looks really homely now that Jack has moved all his furniture in.'

Teresa tilted her head to the side. 'What made you decide to sell your house, Jack? '

'Has everyone finished?' Molly asked brightly, jumping to her feet. It was none of her mother's business, and neither was it any of Molly's, although she was dying to know. But she could tell that Jack felt uncomfortable, so as she reached across to pick up his empty plate she hissed in his ear, 'You don't have to answer that.'

Jack gave her a grateful look, and he also got to his feet. 'I'll help you clear up.'

Molly smirked. If there was one thing guaranteed to get her mum on her high horse, it was the thought of guests messing about in her kitchen.

'No, you won't,' Teresa commanded. 'You sit back down. Molly and I can manage. Have you got room for some apple crumble and custard?'

'Yes, please,' Jack said.

'Not too much for me, Teresa,' Granny said.

Molly and her mum exchanged glances. Molly knew full well that despite her granny's protestations, the old lady could pack away a fair amount of food when she had a mind to.

She followed her mum out to the kitchen, dishes in hand, and popped them on the counter next to the sink. She was about to go back into the dining room for some more, when her mother grabbed hold of her arm.

'I can see what you see in him,' Teresa smirked.

'Pardon?'

'He's a bit of alright, isn't he?'

'What on earth do you mean?'

'He's not bad looking.'

'Is he? I hadn't noticed.'

'Don't give me that, Molly Brown,' her mum said. 'I saw the way you were looking at him. You fancy him.'

'I do not,' Molly objected, then blushed furiously. Even as she was denying it, Molly knew she wasn't being entirely truthful. That was precisely what she had been doing this morning – fancying him.

'I think he likes you, too,' her mother continued, ignoring Molly's stricken expression.

'I doubt that very much.'

Teresa gave her a knowing look. 'He can't take his eyes off you.'

'That's probably because he's trying to subconsciously beg me to get him out of here,' Molly retorted. 'I can't believe you questioned him about whether he had a wife or a girlfriend.'

'I wouldn't have had to ask him at all, if you had given me more information.'

'It's none of our business.'

'You don't know either, do you? And it *will* be your business when you get all jiggy with him.'

'*Mum!*'

Her mother pulled a face. 'Take my advice – get to know a bit more about him before you hop into bed with him.'

'I have no intention of hopping into bed with him,' Molly hissed, keeping her voice low. She'd be mortified if Jack heard the way they were talking about him.

Her mother looked disappointed, and Molly pointed out, 'I thought you weren't too keen on him?'

'That was before I met him. He seems nice enough.'

'He is nice, but that doesn't mean I want a relationship with him. He's not my type.'

Her mother was looking thoughtful. 'I suppose when the renovations are completed, you will have to start charging him rent.'

'Don't worry about that; there will be plenty for him to do. I've got plans for him to help me with the park.'

'I thought the council couldn't afford it?'

'Apparently they can't, but what I'm thinking of won't cost money – not much anyway. It will take an awful lot of hard work, though. Jack doesn't know it yet, but as long as he's living in my cottage, he's going to help me make Sweet Meadow Park beautiful once more.'

CHAPTER 17

Jack dropped his pen onto the desk and leant back in his chair. Thank God it's Friday, he thought. He was shattered. He also couldn't believe it was exactly a week today since he'd moved into Molly's cottage. He felt like he had been living there for a lot longer.

Mind you, that wasn't surprising considering the amount that had been achieved in those seven days. The fence around the cottage had been completed and the wooden gates had been hung, and they looked good, even if he did say so himself. This weekend they planned on giving the fence a coat of wood preserver, but first there was plenty of painting to be done inside now that the skirting boards had been put back on and the dado rails had been re-attached to the walls. That had been one hell of a learning curve. Before moving into the cottage, Jack hadn't even known what a dado rail was, and he'd had to dig deep into his high school education to remember how to work out angles, because the first few attempts at cutting the wood beading to fit into a corner had been an absolute disaster. Still, between them he and Molly had managed it. He had used the same principle when putting the coving up on the ceiling, and although it wasn't perfect, once it was painted no one would notice.

He was looking forward to going home, he thought, lifting his arms above his head to ease out the kinks in his back and shoulders. Then he caught himself.

Home – he had just referred to the park keeper's cottage as home. He supposed it was only natural considering he was living there, but he did feel as though it was his. He had invested so much time and energy into it over this past week, and he knew every nook and cranny that he felt as though he owned it: apart from Molly's bedroom, which he hadn't ventured into yet because they wouldn't tackle the upstairs until the downstairs was done.

It was odd, but he couldn't imagine living anywhere else now, and when he tried, his heart sank. Despite having only lived there for a week, the thought of leaving the cottage made him feel incredibly sad.

But was it the thought of living somewhere else that bothered him, or the thought of not living with Molly?

He loved waking up in the morning, knowing he wasn't alone in the house, and that she was just across the landing. He loved joining her on her early morning walks, and he didn't even mind litter picking with her. Over the course of the past few days, it had become a competition to see who could collect the most rubbish. Even Jet joined in, rooting around in the undergrowth and bringing back plastic bottles which he obediently dropped into the nearest refuse bag. However, because they were doing it on a daily basis, there wasn't much to collect these days.

Although he never would have believed it possible, Jack found it quite invigorating to go out for a walk before breakfast. When he'd lived in his old house, as soon as the alarm went off he had pressed the snooze button, often more than once, until he would eventually roll out of bed and into the shower, bleary-eyed and reluctant, before forcing a cup of coffee down his throat and stumbling out of the door.

These days he needed no encouragement to get out of bed. He was often awake before the alarm, although he still didn't dance into work. The reluctance hadn't gone away, but it was more to do with not wanting to go to work because there was so much to be done in the cottage, rather than a reluctance to start his day. He often even managed to eat some breakfast, which had confused Sue in the canteen, because as a consequence he had been taking his break later than usual and he hadn't had a fried breakfast at all this week.

He couldn't wait to go home this evening, and he relished the thought of two whole days stretching out in front of him. He knew he wouldn't be using them for rest and relaxation, because Molly was a little dynamo. She didn't stop from the minute she got up, to the minute she went to bed, and he couldn't sit there and watch her work, could he? He had to get involved, and if that meant gluing on coving at ten-thirty in the evening, then so be it.

It wasn't only working with his hands that he was enjoying: it was spending time with Molly, and he was looking forward to seeing her later. He'd probably arrive home before her as he liked to finish early on a Friday, although he intended going for a run. The last time he went, he'd taken Jet with him. Jack had been apprehensive at first, wondering whether the dog would get caught up in his feet or would try to run ahead and pull on his lead, but Jet had behaved impeccably, and Jack had enjoyed himself. He hadn't gone very far because he wanted to see how Jet would cope, but now that he was more confident about the dog, he'd attempt a longer run today. And if he returned before Molly arrived home, he'd start the evening meal. If she was home first, she would begin cooking.

It was like being married, but to his surprise the thought didn't fill him with horror – not like the way he'd felt whenever Chantelle had dropped hints about them getting engaged. He had shied away from that idea pretty sharpish. But he didn't feel like that where Molly was concerned. He loved living in the cottage, and he loved living in it with Molly. Maybe he also loved Molly a little bit, too…

Before he could fully grasp that thought, Chantelle appeared in the doorway and rapped out a knock with her knuckles.

'You look miles away,' she said.

Jack blew out his cheeks. He had managed to avoid his ex-girlfriend since last week, so he wasn't too pleased to see her today. He'd hoped she had finally got the hint to leave him alone. He wasn't happy with her invading his office, as she sauntered forward, kicking the door shut behind her.

Feeling cornered, he picked up his pen and leant forward to peer at his computer screen. 'I was thinking,' he said.

'Do you always have a smile on your face when you're thinking?' she asked, coming even closer to perch her bottom on the corner of his desk.

Jack shuffled away a few centimetres, trying not to make it look obvious. 'Depends what I'm thinking about,' he said.

'Something nice, by the look of it.' Chantelle pouted at him.

'What can I do for you?' His tone was brisk.

'I'm sure I can think of something,' she said suggestively, her head low as she gazed up at him from underneath her lashes. 'But that's not why I wanted to speak to you. Your house is on the market.'

'You knew I was putting it up for sale.'

'I didn't realise you had already moved out. I've seen the photographs online – the house is empty.' She sounded almost accusatory.

'So?'

'So… where are you living now?'

'Sorry, Chantelle, but do you really need to know?' He was tempted to tell her to mind her own business, but thought he'd better not. The last thing he wanted was for her to cause a scene, which she was perfectly capable of doing.

Her lips narrowed in annoyance. 'Actually, yes, I do. HR has been requested to ensure all postal addresses are up to date, so I'm afraid I *do* need your address.'

'Why?'

'There will be a letter going out soon from the Chief Exec to all council staff.'

Jack's stomach turned over. 'What's it about?'

'You know I can't tell you that,' Chantelle simpered at him. 'You'll have to read it.'

Oh dear, that didn't sound promising. If it was good news, she wouldn't have hesitated to tell him, so that meant it was bad. He hoped it wasn't *too* bad.

With a sigh, Jack grabbed a sticky note and scribbled his address on it then handed it to her.

Chantelle read it with raised eyebrows. 'You're living in the middle of Sweet Meadow Park?'

'It's only temporary. I'm renting for the time being.'

'Thank goodness for that. You do realise that's where all the yobs hang out?'

'I can't say I've seen much evidence of that,' he said. Except for the litter and a bit of shouting in the evenings, which he hadn't really been aware of, he hadn't been unduly bothered by any of the visitors to the park; apart from the fox, although the creature's unholy shrieking didn't disturb him as often now as it had when he'd first moved into Molly's cottage.

'I'll have to pop by and see it sometime,' she said.

'I wouldn't bother.' Jack hurriedly tried to put Chantelle off. 'Let me move in properly first.'

'I thought you had?'

'Yes, but it needs a bit of work doing. '

'Surely your landlord should have done that before you moved in?'

'Maybe… perhaps… it's complicated.' Jack was aware he was blustering, but he didn't want Chantelle to know his private business, and certainly not where it concerned Molly and his arrangement with her.

'Next time you move,' Chantelle said, tapping the sticky note with her finger, 'make sure you let HR know immediately.'

'Of course. Sorry, I didn't think of it. Too many other things on my mind.'

'I hope you settle in soon, and when you do you'll have to have a house-warming party.'

Jack was horrified. A party was the last thing he wanted. He simply couldn't imagine Molly and Chantelle in the same room. Chantelle would eat Molly alive. And although nothing was going on between him and Molly, he knew without a shadow of a doubt that Chantelle wouldn't see it that way.

He waited for his ex to leave, her heels echoing down the hall, before he risked peeking out of the door. The coast was clear, so he hurried towards the water cooler near the lifts. His mouth was dry and his stomach was churning, and he didn't know whether it was because of the imminent letter from the Chief Executive, or because Chantelle knew where he lived. He prayed to goodness she wouldn't turn up on his doorstep with a housewarming present. It would be just like her.

The lift pinged and he froze, hoping it wasn't Chantelle coming back because she'd forgotten something, and he exhaled in relief when he saw it was Pete.

'What's wrong?' his colleague demanded. 'You look like you've seen a ghost.'

'I've just had Chantelle in my office.'

'Ah, I see. That explains it.' Pete knew all about Chantelle. 'What did she want?'

'I told you my house is on the market, didn't I?'

'You did.'

'Chantelle saw it online and realised I'd moved out. She wanted my new address.'

'Did you give it to her?'

'I had to. She does work in HR after all, so she is entitled to ask for it and I'm obliged to give it. Anyway, she said HR has been tasked with ensuring all the postal addresses they have on file are up to date. Apparently, there's a letter coming out from the Chief Exec.'

'That's no surprise, although I hadn't heard about any letter,' Pete said, refilling his water bottle. He began walking towards his office, and Jack fell into step beside him.

'What have you heard? I tried to ask Chantelle but she wasn't giving anything away.'

'What *haven't* I heard,' Pete grunted, shrugging his shoulders. 'Everything from the council moving to new offices—' he barked out a laugh '—unlikely considering the amount they've spent on this place, to rumours that Parks and Highways are going to amalgamate with Waste Management, or maybe even Property Services.'

'What do you think is going to happen?'

'No idea, but they do this to us every now and again, don't they? Last year there were rumours they were closing libraries and leisure centres, but the public kicked up such a stink they thought they'd better not. So I suppose this is a new initiative to try to claw back some money by doing away with people's salaries. Anyway, I'd better get back to work, I don't want to be accused of slacking, not in the current climate.'

Neither did Jack, but as he sat down and stared at the spreadsheet in front of him, he wasn't able to concentrate. The last thing he needed right now was further worry about his job. For the past week he had managed to push it to the back of his mind, but it was very much in the forefront again, and he pulled a face. Maybe it was time to start looking for a new one?

***

'Got anything nice planned for the weekend?' Astrid asked as Molly switched off her computer.

'Painting the living room and the snug,' she said. 'And possibly the hall and the stairs if we've got time.'

'Listen to you, *if we've got time*. You sound like a proper married couple.'

'Don't start that again. You've done nothing but tease me about Jack ever since he moved in.'

'That's because you haven't stopped talking about him,' Astrid pointed out. 'It's been about a week, hasn't it?'

'A week today.'

'And you've mentioned him every single day, several times.'

'That's because he's doing such good work in the cottage,' Molly protested. She didn't talk about him *that* much, did she?

'I can't wait to see it,' Astrid said. 'The last time I was in the park, the cottage was a right mess.'

'It's looking very different already,' Molley said with pride.

'Living there seems to suit you. You're positively glowing. Or is that because of the delectable Jack?'

'How do you know he's delectable? You haven't even met him.'

'I've seen the official council photo of him you sent me, and you clearly think he is. Have you got any more? And don't try to tell me you haven't taken any of him, because I won't believe you.'

Molly's cheeks burned. She had taken several photos of Jack, but he wasn't aware of it. She'd taken them on the pretence of logging the work that had been done so she could look back on it and marvel at how far they'd come. It was a coincidence Jack had happened to be in the frame when she had taken the picture.

With a sigh, she fished her phone out of her bag and scrolled through it, before handing it to Astrid.

'Flipping heck, he's not bad looking, is he? You've landed on your feet there, girlie.'

'I keep telling you, he's my lodger.'

'Doesn't mean to say you can't have one that's nice to look at, does it?'

Molly frowned. 'We shouldn't be talking about him like that. I would hate it if the shoe was on the other foot and he was showing photos of me to his mates and they were saying the same sort of thing.'

'He probably is,' Astrid said. 'You're stunning.'

Molly's blush deepened. 'Stop it, I'm nothing of the sort.'

'I bet your lodger is thinking he's landed on his feet,' Astrid persisted. 'Rent-free and with a gorgeous woman like you? Has he kissed you yet?'

'No, he has not! And would you be saying the same sort of thing if he happened to be a woman?'

'I would if you were gay,' Astrid countered.

'You've got sex on the brain,' Molly said sniffily.

'Not sex, girlie, luurve. It's about time you found Mr Right.'

'Jack Feathers is certainly not Mr Right.' She picked up her bag and headed for the door.

'If he isn't, then we'll have to go out and find him. We haven't had a proper night out in ages.'

'We haven't. I'm a bit tied up this weekend,' Molly said, 'but I promise we'll do it soon and have a good gossip.'

'It's a date,' Astrid called as Molly opened the door and slipped through it. Her friend's final words, 'Unless you already have one with Jack,' followed her outside.

Molly shook her head and rolled her eyes. Astrid was incorrigible, but Molly loved her to the moon and back. She was good fun to work with, and even more fun on a night out, and Molly was looking forward to having a drink and a catch-up. She'd been so busy with the cottage lately, that it would do her good to take some time off. Not this weekend though, because she wanted to break the back of the painting and decorating.

Her head was full of what she had to do as she drove home, and as she approached the park she noted with pleasure that the main gates were already open, which meant that Jack had arrived home before her. True enough, his car was on the driveway, but when she tried the front door and discovered it was locked, she guessed he'd gone out for a run.

Molly took a moment to survey the cottage, marvelling at how much it had changed in just a few weeks. The front garden still needed some serious work, and the recent lovely weather hadn't helped when it came to the proliferation of weeds, but the picket fence was now in place, and the cottage was beginning to look loved and lived in.

And when she went into the living room, her heart soared. It was no longer the gloomy, grimy room it had once been. The dried-out plaster on the walls was a pale pinky-peach, and the room was flooded with light. The tiled floors still needed some attention, and she would get to that in time, but the squashy sofas lent an air of cosiness, as did the fireplace. It still needed to be swept, but the old wood burner had been treated to a coat of some yucky black stuff that had completely transformed it. It looked almost new, and gleamed blackly in the chimney breast, and she imagined what it would look like on a dark and stormy night, with a fire burning in its depths. For now though, she would have to settle for some fairy lights draped over the top of it, and she made a note to pick some up the next time she was out shopping.

With a spring in her step, Molly went into the kitchen and hung her bag on a peg on the back of the pantry door, feeling so happy she could burst. The only thing missing was her dog. And Jack.

Suddenly the conversation with Astrid popped into her head and Molly had an image of Jack's lips, his head bent to kiss her.

Back off lady, she told herself. *Jack doesn't need you drooling all over him.* And with that she went upstairs to change out of her work clothes, before she began preparing their evening meal.

Wearing an old pair of jeans and a T-shirt covered in paint, and with her hair piled on top of her head in a scruffy bun, she didn't feel the least bit attractive, so hopefully that would drive any thoughts of Jack kissing her right out of her head.

CHAPTER 18

Jack jogged through the little gate at the other end of the park and slowed as he neared the bandstand. A couple of youngsters had already gathered there, and a vague whiff of cigarette smoke wafted up his nose as he went past. More fag ends for him to clean up in the morning, he thought. And he also caught a glimpse of a can being passed around and guessed it would be dumped on the grass by the end of the evening.

He slowed to a walk to give Jet a chance to cool down before they reached the cottage. The dog was panting heavily but he still had a bounce in his step, so Jack wasn't unduly concerned. The pooch had coped well with the extra distance and was padding nicely by his side.

Jack put a hand on the silky head. 'You're a good boy,' he murmured, surprised at how much he enjoyed the dog's company on his run; it was like running alone, only better.

Jack's breathing was quickly returning to normal and his pulse was slowing nicely he saw, as he examined the app on his watch, angling it so he could read it properly; but when he looked up from the screen his heart gave a nasty leap.

There was a woman standing outside the newly hung gates, staring at the cottage.

'Chantelle,' he growled, and Jet nudged his hand and whined.

She hadn't seen him yet and Jack wanted to make sure she didn't, so he slowly moved towards a large beech tree and sidled around it, keeping his eyes on her.

He knew it had been a mistake to give her his address, but what else could he have done? And he certainly hadn't expected her to turn up a few hours later. He wondered how long he could stay outside: she must have seen his car, so she probably knew he wouldn't be far away.

Hoping she hadn't already knocked on the door, he leant up against the trunk, feeling the rough bark through his Lycra top, and rested his head against the tree.

'Please go,' he muttered, and Jet whined again.

Jack stayed in the same position for a few minutes before eventually risking a quick peep.

His relief when he saw Chantelle heading towards the main gate was immeasurable. He felt as though he had dodged a bullet. Hoping to goodness she hadn't spoken to Molly, he waited until she was no longer in sight, then hurried towards the cottage.

'Molly?' he called, opening the door, Jet bounding ahead of him. The smell of frying onions and garlic was in the air.

'I'm in the kitchen. Dinner will be half an hour,' she called back, and he was pleased to hear she sounded normal. Maybe all Chantelle had done was come for a look-see? He hoped that was the case.

As he climbed the stairs, taking them two at a time, he heard Molly making a fuss of the dog and he smiled. However, the smile didn't stay on his lips for long, as he grabbed his phone and fired off a quick message.

But after he sent it, he wished he hadn't. He should have waited until he calmed down a little, but he was furious. How dare Chantelle come to his home.

However, when he thought about it logically, he realised that technically, she hadn't. She had every right to be in the park, which was an extremely public place, so sending her a message telling her to butt out and leave him alone probably wasn't the wisest thing to do. He wished he could take it back, but it was too late now.

Oh well, he reasoned, at least he had made his feelings clear. He'd pussy-footed around her for far too long, not wanting to hurt her feelings, and he had tried letting her down gently, but that hadn't worked, so maybe this would.

Hastily Jack stripped off his running gear and jumped in the shower. He would no doubt need another later after wielding a paintbrush, but he didn't want to sit opposite Molly at the dinner table when he was all hot and sweaty. He told himself he was simply being considerate, and ignored the little voice in his mind hinting it was because he wanted to look and smell his best.

'Anything I can do?' he asked, walking into the kitchen a short while later and sniffing the air appreciatively. He noticed his mobile on the counter next to Molly's, and seeing the two phones sitting side by side gave him a warm, fuzzy glow.

'You can lay the table,' she suggested.

He got the knives and forks out of the cutlery drawer, sneaking glances at her out of the corner of his eye as he did so. Every time he looked at her, he saw something new – such as the freckle on her earlobe, for instance. Then his gaze was drawn to the pale skin beneath it, and he wondered whether it was as soft as it looked.

The urge to find out was almost overwhelming, and he might have done something stupid but for the sudden harsh tune blaring from his phone that dragged his thoughts away from nibbling her neck.

He dropped a knife on the floor with a loud clatter and bent to retrieve it before he reached for his phone, gritting his teeth when he saw Chantelle's name and photo on the screen.

'Excuse me – I have to take this,' he said. 'I won't be long.'

Jack hurried outside, knowing if he dropped the call or turned his phone off, he'd risk the possibility of Chantelle turning up at the cottage again.

'Chantelle,' he said sotto voce, as he stepped into the garden. 'What are you playing at?'

'I don't know what you mean.'

'You know perfectly well what I'm talking about. What were you doing in the park?'

'I went for a walk.'

'You never go for a walk.' Chantelle wasn't a "going for a walk" type of woman. Which was why he had been so taken aback when she had told him that she wanted to go running with him. It wasn't the sort of thing she'd ever expressed an interest in. Looking back, that had probably been when he'd realised she was being far too controlling for her own good. And for his.

He could almost hear her shrug over the phone. 'Well, I did today,' she countered. 'It looks nice, your cottage. The garden is a mess, though.'

Jack stared at the back garden, which was even more overgrown than the front, and didn't say anything.

'Are you planning on staying there long?' she tried again.

'No idea.'

'Look, Jack, I was curious, OK? There was no need to send me such a snotty message.'

'Sorry, but I thought that after the conversation we had when you came to mine the other day, you would have…' He was going to say "got the hint", but he thought it sounded a bit harsh.

'Did you enjoy your wine?'

'I haven't opened it yet.' He had given the bottle to one of his neighbours. He wouldn't have felt right drinking it himself.

'You could save it for your moving-in party,' she suggested.

He took a deep breath and blew out his cheeks. 'I'm not having a moving-in party.' He changed the subject. 'Have you moved into *your* new place yet?'

'Er… no, not yet.'

Jack shook his head. He didn't for one minute think she had another place lined up – or another boyfriend, despite what she'd told him.

'Jack! Dinner is ready!' Molly's voice carried from the kitchen, and he saw that the window was open.

'Who was that?' Chantelle's voice was sharp.

'No one.'

'You've got someone else!' she accused. 'No wonder you couldn't wait to get rid of me. Moved in with her, have you?'

'Chantelle, you've got it all wrong. Molly is my landlord.'

'Huh! You must think I'm stupid.' Her voice was a snarl.

'I don't—'

'I hope she makes you happy,' she spat, her tone suggesting she hoped the exact opposite. 'Scumbag!'

Jack was about to explain the situation to her, when he realised he was holding a dead phone.

'Jack! Dinner!'

'Coming.' Sadly, he slipped his phone into a pocket and went inside. He hadn't wanted to hurt Chantelle and it wasn't his fault her jealously had made her jump to the wrong conclusion, but he still felt bad. He wished she didn't love him as much as she did, and he hoped she would one day find someone worthy of her love, but unfortunately that someone wasn't him.

'Everything OK?' Molly was staring at him in concern.

He didn't want to go into detail, but he had to say something. 'That was my ex. We broke up a few months ago. It hasn't been easy.' He grimaced.

'There's no need to explain,' Molly said. 'Shall we eat?'

'I think we'd better.' The table now held two plates of food. 'It looks lovely.'

It really did, but Jack had lost his appetite. And from the way Molly pushed her meal around her plate, she didn't appear to be hungry, either.

***

What had that been about, Molly wondered as she picked at her food. Jack hadn't looked happy when he came in from the garden and he continued to look miserable as he prodded at his meal.

Considering he had left his phone sitting next to hers, she hadn't been able to help see the name of the caller flash up on the screen, and she couldn't have failed to notice the accompanying photo.

Chantelle was gorgeous, Molly thought. Long, blond hair, classically pretty features, perfect makeup… No wonder Jack was sad they were no longer a couple. Molly bet they would have looked good together.

Who had broken up with whom, she wondered?

From the woebegone expression on his face, Molly guessed that Jack was the dumpee and his ex had been the dumper. As he had said, he hadn't found it easy, and her heart went out to him. She'd never been in love so she had no idea what he must be going through, but she could imagine, and she wished she could do something to make him feel better.

No wonder he had been so reluctant to put his house on the market: he must have been hoping for a reconciliation.

Molly wished she knew what the conversation had been about, but he had clearly said all he was prepared to say and she didn't want to pry.

Not only was her heart bleeding for him, it was also bleeding for herself. She didn't stand a chance with him, not after seeing what he was missing. Molly couldn't compete with the likes of Chantelle: she was nowhere near as pretty and she definitely wasn't as polished. Look at her – scraped back hair bundled on top of her head, paint-splattered T-shirt, mucky ripped jeans (properly ripped by a rusty nail, and not artfully ripped in the factory before they even reached the shop). Molly was under no illusion that she looked a mess. She was also under no illusion that Jack would ever be interested in her romantically. And especially not when he was pining over someone as gorgeous as Chantelle.

As they cleared away the dinner things and got started on the decorating, Molly's thoughts kept returning to the phone call, and she wondered why Chantelle had phoned. It was probably something to do with the sale of the house, but Jack hadn't mentioned anyone else had a stake in it. Maybe Molly should have asked, because if Chantelle was a co-owner, in order for a sale to go through all owners had to sign the paperwork. Then again, that was something for the solicitors to sort out, not her.

Whatever the reason, Jack and Chantelle had unfinished business, and despondency swept through her.

Molly grew even more morose as she thought about what would happen when the sale of his house went through. It wouldn't be long before he had an offer on it, and there had been some interest, the property already having had a couple of viewings – although she hadn't told Jack about them yet. There wasn't any point until someone made an offer, or unless the prospective buyers all had the same negative comments to make, in which case she would be obliged to share them with him. So far, the three prospective buyers who had been shown around the house had been complimentary, and she was quietly hopeful one of the viewings would result in a second.

Actually, she wasn't hopeful at all. She was dreading it. If his house sold as quickly as she suspected it would, Jack might move out sooner rather than later. Even in this short amount of time, she had got used to him and would hate to see him go.

The thought of Jack not living in the cottage made her incredibly sad.

CHAPTER 19

Jack straightened up and put the palm of his hands in the small of his back to ease the ache. He felt as though he'd been bending over for half the afternoon, but even if he had, the flower bed he and Molly had been working on had been worth it. It was totally transformed.

Only yesterday the edges had been undefined and it had been hard to tell where the grass ended and the flower bed began. Between them, he and Molly had sharpened the edges and removed all the weeds: to be honest, he thought they may have removed some perennials as well, but neither of them knew enough about plants to be confident that they hadn't. They had also dug over all the exposed earth and had trimmed any straggly and overly-bushy bushes, before finally planting a carpet of small bedding plants. Some of them had already begun to flower, so clusters of pretty blooms were scattered throughout the beds.

All it needed was a good watering and they could call it a day.

Three flower beds done, about twenty to go.

Even now, six weeks since he had moved into the cottage in Sweet Meadow Park and a considerable amount of work later, he couldn't believe how easily Molly had roped him into helping make her vision for the park become a reality.

She had been quite clever and rather ingenious in the way she'd gone about it, but he hadn't minded. Once the interior of the cottage was done (as much as it could be when it still needed a new bathroom suite), and the gardens, front and back, had been mowed, weeded and pruned into submission, he supposed it was inevitable that Molly would give the park her full attention and persuade him to give her a hand.

It had started innocently enough, with him accompanying her on her morning walks as she collected up any rubbish from the day before. He could hardly stand by and watch, so he had joined in; the crunch time was when she'd presented him with his very own litter picker. At that point he'd guessed he didn't have any option, other than to help.

Then had come the snippers. They were called secateurs, but Jack preferred the word 'snippers'. On those evenings when he didn't go for a run, he usually went out for a walk with Molly. One day Molly had produced a pair of snippers from her pocket with the same degree of flourish as a magician taking a rabbit out of a hat. When she'd told him why she was carrying them and what she had intended to do with them, he couldn't in all conscience refuse to help with that, either.

Despite more thorns in his hands than he could shake a blackberry at, and more scratches than he cared to count, they had made some progress in clearing a path through the woodland. The only complaint he had was that if they happened not to do any snipping for a few days, the damned brambles grew back almost as densely as they had been at the start.

Jack hated brambles with all his heart.

Working on the flower beds had come about because of Teresa. Molly's mum had arrived at the cottage one Saturday morning a couple of weeks ago, with tray after tray of tiny plants. She'd claimed to have grown them from seed for her own garden and had donated them to Molly, but the sheer number of seedlings hadn't all fitted into the cottage's garden, so Molly had innocently suggested popping a few of the baby plants into one of the flower beds in the park itself. And that, as they say, had been that.

Three flower beds later, and Molly wasn't showing any signs of easing up on her project.

Jack had to admit that the main entrance to the park with its impressive wrought iron gates, was looking very welcoming now that the beds to either side were neat and tidy and were brimming with early summer blooms.

Of course, there was much more to do, but Jack had no doubt that Molly, with her determination and inability to take no for an answer, would get it done.

'It looks good, doesn't it?' she asked, threading an arm through his.

A shot of desire stabbed him in the gut, as usual. Whenever they touched, he had the same reaction – longing, with the addition of a substantial amount of… Jack wasn't sure what to call it. He was undeniably attracted to her – that went without saying – but what he felt for her was far more than pure lust. He looked forward to seeing her in the morning, he looked forward to seeing her when he came home from work. He looked forward to seeing her, full stop. She filled his mind when he wasn't with her, and she filled his mind when he was. She was in his head, and no amount of wishing that she wasn't, could budge her from there, leading him to suspect he might be half in love with her.

The past six weeks had been some of the happiest of his life. He should be feeling anxious – his job situation was the same as it had been when he'd first met Molly (although the letter that Chantelle had warned him about had yet to materialise), he still hadn't had an offer on the house, and he still didn't know where he was going to live long term. He was in a state of flux, and by rights he should be having a minor panic. Instead, he felt more contented than he had ever been. He could have told himself the reason was that he loved living in the cottage and he loved living in the park. He could also tell himself that he had fallen head over heels with a daft black hound. And although all that was true, it wasn't the real reason.

The real reason was Molly.

'Penny for them?' she asked, nudging him.

'Eh? Oh, sorry. Miles away. Yes, they do look good.'

His heart skipped a beat when she smiled up at him, and he ground his teeth together to stop himself from kissing her. She had the loveliest lips…

'Shall I get us a drink, then we'll clear up?' She indicated the rake, spade, trowel and assorted implements they had used to smarten up the bed.

'That would be lovely,' he said, wincing as she gave his arm a squeeze before going back to the house. Every time they touched, bolts of electricity shot through him, and his whole arm continued to tingle for minutes after she'd released him.

He gathered everything together while he waited for her to return, and stowed it in the wheelbarrow.

'Here you go.' She handed him a glass of cold lemonade with ice.

'Thanks.' He took it from her, his fingers brushing against hers, and grimaced at the way his pulse soared.

How much longer could he go on like this?

'Cheers!' she said.

As their eyes met over the rim of their drinks, he was unable to look away, leaving it up to her to break the connection. As far as he was concerned, he would happily drown in her gaze for the rest of the day.

Molly, however, had no such inclination. She smiled at him and took a deep draft of her drink. 'Ooh, I needed that. Gardening is thirsty work.'

'It looks grand,' a voice from behind said, and Molly turned around.

Jack continued to stare at the newly planted flower bed and tried to compose himself. It would do no one any good to let his feelings for her show. He was fairly certain she didn't feel the same way, so there was no point in making things awkward between them.

'Hi, Bill, how are you?' Molly sounded pleased to see the old gent.

'Not so bad. You'd better water them flowers.'

'We intend to, as soon as we've tidied up.'

Bill sniffed. 'Told you she would get you dancing to her tune.' This was addressed to Jack.

Not to be rude, Jack smiled. 'You certainly did.' He couldn't recall the old man saying any such thing. 'Molly, I'll take this lot back to the shed—' Jack pointed to the wheelbarrow '—while you have a chat with Bill.'

He left them to it and wheeled the barrow around the side of the cottage. As he put the tools back where they belonged, he thought about what Bill had said and realised how accurate it was – he most definitely did dance to Molly's tune, and he didn't begrudge her a single step.

More fool him.

***

'Drink up and I'll get us another.' Astrid downed her vodka and grapefruit juice and waited for Molly to finish her gin and ginger beer.

'Same again, please,' she said. 'Lashings of ginger beer, this time. I don't want to go home drunk.'

'Why? Worried you might lose control and jump Jack's bones?' Astrid teased.

'Certainly not!'

'I think the lady doth protest too much,' Astrid chortled as she grabbed Molly's empty glass and walked over to the bar.

She was still chortling when she returned with fresh drinks.

'Stop it,' Molly said crossly.

'Because I'm right?'

'No. Yes. I don't know.'

'I do. You've got the hots for him.'

'Maybe I have, but he doesn't feel the same way about me.'

'Are you sure?'

'As sure as I can be. I've been dropping hints for weeks, but he ignores them.'

'They're probably too subtle and are going straight over his head. You know what men are like – you've got to bash them on the bonce with it before they notice. Why don't you make it clearer?'

'How?'

'What are you doing now?'

'Sending him sultry looks, putting my arm through his, stroking his back when I walk past… That kind of thing.'

Astrid waved a hand in the air. 'That's no good. You've got to be more direct.'

'Such as?'

'Snog him.'

'Like, walk up to him and just kiss him?' Molly's eyes widened.

'Yep.'

'Without any build up?'

'You could try candlelight and wine, but I wouldn't bother.'

'But what if he doesn't like me like that? Anyway, I think he's still in love with his ex.'

'He told you that, did he?'

'No…'

'Has he had any more phone calls from her?'

'Not since the one I told you about. At least, not to my knowledge.'

Jack could be speaking to Chantelle several times a day for all she knew, but if he was, he hadn't mentioned it. But then again, why would he? Molly was just his landlord. The fact that he was helping her around the park now that the cottage was finished was because he felt obliged to. Once or twice he had brought up the subject of paying her rent, but she'd told him not to be so silly. So of course he'd try to pay her in whatever currency he could, because he was that type of person. Over the weeks that he'd been sharing her house, she had come to know him, and her first impression of him being a jobsworth had long gone. She now understood he was operating under certain constraints, and that rules and regulations had to be adhered to. She also knew that if he could have helped in a formal council capacity, he would have.

'Has he been seeing her?' Astrid persisted.

'I don't know. I'm not with him every second of every day.'

'Keep your hair on. Blinking heck, you have got it bad. I've never seen you like this.'

'Sorry.' Molly was contrite. Astrid was only trying to help, and here was Molly taking her frustration out on her friend.

'What does he do in the evenings?' Astrid asked, waving the apology away. 'How often does he go out?'

'Erm… now you come to mention it, apart from going for a run a few times a week, he doesn't go out very often.'

'Ah ha! That proves it.'

'Proves what?'

'That he can't be seeing his ex.'

'It doesn't mean to say he's not pining for her.'

'True…' Astrid ran her finger around the rim of her glass. 'Why don't you ask him?'

'I don't think that's a good idea. We don't have that kind of relationship.'

'And you never will if you don't pull your finger out,' Astrid warned.

Molly knew that her friend was only trying to help, but there was no way she could ask Jack straight out how he felt about his ex, and she most definitely wouldn't kiss him without any indication of whether he would appreciate it. He might be horrified. And even if he wasn't, he still mightn't like being leapt on by his landlord, and it might well sour their relationship. They were getting on brilliantly at the moment, so there was no point in rocking the boat.

No, she would leave things as they were, and carry on with her subtle hints and see if there was any response.

The last thing she wanted was to drive him away.

***

'Did you have a good time?' Jack asked as Molly walked into the living room. She was swaying a little, so he guessed she must have.

'I did, thanks. It was good to catch up.'

'You see Astrid every day at the office,' Jack pointed out with a chuckle.

'It's not the same.' She hiccupped loudly. 'Oops!'

'Come on, let's get you to bed.'

'Yes, please.'

Molly's voice sounded odd – breathy and sultry – and he wondered how much she'd had to drink. She was certainly the worse for wear, and he thought how cute she was with her unfocused eyes and her hair all mussed up. She had a pouty smile on her lips, and it suddenly occurred to him she might not have met Astrid on her own. They might have had a double date.

Molly hadn't mentioned a man, but it didn't mean to say she hadn't met up with one this evening, or she could have been chatted up by a guy when she had been in the pub. It would explain her strange demeanour.

Deflated, he took her elbow and guided her towards the stairs. 'You need a couple of paracetamol, a pint of water, and a good long sleep. Do you need any help?' he asked.

'I can manage.' It was her stock response, and her tone was abrupt – a distinct contrast to a minute ago.

She shook off his hand and he wondered what he'd done to upset her.

'Molly… I…' he began.

She paused, one hand on the doorframe, her expression wary.

He was close enough to kiss her, and he wished he had the courage, but he didn't want to ruin what they had – they were good friends and if he made a move on her and she didn't want to know, he would lose that. He would also have to leave because there was no way he could carry on living here after he'd made a fool of himself. Anyway, she was half-cut, and he wasn't the type of bloke to take advantage of an inebriated woman.

Instead, he tucked a wayward strand of hair behind her shell-like ear, and stroked her soft cheek with the back of his hand. 'Sleep tight.'

'You, too.'

Then she was gone, and he was left listening to her footsteps on the floorboards above his head and wishing he hadn't let her go.

***

Sleep was a long time coming. Jack tossed and turned, got up for a drink, then tossed and turned some more. He had gone to bed shortly after Molly, at around a quarter to eleven, and so he probably wasn't particularly sleepy despite the gardening he'd done today.

He should have gone for a run this evening to help burn off some of his excess energy, but he'd stayed at home instead, wondering whether she was having a good time.

It seemed she'd had a very good time indeed…

He was still lying there, staring irritably at the ceiling, when he heard a noise coming from outside. It wasn't the usual sound of kids messing about. The noise was closer for a start, and he guessed it wasn't coming from the bandstand which was where the teenagers normally gathered in the evenings. Not only that, it was nearly midnight and the youths were generally long gone by now – probably because they had run out of booze and fags.

He could hear voices, but they were muffled, and there was a kind of scuffing sound. Having no idea what it could be, he slipped out of bed and walked over to the window. But before he could pull the curtain aside, a volley of barks from Molly's bedroom made him jump.

'Molly? Are you OK? *Molly!*'

She didn't answer.

Jack raced across the landing and came to a skidding halt outside her door. Jet was still barking so perhaps she hadn't been able to hear him above the noise the dog was making.

He called her name again, then knocked.

Still no response.

Bugger it – he was going in.

With his heart in his mouth, he turned the handle and pushed the door open. He wasn't sure what he was expecting to see, but it certainly wasn't the sight of Molly standing in front of the window, staring across the park.

And when she turned towards him and he saw the glistening track of tears on her cheeks, he was by her side in a trice.

'What is it? What's wrong?' he cried, gathering her stiff body to him and holding her close. He could feel her trembling and he wondered what could have upset her so badly.

'Look.' She pointed through the window.

It took him a moment to understand what he was looking at, and when he did white-hot anger surged through him.

Those little scroats had only gone and torn up the bushes and plants in the newly-created flower beds.

With a muffled oath, Jack released Molly, charged out of the bedroom and down the stairs, taking them two at a time. He was out of the door and racing down the drive before he realised he didn't have anything on his feet and was only wearing pyjama bottoms.

He didn't care. He was far too concerned with catching those responsible: he could see the horrible little gits haring through the gate and tearing off down the road.

Jack realised he didn't have a hope in hell of catching them, and cursed himself for not taking the time to jam his feet into his trainers. If he'd have been wearing those he would have caught them without any trouble and—

And what?

With a heavy heart, he checked the damage.

It was difficult to see the full extent of it in the dark, but he was fairly certain many of the plants that they had put in over the past few days had been pulled up and flung across the path. The remainder of the bedding plants had been trampled, as had some of the well-established bushes. Several had stems and branches missing, which were also strewn across the ground.

From what he could see, Jack thought the flower beds he and Molly had so painstakingly tended, looked worse now than they had originally.

It was a heart-breaking blow and a kick in the teeth for all their hard work.

Sadly, Jack turned his back on the mess and went inside to comfort Molly.

***

Molly didn't need comforting, Jack soon discovered. Molly was furious.

What Molly wanted was vengeance, but she wasn't going to get it.

When Jack returned to the cottage, it was to find her pacing the living room, Jet at her heels (thankfully the dog had stayed inside), ranting about what she would do to the little darlings when she got her hands on them.

The tears of earlier, Jack soon discovered, hadn't been tears of sadness: they had been tears of anger. Molly was absolutely fuming, and Jack didn't blame her. He was mad, too.

All that hard work, and nothing to show for it.

'They don't deserve to have anything nice,' Molly cried. 'They've got no respect for anything. All they want to do is to destroy things. I've seen better-behaved chimps in the zoo! And where are their parents, that's what I want to know. Those kids should be home in bed, not wandering the streets at midnight. Goodness knows what other mischief they've got up to. And people wonder why crime rates are soaring! Maybe they should look closer to home and check on what their offspring are doing.'

Jack agreed. This was one of the reasons why he hadn't felt able to commit council funds to restoring Sweet Meadow Park, but now wasn't the best time to remind Molly of that. He was gutted that she had to find out for herself. He had been hoping to have been proven wrong for once.

'That's it – I'm done!' she announced. 'I've given it my best shot, but if nobody appreciates it, I don't know why I bother.'

'*I* appreciate it,' Jack said softly.

'If people want an eyesore of a park, then they can have one. As long as they stay away from my cottage that's all—' She stopped. 'Pardon?'

'I appreciate it,' he repeated, then his heart melted as her face crumpled.

Molly sank to her knees and sat on the floor, and this time her tears reflected misery instead of anger.

Jack sat down next to her and put his arms around her shoulders, letting her cry as he stroked her hair. Her head was on his bare chest and tears trickled down his stomach, and only when her sobs finally turned into hiccupping snivels did she pull away.

'I'm sorry,' she sniffed, trying to wipe the dampness from his skin with the sleeve of her pyjamas.

'There's nothing to be sorry for.'

'But all that work and me making you help...' She trailed off.

'You didn't make me,' he told her. 'I did it because I wanted to. Helping in the park was never part of our rental agreement.'

Molly sniffed loudly. 'I expect you'll want to move out now. I would if I could, but who would want to live in a place like this? Who would want to buy it?'

'I still want to live here. And I believe you do, too.'

Molly shrugged, then sat up straighter. 'I don't know what I want,' she admitted. 'I thought I did – but I was being naïve in thinking if people saw how nice it could be, they would respect it and care for it. How stupid.'

'It's not stupid. You want to see the best in people, that's all. And you want what's best for the park.'

'What I want and what I'm going to get, isn't necessarily the same thing.' Her gaze was candid.

'It still could be.'

'How?'

'We can't turn the park around on our own – it's too big a job for two people. We need an army.' Bill had said the very same thing, and he had been right.

'An army?' Molly was looking at him like he'd lost his mind.

'I think we ought to ask for volunteers. Besides, the more people from the community who are willing to help, the more the word will get out that people care about the park, and maybe there will be an end to this senseless vandalism. After all, the park is a community space, it should be up to the community to look after it.'

'That's a brilliant idea! Why didn't I think of that? I could kiss you.'

'There's something else,' he said, before she got carried away. He blew out his cheeks. He knew that what he was about to do was wrong and he could land himself in a whole heap of trouble for doing it, but if Molly was to carry on with her vision for the park, it would have to be done. 'I'm going to lock the park gates between the hours of eight in the evening and six in the morning.'

'I don't understand. The gates are already locked – all the time.'

'I'm not talking about the big ones; I mean the small ones. There are five around the perimeter. I'm going to lock them all, starting with right now.'

Molly's eyes were wide. 'Can you do that?'

'The keys to all the gates are on the big key ring in the pantry.'

'I wondered what they were for.'

Jack looked away. Thankfully Molly hadn't asked the right question. It wasn't a case of *could* he lock the gates, rather, was he *allowed*. Probably not, but as the Parks and Highways Officer he would take his chance. After all, if anyone objected, the complaint would land on his desk.

'You'd do that for me?' The look in Molly's eyes took his breath away.

'For you, and for the park,' he said softly.

Their faces were centimetres apart. He could feel her gentle breath on his cheek. Their knees were touching, and the heat of her nearness made him weak with longing.

If he leant a fraction closer, his lips would be on hers and he'd be able to taste her…

Abruptly, Jack got to his feet. 'I'd better make a start,' he said. 'Those gates won't lock themselves.'

He was as aware of her gaze as he would have been had she touched him. It was as much of a physical caress as when he had stroked her cheek earlier. He could feel the weight of it, dragging him back down, and he would have loved nothing better than to join her on the floor and kiss her until morning.

But just as he didn't want to take advantage of her when she'd had too much to drink, neither would he attempt to kiss her when she was so upset.

He would give it a few days, let the dust settle so to speak, and after that, if the opportunity arose, he'd seize it with both hands.

CHAPTER 20

Molly stared at the three people standing in front of the bandstand the following Monday evening and disappointment swept through her. She had been hoping for a better turn-out, but beggars couldn't be choosers, even if one of those people was Bill and he was only there out of curiosity. The second was a middle-aged lady with wiry grey hair and a slash of pink lipstick on her mouth. She was clutching a canvas bag-for-life to her chest, and her eyes darted nervously from Molly to Jack and back again.

The third was a guy aged about thirty, with tanned skin and bright brown eyes. He had heavy work boots on his feet and the sort of trousers hikers wore, with lots of pockets. He also had a bag with him, a well-worn rucksack on the ground between his feet.

'Er... hello,' she began, conscious of a tick beneath her right eye and hoping it wasn't obvious. 'Thank you for coming.'

'Where's the band?' the woman piped up.

'What band?' Molly sent Jack a confused look, and Jack shrugged and made a face.

'The one that's supposed to be here,' the woman said.

'There isn't any band.' Molly frowned.

'There is! It said so on the leaflet. I've got it right here, so don't try to deny it.' The woman delved into her bag and pulled out a crumpled piece of paper. 'See?' She jabbed at it with a finger.

'Sorry,' Molly said, realising where the woman's confusion had arisen from. 'It says to meet at the bandstand, not that there will be a band.'

The woman huffed out a cross sigh. 'You've got us here under false pretences. I ought to sue you for wasting my time.'

'You're as daft as a box of frogs, Fiona. Read what it says!' Bill rolled his eyes and tutted.

'And you are a miserable old git,' the woman retorted. 'I thought a band was too good to be true. This park is a disgrace.'

Molly watched her stalk away and took a deep breath. It looked like she was left with one potential volunteer to help tidy up the park: hardly the army of helpers she had been hoping for when she'd put up those fliers around the town. Maybe she had been a bit hasty and should have given it more time, but after the vandalism of the other night she'd wanted to strike whilst the iron was hot, so had printed out several requests for volunteers the very next morning. Maybe if she had arranged the meeting for a week or two later, the call for volunteers would have garnered more interest? After all, this wasn't going to be a one-off thing – it would be a regular occurrence because it would take more than an afternoon to make any impact.

'I'd better be off,' Bill said. 'I only came to see how many bothered to turn up.' He shook his head as though he hadn't expected any more than this, and tugged on his dog's lead. 'Come on, Patch. I thought it would be a waste of time and I'm right. Talking about a waste of time, this lot no doubt want their bandstand back.' He jerked his head at a group of teenagers making their way towards them.

'Yeah, shove off, grandad,' one of them shouted at Bill's retreating back.

Bill stuck a middle finger in the air but didn't turn around.

Molly had been studiously ignoring the youngsters who were lingering on the path several metres away, because she guessed they weren't here to volunteer for anything.

That left the guy with the rucksack. Feeling self-conscious Molly stepped down from the dilapidated bandstand and walked over to him.

'Hi, I'm Molly and this is Jack. Don't tell me you were expecting live music, too?'

'Absolutely not! I'm here for the newts.'

'Pardon?' Molly blinked.

'Great crested newts. I'm also here for the other wildlife, of course.'

'Newts,' she repeated, risking another confused look at Jack. He appeared to be as bemused as she, as he pulled an "I've no idea what he's on about" face.

The guy said, 'This park has got the ideal habitat for them – pond, grassland, woodland. They are a protected species, you know.'

'No, I didn't know.' Molly stared at him, not thinking about newts at all. She was thinking that this guy was seriously good-looking. He had dark hair which was caught up in a bun on the top of his head, and a beard, but it was his eyes that commanded her attention. She'd heard the phrase *arresting* before, but she hadn't realised what it had meant until now. They were incredibly intense, and she could feel herself being sucked into their depths.

'I'm Reuben, by the way.' He held out a hand and Molly shook it. His grip was firm, his palms rough, and she guessed he worked with his hands.

If Astrid had been here, Molly knew what she'd have said – that he could work on her with his hands any day – and she almost snorted. Wait 'til she told her about him: Astrid would volunteer like a shot.

Despite his good looks and rather fit body, Molly wasn't attracted to him in the slightest. He was too extravagant for her liking – and anyway, she had Jack.

Or rather, she *didn't* have Jack, but she was working on it.

She'd thought he had been about to kiss her the other night after he'd chased the vandals away, but he hadn't: much to her disappointment. Instead, he had rushed off to lock the park gates, and she'd taken herself back to bed.

A few days later and she was still trying to get close enough to replicate the situation but, as she had explained to Astrid, her attempts at flirting with Jack seemed to go over his head, making her all the more convinced that he wasn't interested in her romantically.

'I saw your call for volunteers, so I thought I'd chip in, and I can search for newts at the same time,' Reuben was saying.

'So you don't know for sure that there are newts here?' Molly asked.

'There'll be newts alright. Smooth newts, more usually called common newts because they are… well… common – and there might be palmate newts, although they're rather less common.' He laughed at his own joke. 'As I said, what I'm looking for is the rare great crested newt.'

'Okaay.' She honestly didn't know what to say to that. She needed people to help clear the path through the woods, remove trolleys from the pond, and restore the damaged flower beds. She didn't need people grubbing about in the mud, looking for weird amphibians. 'There's a fox in the park,' she said. 'And rabbits. Squirrels, too, and loads of birds.'

'Anything unusual?'

'Er, I'm not sure.' Molly could recognise a few species, such as pigeons, blackbirds and sparrows, but that was about it.

'No worries. I'll keep an eye out, and if I see anything of significant interest I'll report back. Now, what do you want me to do today?'

Ahh, that was better, Molly thought. 'I was hoping we could start with the flower beds near the main entrance.'

To her surprise, Reuben's face fell and he said, 'I don't do flowerbeds – unless we're scattering flower bombs or wildflower seed. Most beds are filled with non-native species, and many are useless to bees and butterflies.'

'Right.' Oh dear, this wasn't going so well. 'How about you tell me where you think you can help?' Molly suggested.

'Great idea! Do you want to show me around the park?'

Molly looked at Jack. He hadn't said much and she wondered what he was thinking.

'Go ahead,' he told her with a shrug. 'I'll carry on with repairing the damage from the other night.'

They had already done some tidying up, such as sweeping up all the destroyed plants and trying to salvage what little they could, and they had cleared away all the stems, twigs and branches from the decimated shrubs and bushes, but it would take a while before they looked as good as they should.

Jack began walking in the direction of the cottage without saying anything further, leaving Molly perplexed.

'Partner?' Reuben asked, when Jack was some distance away.

'Lodger.'

Reuben's eyebrows rose. 'Oh, sorry, I assumed—'

'It's OK,' Molly interrupted. 'I own the former park keeper's cottage, and Jack is renting a room. For the time being.' She was all too aware that it wouldn't be forever.

'Did I step on any toes?'

'How do you mean?'

'He seemed a bit put out. Should I have asked *him* to show me around?'

'Because he's a man and I'm not?' Molly shot back.

'Because he... Look, never mind. It's none of my business. Shall we get started?'

'Yes, let's.' Molly began walking towards the pond and the meadow, feeling irritated. She had no idea why Jack had stalked off, and so far she wasn't impressed with Reuben, either. The park might be in dire need of all the help it could get, but she could do without a sexist bloke, thank you very much!

***

Jack stomped along the path, his heart thumping, dismay flowing through him, and it wasn't due to the lack of volunteers. He *was* disappointed about that, of course, but he was more perturbed about the one who had turned up.

Reuben was everything Jack wasn't: handsome in a hippy sort of way, outdoorsy, fit, and knowledgeable about nature. The man was also willing to get stuck in and get his hands dirty. Jack guessed that, for Molly, the combination was a very attractive one.

He could tell she was enamoured. She hadn't been able to take her eyes off the guy. And when Reuben had asked to be shown around the park, Molly had sent Jack a look that told him she wanted to do this on her own. He hadn't wanted to go with them anyway; he didn't need to watch her simper over this guy any more than he'd witnessed already.

Thank God he hadn't acted on his impulse to kiss her the other night. He might have got his face slapped. It had been wishful thinking on his part when he'd hoped she was attracted to him. She wasn't and would never be – Reuben was much more her type.

Even Jet had abandoned him to go with his mistress and this new bloke, trotting behind them without so much as a glance in Jack's direction.

Savagely Jack picked up a shovel and stabbed it into the soil. The earth had been compacted where it had been trodden on by the yobs the other night, so before he attempted to replant anything he thought it best to loosen the ground and give it a good raking. As he did so, he imagined it was Reuben's head he was attacking, but it didn't make him feel any better.

But what was playing on his mind more than Reuben's good looks was what Molly had said to the man when he had asked her if Jack was her partner. Her brief and succinct reply had cut him to the quick.

Lodger.

That was all he was to her – the guy who rented a room in her house.

He hadn't been able to hear anything else because by then he'd taken a few more steps and was out of earshot, but at that point he hadn't wanted to hear any more anyway. He had heard enough.

Jack felt like kicking himself. He had honestly thought she was starting to consider him more of a friend than a lodger, and he'd even managed to convince himself she was developing feelings for him.

He must have imagined the lingering looks, the brush of her hand, and the way she peeped up at him from under her lashes. If he'd have Googled *how can I tell if a woman fancies me?* Jack was fairly sure those things would be on the list. She also giggled at his jokes (not many people did) and played with her hair a lot when she was talking to him.

But did all those things add up to her fancying him?

Evidently not. Not after the way she had gone all gooey-eyed and tongue-tied the second she'd set eyes on Reuben.

Jack couldn't believe he had got it so wrong.

Or maybe he could – he'd got it wrong with Chantelle too. Except in a different way: he hadn't realised Chantelle was so into him.

It was obvious that he was hopeless when it came to reading women.

Even so, he could read Reuben well enough. The guy hadn't wasted a second on checking whether Molly was single. And she had made it clear to the man that she was.

Jack dug the spade into the ground and leant on the handle.

As far as he could tell, he had two options – he could fight for her, or he could withdraw gracefully.

Maybe if Jack had kissed her, he could have made a case for fighting for her. But he hadn't, and he had a feeling it was too late now. It would seem a bit weird that he hadn't shown her how he felt up to now, and yet was suddenly declaring his undying love as soon as a rival appeared on the scene.

He could hardly—

Wait a minute… *He loved her?*

Surely not? He couldn't be in love and not realise it, could he? That kind of thing only happened in the movies.

But if it wasn't love he was feeling, what was it? Desire, certainly, that went without saying, but his feelings ran much deeper than wanting to jump into bed with her. And he didn't want to *jump*: he wanted to make love to her. Long, slow, meaningful love, where he gave her everything he had, body, heart and soul.

Flippin' heck! He *was* in love!

How the hell had that happened? And when? There must have been a time when he was on the cusp between friendship and love, so how hadn't he noticed that his feelings for her had deepened to the point of no return? And why hadn't he become aware of this before Rampant Reuben had shown up?

Great, wonderful, brilliant, he thought sarcastically, shaking his head at his stupidity. And what was worse was the sight of Molly and Reuben sauntering past the children's play area, so close that they might as well have had their arms wrapped around one another, smiling fit to burst, and quite evidently very happy in one another's company.

His eyes narrowed when they halted and Reuben showed her something on his phone. Their heads were practically touching as they huddled even closer to stare at the screen. All that was needed was for one of them to turn their head a fraction and they would be kissing.

Stifling a groan of despair, he left the shovel where it was and dashed towards the cottage. He would have a quick shower and go to the pub. He could hide there and drown his sorrows at the same time.

***

The most natural thing in the world would be to tell Jack about Reuben's hope that there might be rare great crested newts living in the park, but Molly didn't want to jinx anything. If it was confirmed, he would be the first to know – after Reuben and herself, of course.

Reuben told her that finding a newt could be a bargaining chip to help twist the council's arm and persuade them to do a better job of maintaining the park, and this was another reason for not sharing the news with Jack; she didn't want to put him in an awkward position.

On his tour of the park, Reuben had shown her a whole load of things that she hadn't noticed previously – insects and plants, mostly – and she had quickly revised her initial opinion of him. He was knowledgeable about wildlife and conservation, and although that wasn't her main reason for wanting to restore the park, the longer she lived here, the more invested in its various inhabitants she was becoming.

Molly loved that Reuben shared her view of keeping the pond and meadow wild – although how she was going to do that, having no experience of pond or meadow management, was beyond her – opening up paths through the woodland for everyone to enjoy.

Reuben was keen to get started on that as soon as possible, and he had mentioned something about using a machete, but Molly hadn't wanted to enquire too closely. How he cleared it was up to him, and she trusted him to do it properly.

He told her he would start first thing in the morning, and she could only admire his dedication and wonder what he did for a living, considering tomorrow was Tuesday and she and Jack would be at work. When she'd advised Reuben of this, he'd shrugged and told her he would bring whatever he needed with him, plus food and water, so she needn't worry as he was used to roughing it.

None the wiser, she'd said goodbye and went to find Jack. She could have sworn she had seen him digging over one of the trampled flower beds, but he wasn't there now.

'Jack?' she called as she barrelled through the front door, Jet at her heels.

The dog barged past her and bolted up the stairs, so she guessed Jack must be up there.

'Jack?' she called again, trotting up the stairs after Jet. Even without the newt news, she had so much to tell him, and she had a feeling Reuben was going to be invaluable. He could concentrate on the woodland and the area around the pond, leaving her and Jack to tend to the more manicured parts of the park. Not that they were manicured at the moment, but they could be, given time and effort. And a lack of vandals.

So far, locking the gates at night was proving to be a success. Bill had informed her that he had heard a few people complaining, but he'd told them it was their own fault for not being more respectful, and the council were only doing what they had a right to do. Molly had bitten her lip and thought it best not to enlighten Bill. If he assumed the council were behind the gate closures, then so be it. In a way, it was – but only in so far as the man who locked them every night and unlocked them every morning happened to work for the council. She'd wondered whether Jack was exceeding his authority, and she hoped he knew what he was doing.

She found Jet on the landing, staring expectantly at Jack's closed bedroom door.

'Jack? Are you in there?'

'I'll be out in a minute,' he called back, and Molly debated whether to wait for him here or to go downstairs.

She opted for the kitchen and had just put the kettle on when he appeared.

Molly did a double take. She was used to seeing him in either a suit and tie, or scruffy gardening clothes, but this evening he was dressed in a smart pair of chinos and a pale green linen shirt.

He looked gorgeous and she almost drooled when he casually rolled the sleeves up to reveal his strong forearms.

Oh, my…

'Tea?' she managed to force out, her voice squeaky. She felt very unkempt and dishevelled: her hair was in a hasty ponytail, her face was makeup free, and her jogging bottoms were baggy and had grass stains on them.

'Not for me, thanks. I'm going out.'

'Oh?' It came out even squeakier, and she cleared her throat. 'Somewhere nice?' God, she sounded like her mum.

'Just the pub. Did you want me for anything in particular?'

'Er, to give you an update on Reuben. He says—'

'Can it wait? I'm already late.'

'Oh, yeah, sure. No worries.'

'OK. Bye, then.' And with that he was gone, leaving Molly feeling strangely bereft and more than a little confused.

He hadn't mentioned he was going out. Before the disastrous meeting earlier, they had discussed showing the volunteers what needed to be done – that was when they'd assumed they'd have a few volunteers to show. But now, just an hour later, Jack had gone out.

Molly couldn't help wondering who he was meeting.

He'd looked scrumptious and he'd smelt divine. His aftershave lingered in the air, taunting her. It wasn't one she remembered him wearing before, and she wondered whether it was new, and who he was wearing it for.

Feeling abandoned and rejected – which was ridiculous considering he was only her lodger and they weren't supposed to be living in each other's pockets, she phoned Astrid.

'It's not like him to go out,' Molly concluded after she'd told her friend about his abrupt departure and strangely distant attitude.

'Do you think he's on a date?' Astrid was crunching loudly.

'What are you eating?'

'Salt and vinegar crisps. I've got a glass of pop, too, and I'm feeling very guilty. The kids are in bed, and because I don't allow them to eat this crap, if I want to indulge I have to do it in secret.'

'Oh, right. Enjoy.' Molly considered the question. 'I'm not sure. He didn't say anything earlier, so if he is, it's sudden.'

'Maybe he didn't think it was any of your business?'

'Ouch.'

'Well, it isn't, is it? Not unless you've managed to snog his socks off – and then maybe it would be.'

'We've not kissed,' Molly sighed. 'He's either dumb, or not interested.'

'What's your gut feeling?'

'Not interested.'

'Yet you don't think he's on a date?'

'Only because it was so sudden,' Molly repeated. 'We were supposed to be meeting with the volunteers this evening.'

'So you were. How did it go?'

'Not good. Only one person showed up – two if you count a woman who thought there'd be a band on. Don't ask. The other person is good, though. His name is Reuben and he's into conservation. He's getting started on clearing some of the undergrowth in the wood tomorrow. But that's the reason why I'm pretty sure Jack's date wasn't pre-planned.'

'Unless something came up?' Astrid suggested. 'Maybe his ex?'

'That had crossed my mind, too.' Molly wrinkled her nose. 'I'm fairly certain it can't be anything else. As I said, he hardly goes out – just for a run a couple of times a week. And he goes to work, obviously. So he must be meeting Chantelle. Maybe it's something to do with the house—?'

Molly froze. There was a niggle at the back of her mind, an itch she couldn't quite scratch. Something about the name of Jack's ex… Chantelle wasn't a common name, but Molly could have sworn she had come across it prior to seeing the name flash up on Jack's phone. But where…?

Ah ha! She had it, but even as she remembered, her heart sank.

'Can I call you back?' she said. 'I want to check something.'

'Of course. Take care, sweetie. I'm sure you're overthinking it.'

Molly was certain she wasn't. Because she remembered where she'd seen the name before: the council website. And when she checked the list of employees, Molly knew she was right. Staring back at her was the same perfectly straight blond hair and the same immaculately made-up features, that she had seen on Jack's phone.

Chantelle also worked for the council. Jack didn't need to make any special arrangements to see his ex because he worked with her. He could see her any time he bloody well pleased!

CHAPTER 21

'Are things any better between you and Jack?' Astrid asked. Today she was ploughing her way through a tube of Pringles, with a Revels chaser. 'Want one?' She offered the packet of Revels to Molly, who shook her head.

'No thanks. I can't stand the orange or coffee flavoured ones – it's like playing Russian Roulette with chocolates. Why don't they make them different shapes or something, so you can tell which is which?'

'Sadists,' Astrid mumbled around a toffee. 'Well?'

Molly pulled a face. 'He's not speaking to me,' she said, then added, 'He *is*, but not the way he was speaking to me before. He's gone all distant and polite. It's been three days now, and I'm not sure I can take any more of it. It's like living with a cardboard cut-out. Thank goodness for Reuben – at least with him there in the evenings I've got someone to talk to besides the dog. Jack's still helping with the flower beds, but I can tell his heart isn't in it, so I'm leaving him to it and sorting out the woodland with Reuben instead. He's doing brilliantly! He's already created a path wide enough for two to walk abreast, and today he said he was going to source some fallen logs and dot them along the path for people to sit on and enjoy the peace.'

'Aren't you worried they'll sit around drinking and smoking instead?'

'That is a concern,' Molly agreed, 'but at least they can't do it in the evenings.' She rose, deciding to put the kettle on. Seeing Astrid eating her own weight in crisps and chocolate was making her hungry, but lunch was a good hour away, so she would have to make do with a cup of tea and a custard cream.

'Is Jack still locking the gates?'

'He is, and there has been a definite reduction in the amount of litter since. The youngsters aren't happy, of course, and we've both had some abuse shouted at us – Jack more than me. He's the one who tells them they have to leave because he's about to lock up.'

The phone rang, and Astrid pointed frantically at her mouth, having loaded it with another chocolate.

'I'll get it,' Molly said, sitting back down. 'Watkin and Wright, how may I help?' She automatically picked up a pen in case she needed to make a note, but she dropped it onto the desk when she heard what the caller was saying.

Astrid looked at her in concern. 'Is everything OK?' she mouthed.

Molly nodded.

But it wasn't OK, because the person on the other end of the phone had given her the news she'd been dreading.

Jack had an offer on his house.

***

'Jack, I've got something to tell you,' Molly said, as soon as she walked into the cottage later that afternoon.

Jack was on one knee in the hall, tying his laces ready to go for a run, Jet at his side.

The dog bounded over and gave her an enthusiastic welcome as Molly crouched down and ruffled his ears. Sadness pricked her when she thought how much the dog would miss Jack. Jet adored the guy almost as much as he adored her, and he loved accompanying Jack on his runs – the exercise did him such a lot of good. Maybe she'd have to take up running after Jack moved out…

She was under no illusion that as soon as contracts were exchanged Jack would be off. This was only ever meant to be a temporary measure, despite her praying that he might stay on. And the way he had been behaving lately, she knew he couldn't wait to leave.

'What is it?' he asked, looking up as he tied the last lace.

She waited for him to straighten up because she wanted to see his face when she gave him the news, even though she already guessed he would be over the moon.

'You've had an offer on your house for the full asking price,' she told him.

Jack's mouth dropped open and his eyes widened, and for a second he looked taken aback, then a smile spread across his face. 'That's brilliant. Wow! I'd better make some calls. How long do you think it will take until the sale goes through?'

Molly exhaled slowly. 'There's no chain on their side, so it depends on how fast the two sets of solicitors work. The other party will have a survey undertaken, which usually takes a few weeks, and their mortgage company will come out to value it, and then there are the various searches that have to be done, so… hopefully not more than three months?'

Molly didn't miss the disappointed expression that flitted across his face.

'It could be less,' she added, trying to reassure him, despite her heart feeling as though someone was sticking pins in it.

Pull yourself together, she thought. It wasn't his fault she was in love with him.

She hadn't realised how deeply she felt until Jack had started to withdraw from her, and now she was in a right pickle. Fancy being in love with the guy you live with, and him being utterly oblivious! Even worse, Molly suspected he was still in love with his ex – who she also suspected was no longer an ex at all.

'That's good news, isn't it?' she said, with false cheer. There was no way she was going to let Jack know how heartbroken she was at the prospect of him moving out.

'It sure is.' He nodded, the smile back on his face, and Molly's heart sank even further.

Look at him – he was thrilled to bits at the news, and it was obvious he couldn't wait to leave.

'I'd… er…' He pointed to the front door.

'Sorry.' Molly stepped to the side to allow him to pass, careful not to touch him. The friendly, flirty strokes on his arm, the accidental (on purpose) brushing against him was no more. These days she was extra careful to keep her distance.

After she had closed the door behind him, she leant against it sadly. He'd hardly stepped outside before he'd removed his phone from the zippered pocket of his running shorts and she guessed he couldn't wait to pass on the good news to Chantelle.

There was one thing preying on her mind though, and that was… if he and Chantelle had indeed got back together, why was he so pleased about having an offer on the house? Surely it would make more sense to take it off the market and for them to move back in together?

Or did they want to make a fresh start somewhere new?

Molly pursed her lips: with her and Jack's formerly friendly relationship now decidedly frosty, it was too late to ask.

***

That's it, Jack thought as he scrolled down the list of contacts on his phone and pressed Della's number. The sale was really going through.

Even though he had moved out and was living in the park keeper's cottage with Molly, he still hadn't truly believed that sooner or later his house would belong to someone else, that another bloke would mow the lawn, that another—

'Della? It's me, Jack. I've got good news.'

'I was about to phone you,' his sister said.

'Oh? Why?'

'I'll tell you in a minute – you go first.'

'We've had an offer on the house, for the full asking price,' he announced.

'That's brilliant!'

'Isn't it!'

He couldn't have sounded very convincing because Della was immediately contrite. 'Sorry, Jack, I know how hard this must be for you.'

'It's just a house.'

'But it's your first proper home.'

'Yours, too,' he pointed out. He glanced back at the cottage as he lifted the latch on the gate to allow Jet to go through ahead of him. There was no sign of Molly, and he wondered whether she was in the kitchen cracking open a celebratory bottle of Prosecco. He paused, one hand on the nearest post; he couldn't begin his run until he'd finished his conversation and put his phone away.

'Yeah, but I moved out ages ago,' his sister said. 'I know you were hoping you would be able to buy me out.' She hesitated. 'We don't have to go through with it, you know. I don't want to turf you out of your home. I can raise the money another way.'

'Such as?'

'I don't know – I'll think of something.'

'The house was never meant to be a permanent home,' he reminded her. 'All it was ever supposed to be was the first rung on the property ladder. It's about time we both climbed to the second rung.' Unfortunately for Jack, there would be no second rung any time soon. He would most likely be standing on ground level again before too long. But Della didn't need to know that. If she did, she would insist on taking the house off the market and demand that he continued to live in it. Her dream of owning the guest house in Alaska where she worked with Scott, would be seriously compromised.

'Speaking of homes… how is the lovely cottage in the park?' she asked. 'I can't wait to see it.'

'I've sent you loads of photos. You *have* seen it.'

'Not in the flesh. And I can't wait to meet Molly.'

'That's unlikely to happen,' Jack said.

'Oh, but it is, big brother. That's why I was about to phone you. I thought I would pop over and say goodbye to the house, and no doubt there'll be things to sign now. Plus I want to see you and Mum.'

'I've only just heard about the offer. I haven't even appointed a solicitor yet,' Jack told her.

'You'd better pull your finger out then, hadn't you?'

'Molly says it could take three months for contracts to be exchanged,' Jack pointed out. He dearly wanted to see his sister, but he didn't want her to waste money on airfare when she'd only have to fly over again when it was time to sign on the dotted line. And neither did he want to show her around the cottage, because it wasn't *his* pride and joy: it was *Molly's*.

He also didn't want Della to meet Molly. His sister was very astute – she would be able to see how he felt about his landlord in a flash, and that would never do.

'Jack, what's wrong? And don't say nothing, because I know there is.'

Darn it: Della was as bad as their mother when it came to female intuition. 'It's Chantelle,' he blurted, without thinking.

'Jack? Jack? You're breaking up. What did you say?'

'I said, it's Chantelle,' he repeated, raising his voice.

'What?'

'Chantelle.' He shouted the name, then wished he hadn't when he saw Molly's face at the window. He turned around, so his back was to the house.

'Did you say "Chantelle"? What's she done?'

'Can you hear me now?' Jack asked.

'Yes, that's better. I asked, what's Chantelle done? I thought you had finished with her.'

'I have. Just a problem at work, that's all. Nothing for you to worry about.'

'Good. I never thought she was right for you.'

'You've never met her,' Jack said.

'I didn't need to.'

'Are you still coming to the UK?' he asked, changing the subject. 'You might want to wait until the paperwork is ready for signing.'

'Absolutely, I do! It will only be a quick visit to you though, because I want to spend as much time with Mum as I can, if that's OK with you?'

'Of course it is. I'm just delighted to see you.'

'Are you free on Thursday? My flight lands at Heathrow at around eleven in the morning, so I thought I'd hire a car at the airport, see you first, then drive on up to York afterwards.'

'I'll make sure I'm free,' Jack promised.

'Fantastic! Maybe I can pop in to see the house one last time, then you can treat me to an early dinner?'

Jack turned back to the cottage, wondering if Molly was still watching him, but there was no sign of her. 'Of course.'

'Love you, big bro.'

Jack smiled. 'Love you, too.'

The call ended and his smile quickly faded. He should have said those three little words to Molly when he had the chance. At least she'd have known how he felt, even if she didn't feel the same way. But he had left it too late, and now another man had claimed her heart.

As Jack called the dog to him, he caught a glimpse of his rival in the distance and scowled.

That's what Molly had been doing at the window, he thought – waiting for Reuben to make an appearance.

And he was proved right as he heard the unmistakable click of the latch when he was halfway to the gate near the bandstand, and glanced behind to see Molly rushing off in Reuben's direction.

**

It might be silly to cry over someone who had never been hers in the first place, but Molly couldn't help it. Jack mightn't be her boyfriend but in the few short weeks since he'd moved in she felt closer to him than she had ever felt to any man – even without ever having kissed him.

However, the Jack she'd come to know and had fallen in love with, was a different Jack to the man who had been so delighted to be told his house had been sold.

And she knew why – *Chantelle*. He had phoned her barely a minute after Molly had told him the news, and although she hadn't *heard* him tell Chantelle that he loved her, Molly had been able to lipread well enough. Even if she hadn't, the soppy look on his face would have told her everything she needed to know. Jack was still in love with her.

Whether or not they were a couple again, Molly wasn't certain, but it was only a matter of time she thought, as she hurried to catch Reuben before he knocked off for the day. She was dying to see if he had managed to find any suitable logs, and where he'd placed them. Then once he'd gone, she'd sit on one of them and have a good cry.

The only consolation was that Jack didn't realise how she felt about him, because if he did things would be even more unbearable than they already were.

CHAPTER 22

'…and Reuben has identified several endangered species of plants and insects, and he's shown me some weasel droppings.' Molly knew she was prattling but the atmosphere in the cottage was so tense lately you could cut it with a knife and spread it on toast.

Jack had a face like a slapped arse, as Granny would say, and Molly wondered whether things were OK between him and Chantelle. She didn't think he'd been to work today either, because when she'd taken the opportunity to pop home lunchtime to let Jet out for a wee, she'd found Jack in the living room, watching TV.

Rather than ask him outright why he wasn't at work (it wasn't any of her business anyway), she'd started to prattle, and once she'd started, she couldn't seem to stop.

'You ought to see the woods now,' she continued. 'Reuben has done a brilliant job. He would have done more, but he's had a lot of work on. Did I tell you he's a carpenter?'

Jack shrugged without looking at her.

'I'm sure I did. Anyway, I think we'll get started on the pond next. See if we can find any of those great crested newts he was talking about.' Damn! She hadn't wanted to mention those, not until one put in an appearance. If one ever did…

Finally reining in her wayward mouth and hoping that Jack had been listening as little as he'd appeared to be, she said, 'I was cooking on making steak and chips for tea. Would you like some?'

They still ate the occasional meal together, purely for convenience, but not as often as they used to. It was becoming more and more usual for him to claim that he had eaten a substantial meal at work, so she should go ahead and cook for herself. Which led her to wonder who he was eating that meal with.

He still didn't go out much in the evenings, though, which she assumed he might have done if he was back with Chantelle.

Gah! Who knew what was going on! Molly certainly didn't.

What she did know, was that Jack no longer seemed interested in the park. Gone were the long conversations on what needed improving and how they were going to do it. Gone were the planning sessions. Gone was the working together side-by-side, although Jack still did his fair share – enough to fulfil his end of the rental agreement. He continued to makeover the flower beds, and he carried on locking the park gates at night. But he seemed to have lost his enthusiasm for the job. He was just going through the motions, and it saddened Molly to see it.

'No thanks,' he said, in answer to her question. 'I'm going out soon and I probably won't be back until later. You go ahead: I'll sort myself out if I'm hungry.'

'I see. OK. It's just you and me,' she said to Jet, tears pricking at the back of her eyes.

Maybe it *was* time for Jack to move out: she couldn't take much more of this polite professional treatment.

'Have I done anything to upset you?' she blurted, then clapped a hand to her mouth. God knows where that came from. She'd had no intention of saying any such thing.

'Not at all.' He sounded mildly surprised.

She'd said it now and couldn't take it back, so she might as well pursue it, get it out in the open so to speak, because something was definitely wrong.

'What is it, then?' she persisted. 'You're not the same Jack you were a couple of weeks ago.'

Molly tried to think back to what might have changed, but nothing jumped out at her. Except… maybe he hadn't been as oblivious to her flirting as she had presumed, and this was his way of telling her that he wasn't interested without embarrassing her by actually saying anything.

Her face flamed and she wished she'd never started this flippin' conversation.

After a long pause where she thought he was about to tell her he was flattered by her interest and that she would make some lucky guy a wonderful girlfriend, but he didn't think of her like that, he eventually said, 'It's a work thing.'

'Work?' she repeated in surprise.

'Yeah.'

'Want to talk about it?'

'Not really.'

Molly bit her lip and stared at her hands.

'It's just… There's talk of a restructure of some of the departments and everyone's having their jobs evaluated, so the atmosphere isn't brilliant,' he explained, filling the silence.

'*Your* job is safe though?'

He shrugged. 'No safer than anyone else's.'

Oh dear, no wonder he seemed distant and preoccupied – here he was, worried about his job, and all she could do was prattle on about weasels. It might also explain why he had been so delighted when she'd told him he'd had an offer on his house – he might well need the money.

'I'm sure you'll be OK,' she said, but the expression on his face told her he wasn't convinced, and when she put a reassuring hand on his arm, he flinched as though she had struck him.

'Sorry,' she muttered, heat whooshing into her cheeks at his reaction.

Without waiting for him to respond, she darted into the kitchen on the pretence of making a cup of tea before she had to go back to work.

By the time she had switched the kettle on and lifted a cup off the mug tree, he was gone. No goodbye, no see you later… just the sound of the front door closing and the waft of his aftershave in the air.

***

'It's so strange being back,' Della said as she stood in the centre of the empty living room and gazed around. 'We had such fun, didn't we? Remember when I painted that wall and you said it looked grubby?'

'What was that colour called?'

'Mushroom Fizz.'

'It was… er… how can I put this nicely… the colour of dishwater.'

Della giggled, and Jack smiled at the sound. Gosh, he had missed her!

'Looking back, you were right – it *was* awful. But I thought we were being so stylish.'

He studied his sister as she wandered around the ground floor, running her fingers across the worktops in the kitchen and lowering the blind a fraction.

'You've gone blonder,' he observed. She was also glowing and looked happy and healthy – Alaska and Scott suited her.

'I fancied a change,' she said.

'And you've let it grow.'

'So have you! When was the last time you had a haircut?'

Jack ran a hand through his hair. 'I've been too busy.'

'Ah, yes, manpower in exchange for rent. How's that going?'

'The cottage is done. More or less. It needs new cabinets in the kitchen, and the bathroom suite is a hideous peach colour, but…' He trailed off.

He wouldn't be around to witness the installation of a new bath. As soon as his share of the money from the sale of this house was in his bank account, he would start looking for another place to live. He had been hoping to stay on in Molly's cottage for a few more months so he could save most of his wages, but he couldn't entertain the idea now, not with her so full of Reuben.

Take today, for instance: it had been Reuben this, and Reuben that. She had positively gushed, leaving Jack in no doubt she'd fallen for the guy big time.

And then she'd had the cheek to ask him what was wrong!

Jack gave himself a mental shake. He was being unfair: how was she supposed to know how he felt about her if he'd never told her? As far as she was concerned, they were only friends. If that. He still wasn't convinced that she didn't regard him as anything other than her lodger.

He was fully aware he had been distant of late, but he hadn't expected her to quiz him about it, so when she'd asked, he had blurted out the first thing that had popped into his head.

It was true enough – he *was* worried about his job. Rumours were still flying thick and fast, but no one really knew what was going on. He was tempted to look around for another job, but he wanted to wait until he'd sorted out somewhere else to live first. He would have to apply for another mortgage if he intended to buy, and the mortgage company would want to know how long he'd worked for his current employer before they loaned him any money. Working for the council for nearly thirteen years looked good on paper. And a property rental company would also want to do employment checks – so he was stuck in this job for the time being.

'Are you sure you don't want to take me to see it? We could order food in rather than go to a restaurant. Or you could cook?' Della was looking at him expectantly.

'Another time,' he said. 'Assuming I'm still there. It's only temporary,' he reminded her. 'Plus, Molly is at home and I don't want to intrude.'

'Surely she won't mind you bringing your sister back for a couple of hours?'

'She's not well,' he lied.

Della gave him an odd look, but to his relief she dropped the subject. 'I think it's time to go. Goodbye, house, it was fun living in you.' She turned to him, her eyes glistening with unshed tears. 'Is it silly to feel like I'm giving away a family pet? I haven't lived here for years, yet…'

'Come here' he said, opening his arms wide to give her a hug. 'You're not being daft at all. I feel the same way.'

'Are you sure you don't want to buy me out?'

'Nah, it's time to move on.'

'Have you found anywhere yet?'

'Not yet.' He led her towards the door, and once outside he locked up carefully.

'What sort of property are you looking for?'

Della continued to quiz him all the way to the restaurant, and the more vague his answers became, the more questions she asked until he cried, 'Enough already! You sound like an estate agent. Pull into the car park here,' he added.

'This looks nice,' Della said, gazing at the sign above the restaurant's door. 'The Anatolian Kitchen.'

'It's Turkish. It's only been open a few months and I've heard it's very good, but I haven't tried it myself.' He had a vision of Molly sitting opposite him as they were shown to a table, and he sadly shoved it away. This wasn't the time to be thinking about her – he wanted to savour every second with his sister because he had no idea when he would see her again.

Over a bowl of olives and a starter of goats' cheese wrapped in filo pastry, Della and Jack caught up on their news. Or rather, Della did most of the talking and Jack listened. But during the deliciously tasty main course of melt-in-the-mouth chicken shish (Della had the same), he was aware of her giving him concerned glances.

'There's something you're not telling me,' she said, scooping up a forkful of the fragrant lentils and rice, her eyes half closed in bliss. 'Mmm, this is gorgeous.'

'Isn't it just.' Jack speared a portion of chicken. 'If I say "nothing", will you believe me?'

'Not a chance! Go on, spill, else I'll tell Mum there's something wrong and she'll get it out of you.'

'You wouldn't!' He thought for a second. 'Yeah, you would.'

Della tilted her head, acknowledging the truth of it.

Jack put his fork down and clasped his hands together. 'It's a woman.'

'I might have guessed! Not that awful Chantelle?'

'Molly.' Jack noticed the relieved expression on his sister's face, but thought she wouldn't be so pleased when he explained the situation. 'I'm in love with her.' His smile was sad.

'And she doesn't feel the same way?' Della guessed.

He shook his head.

'Oh, Jack… I'm sorry. It must make things very awkward.'

'It would be even worse if she knew how I felt about her.'

'You haven't told her?'

'What's the point?'

'Duh! Because she might like you, too? How do you know she doesn't?'

'She fancies Reuben.'

'The volunteer guy?'

Jack nodded sadly.

Della stretched out her hand to cover his, giving him a squeeze, her eyes full of sympathy.

'Finish your meal,' he told her, and after squeezing his hand again, she resumed eating.

Jack's appetite had deserted him, but he gamely picked up his fork, not wanting Della to worry, and changed the subject.

With neither of them able to manage a dessert and Della having a long drive ahead of her, they settled for Turkish tea and a tearful farewell.

'Don't leave it so long next time,' Jack said, as they stood outside the restaurant. He pulled her into his arms and buried his face in her hair, his eyes and his heart full.

'You're going to have to come to Alaska,' she urged. 'A visit is long overdue. And I'm dying for you to meet Scott.'

'He sounds like a top bloke, but tell him that if he doesn't treat you right, he'll have me to answer to.'

'You always did look out for me,' Della said, her voice thick with tears.

Jack pulled away so he could see her face, and he tenderly wiped her cheek. 'And I always will,' he promised. 'No matter how far you go.'

She sniffed, her chin wobbling. 'Stop it, you're making me cry. And Jack, you *will* find someone,' she assured him.

Jack couldn't reply, because he already had found someone – it was just a shame she didn't love him back.

***

'Molly? Hi… I, er, hate to be the bearer of bad news, but I thought I'd better phone you straight away. I've just seen Jack and—' Astrid paused then said, 'I'm sorry.'

Molly guessed what was coming. 'What's happened?'

'You know that new Turkish restaurant in town? I saw Jack coming out of it with a woman. They were all over each other.'

Molly's blood turned to ice in her veins. So that was where he had gone – he'd had a date. 'Do you know who this woman is? What did she look like?'

'I only saw her from the back – she was too busy burying her face in his neck – but from what I could see, she was slim with long blond hair. A bit taller than you, but not as tall as Jack.'

'It could be Chantelle. I don't know how tall she is, but she's got long blond hair.'

Astrid said, 'I know I shouldn't, but I took a photo. Do you want me to send it to you?'

Molly did – and she didn't. It was one thing being told that Jack was all over a woman, and quite another seeing it for herself.

Curiosity got the better of her. 'Send it,' she confirmed.

A moment later, she was staring at it and wishing she wasn't.

The woman had her back to the camera, but that wasn't what caught Molly's attention – it was the love on Jack's face. He was gazing at Chantelle with an expression of utter devotion, and Molly felt like bawling.

Her instinct was right: he *was* still in love with Chantelle and from the way the pair of them were clinging together as though they never wanted to let go, Molly knew they were an item once more.

'Thanks, Astrid,' she said quietly.

'Are you going to be OK?'

'I'll be fine,' she said, knowing she wouldn't be fine for a long time to come.

She was in love with Jack, but he was in love with someone else.

How could she ever be fine again?

CHAPTER 23

The cottage was in darkness when Jack returned, and there was no sign of life. Guessing that Molly must be in bed, Jet with her, he swapped his shoes for trainers, grabbed a torch and the keys to the gates, and slipped outside.

He was too strung out to sleep, so the walk would do him good. Besides, it was still relatively early and he knew that if he went to bed now he'd spend the next two hours staring at the ceiling.

After he'd said goodbye to his sister, he had gone back to his old house and had sat in the garden, thinking. But it hadn't done any good. He still had no idea what he should do for the best, so he'd made his way back to the park keeper's cottage and the woman who owned it, his heart heavy.

In a way, he was relieved she was in bed, because he didn't think he could face her tonight, not when he was feeling so raw after seeing Della. Anyway, he hadn't locked the gates yet, so if she had been up he'd have had the perfect excuse to go out again.

He always followed the same route every evening. Starting with the gate located at the far side of the children's play area, he strolled past the woodland (scowling at the newly created path), through the field to the gate at the top, then made his way across the meadow to the pond. The gate there was seldom used, and from the way the grass had grown up through its bars, he guessed it hadn't been opened for a while. He locked it anyway, then followed the edge of the pond and down through the meadow again until he felt tarmac beneath his feet.

This path would take him past the boarded-up cafe and the run-down bandstand, and he'd lock that gate after ushering out any teenagers who were loitering there. Finally, he would lock the small gate next to the large main ones, after which he'd have no excuse to stay out any longer, although he could always sit on a bench if he could find an unbroken one, and look at the stars and contemplate the way his life was slowly falling apart.

'Oi, mister! You gonna kick us out or what?'

Jack was brought out of his musings by the cocky voice of a lad who should have been safely tucked up in bed at home and not showing off in front of his mates – who also had no business being in the park at ten-forty-five on a Thursday night, especially during term time when they probably had school the next day.

'I sure am,' he said, trying not to show his irritation. Did they have to go through the same ritual every evening? He'd tell them he was about to lock the gates, and they'd give him grief. Sometimes it took him twenty minutes or more to shift them.

Tonight, possibly because he was later than normal, they gave him less attitude than they usually did, and left with only a few cat calls, plus a bit of swearing and jeering.

Result!

Maybe they were finally getting the message that no matter what names they called him or how much fuss they made, he was going to lock the gates regardless. In the beginning he'd had to threaten to lock them in to get them to move (that had gone down like a lead balloon – and he was surprised none of them had called his bluff), but as the days had trundled on, they'd come to grudgingly accept his authority.

With the last gate finally locked, Jack went to bed.

***

'Jack? Are you awake? *Jack?*' Molly knocked on Jack's door again. Surely he couldn't still be asleep? Not with Jet whining louder than an old-fashioned kettle on a hob, and her hammering on his door.

When it opened abruptly, Molly stepped back.

Jack wasn't wearing much, just a pair of shorts, and her eyes immediately went to his chest and the smattering of hairs trailing down his stomach.

With an effort, she tore her gaze away and focused on his face. He looked remarkably alert for someone who had been soundly asleep, she thought, but then she noticed earbuds around his neck and his mobile in his hand, and guessed he must have been on the phone to Chantelle, whispering sweet nothings in her ear.

'Sorry, I was listening to music,' he said. 'What's up?'

'I think someone might be in the park.'

'Not that again.' Jack's eyes narrowed and his jaw hardened. 'The little…'

'I'm happy to go,' Molly said, 'but I thought it best to wake you in case I ran into trouble.

'You will not go.'

'I can manage.'

'Against a bunch of yobs?'

'I'll have Jet with me.'

'That's not a good idea. Wait there.' Jack disappeared into his room, reappearing a few seconds later wearing a pair of jeans and pulling a T-shirt over his head. 'I'll go, but if you insist on coming with me, keep a tight hold of Jet. You don't want to risk him getting hurt or biting anyone.'

'He's not got a nasty bone in his body!' Molly was aghast that Jack should think such a thing.

'I know he hasn't, but if things get hairy he might feel he has to defend you.'

Molly hadn't thought of that, so along with the worry about what was happening in the park, she was now also worried about her dog. 'Oh, God… Shall we ignore it? And not go out there?'

'I'll be damned if I'm going to let a bunch of ill-mannered, disrespectful, unruly teenagers destroy what you've done.' Jack pushed past her and hurried down the stairs.

Molly trotted after him. 'What *we've* done,' she corrected.

'Apologies – Reuben's worked hard, too.'

'I wasn't referring to him,' she said, but Jet's whining had turned into deep, rumbling growls and she didn't think Jack heard her.

He shoved his feet into his trainers and yanked the door open, racing outside, Molly haring out after him, one hand wrapped around Jet's collar to stop him from running off.

But there was nothing to be seen.

The restored flower beds were untouched and no one lurked in the shadows as far as Molly could tell. Jack had come to a halt on the path and he was also scrutinising them, a frown marring his brow.

Then his head came up. 'Listen. Do you hear that?'

Molly was about to say that the only thing she could hear was Jet's grumbling, when she heard it too.

'Is someone shouting for help?' she asked and Jet whined loudly, tugging at his collar. 'Where's it coming from?'

'Inside the park, I think,' Jack replied, cupping a hand to his ear. 'Over there.' He pointed towards the meadow.

Molly and Jack arrived at the same conclusion. 'The pond!' she cried, just as he said, 'It's coming from the direction of the pond,' and they stared at each other in dismay.

'It can't be – I locked the gates. And I made sure no one was left inside.'

With a muttered curse Jack broke into a run and sprinted away. Molly tried to keep up with him, but even with Jet pulling her along, she was quickly left behind. All she could do was follow as best she could.

Dreading what she might find, she jogged after him, puffing and panting, and lamenting her lack of fitness, and as she stumbled along the path the cries for help became louder and more frantic.

'Please God, don't let anyone be hurt,' she prayed, her lungs labouring and her legs aching, and a stitch soon had her clutching her left side in pain.

Finally, she was almost there. A three-quarter moon shed silver light on the water, and she squinted, wondering why it appeared to be frothing and not its usual still surface.

Oh, my God! Someone was in the water!

Two someones!

A third person stood on the bank and she recognised him as one of the teenagers who was usually to be found near the bandstand, the one who had said "Make me" when she had asked him to pick his litter up.

'Connor's drowning, mister!' the boy shouted. 'He's stuck on something.'

Molly rushed up to him, her eyes scanning the pond, and she bent forward to catch her breath.

Jack was wading out to the far side, and as she watched he launched himself forward and began to swim. He was heading towards the pale, frightened face of a boy who was splashing ineffectually and barely managing to keep his head above water.

'What happened?' she asked.

The kid standing next to her looked younger than she remembered, and less sure of himself. He was also soaking wet. 'He fell in. He's a shitty swimmer so I went in after him, but he got caught up and I was scared I might, too.' He was close to tears. 'I left him there.'

'Don't worry, Jack will get him out.' She prayed that was true. Jack seemed to be a strong swimmer and she had every faith in him.

Her heart was in her mouth though, and she didn't think she could watch, but neither could she look away. As he drew nearer to the boy, she could hear Jack talking to the lad, but was unable to make out the individual words.

'Have you phoned the emergency services?' she asked.

'I couldn't. I left my phone on the grass before I went in, but I can't find it.'

Molly realised he was close to tears. 'I'll call them,' she said, fear making her hands shake as she reached into her pocket for her mobile.

But just as she was about to dial 999, Jack dove beneath the surface.

Shocked, Molly shrieked, 'Jack! What the hell are you doing!'

At that moment Jet leapt forward, almost yanking her off her feet. Abruptly, she let go of his collar and fell to her knees as the dog bounded into the water.

'Jet!' she screamed, but he ignored her, doggy paddling towards the boy, who was spluttering and coughing.

Terrified for all three, she patted the ground, searching for her dropped phone, and at the very same moment her fingers touched the screen, the boy standing next to her shouted, 'He's got him. See?'

Molly saw, and relief swept through her. Connor was free of whatever it was he had got caught up on, and was clinging to Jack like a limpet, his arms around Jack's neck.

She clambered to her feet on shaking legs. Thank God for—

Wait… Jack didn't seem to be swimming; he was stationary in the water and splashing more than he should.

Something was very wrong indeed, and she guessed the boy must be dragging him down. Jack was floundering badly and wasn't making any progress.

Oh, my God, they were both going to drown!

And they might have, if it hadn't been for Jet.

The plucky dog had reached Jack and the boy, and was circling them. Molly couldn't quite make out what happened, but suddenly the dog was swimming for the bank with the boy hanging onto his collar as Jet towed him along. She could hear the animal's puffed exhalations as he tried to breathe and swim whilst being half-strangled by the scared youngster whose life he was saving, and she prayed he would reach the shallows safely.

But it was Jack who she was more worried about now – he'd disappeared under the water again and he had yet to resurface.

'Don't you dare drown,' she yelled, stooping to remove her trainers. There was nothing for it, she would have to go in. 'You can't die, you stupid man. I love you! Oh, buggering hell!' she cried, feeling sick with relief when she saw his head break the surface of the water, cursing him for scaring her like that.

Jet's paws touched the bottom of the pond, and the boy he was towing realised the water was shallow enough to stand up in.

'Are you OK?' she cried, hurrying into the water to help him and gasping at the cold.

'I'm alright. Cold, though. It's effing freezing in there. We climbed the fence,' he said, his teeth chattering.

Jet shook himself violently from the top of his head to the tip of his tail, sending water droplets through the air, dousing Molly.

The other teenager chimed in, 'We know it was wrong, but we wanted to teach *him* a lesson.' He jerked his thumb towards Jack, who had almost reached the bank.

'We'll discuss that later.' Turning to Connor, Molly said, 'Are you sure you're OK? Do you need an ambulance? I think I'd better call one anyway, to be on the safe side.'

'Don't,' Connor begged, looking frightened. 'Liam, tell her.'

'You can't. His dad will kick off big time if he finds out,' Liam explained.

'I don't care,' Molly began, and was about to make the call when Jack stumbled out of the water, staggering as he reached the bank, where he flopped onto the grass and lay motionless.

'Jack!' Molly left the two boys to their own devices, seeing that Connor wasn't in any immediate danger, and went to tend to the man she loved.

Relieved to find him breathing, she rolled him onto his side.

'I'm OK,' he gasped. He was shivering violently and his breathing was ragged, but he didn't appear to be hurt. 'Cold and out of breath, that's all. I thought I was a goner for a minute.'

'What happened?'

He sat up, his chest heaving. 'The boy's foot was caught in a shopping trolley. I had to dive down to free him, but when I came back up, he practically climbed on top of me and pushed me under again, so this time it was me who got my foot caught.' He shook his head.

'Stupid.' He turned a stricken face towards her. 'Is he OK?'

'He's fine and so is Jet.'

'That dog's a hero. If it wasn't for him…' Jack trailed off.

Molly shuddered. She didn't want to think how badly things could have gone if it hadn't been for the bravery of her dog.

'Right,' she said, taking charge, because someone had to and she was the only one in any fit state. 'I'm going to phone for an ambul—' She stopped and looked around. The two boys were nowhere in sight. They had scarpered, without a thank you or even a goodbye.

There's gratitude for you, she thought, hoping Connor was OK. If she knew his full name or where he lived, she would go to his house to check: but all she could do now was to look out for him or his mate, Liam, at the bandstand tomorrow night.

With a sigh, she put her arm around Jack and helped him to his feet. She needed to get him and Jet home and dried off.

And when Jack went to bed, she would be able to let the tears which she was gamely holding back, flow to their heart's content. Jack mightn't be hers, but that didn't matter any more. He was alive, and she could so very easily have lost him completely.

CHAPTER 24

'I heard that you had fun and games last night.'

Bill's voice made Molly jump and she whirled around to find him standing a few feet away, staring into the calm waters of the pond.

'I thought you didn't come here?' she replied.

'I don't usually, but I wanted to see where your man nearly drowned.'

'He's not my man.'

Bill peered at her with rheumy eyes. 'You would like him to be.'

Molly sniffed and turned her attention back to the pond. She was trying to spot the death-trap of a trolley, but the water was holding onto its secrets.

Bill delved into his pocket and brought out a foil-wrapped parcel. 'That's for Jet. It's a marrow bone. He's earned it.'

Molly took it. 'Er, thanks, but why don't you give it to him yourself?'

Jet was snuffling around in the bushes, Patch by his side.

'Patch will be jealous,' Bill told her solemnly.

'I see. In that case…' She slipped it into the pocket of her fleece. 'What are you doing out so early?' she asked. It was barely six a.m. Her excuse was that she had been unable to sleep, the events of last night flashing across her mind whenever she'd closed her eyes, so eventually she had got up and had taken Jet out for a walk, unlocking the gates as she did so to save Jack having to do it: he needed all the sleep he could get, after last night. But before she'd left, she had eased his bedroom door open to check that he was still breathing.

Seeing him soundly asleep, she had studied him for a moment, her gaze travelling over his peaceful face, then she'd crept into the dawn, her feet taking her through the field and onto the meadow.

'I couldn't sleep,' Bill said. 'It's my own fault. I dropped off in the chair last night, then when I went to bed I was wide awake. I'll finish my walk and have some breakfast, then go back to bed. Old age don't come by itself, you know – it buggers up your circadian rhythm.'

Molly suppressed a smile – circadian rhythm, indeed!

'It looks pretty innocuous, doesn't it?' she said as they continued to stare at the water.

Bill was silent for a while, then he said. 'It's all over town.'

'What is?'

'That your Jack saved a boy from drowning and nearly died himself.'

'How do you know?' Surely no one else was around this early in the day?

'Social media. Sweet Meadow has a group.'

'What does it say?' Dread washed over her. 'Is the boy OK?'

'Oh, aye, he's fine. In hot water 'cause he should have been in bed, but other than that he's as right as rain. There's a bit of a to-do about the gates being locked, though. People are saying that it would never have happened if they'd been left open. They're on about complaining to the council. The father of one of the youffs says he's going to sue.'

Molly was flabbergasted and her heart sank. 'Oh, no!'

Bill grunted. 'It would be a crying shame if that happens. It's about time the council did something about the park and the yobs who hang around here. When I saw your Jack locking up after those little wotsits had made a mess of your flower beds, I felt like cheering.' Bill tutted. 'Damned kids. After this, I expect those liver-lily council officials will bend over backwards to keep them open now. Mark my words, the park will soon go to rack and ruin again – and just when you were starting to make a bit of progress, too. It's criminal, that's what it is.'

'I hope Jack won't get into trouble. I'd better warn him,' she said. 'Thanks, Bill.'

Jack was up and dressed when she hurried into the cottage. He was in the kitchen, cradling a cup of tea, and leaning against the worktop, his expression thoughtful.

Jet trotted over to him, and Jack bent to stroke the dog's ears.

'How did you sleep?' she asked.

'Fine, thanks.'

'No after-effects?'

'None whatsoever,' he assured her. 'I hope the lad is OK.'

'He is,' Molly assured him. 'I know that Connor said he didn't want me to phone for an ambulance last night because he was scared of getting into trouble, but it's all over social media that you saved him from drowning and almost drowned yourself. Sometimes I really dislike people.'

'Why?'

'Because they're saying it would never have happened if the gates had been left open.'

'The ungrateful little…' Jack ground to a halt and shook his head.

She could tell he was hurt, and she didn't blame him. He had risked his life to free that kid, and this was the thanks he got.

'Exactly! You wait until I see those pair again. I'm going to give them a piece of my mind. And their parents, too,' she said.

'It won't do any good,' Jack told her. 'And it might make things worse.'

'You do realise that the gates will have to be kept open from now on? We can't risk anything like this happening again.'

'I know.'

'Jack…?' Molly hesitated. 'Bill seems to think you might get into trouble. He says that the father of one of the boys is talking about suing the council.'

Jack set his mug down slowly. 'He can't do that. It's nothing to do with the council; the gates being locked is down to me.'

Although she hadn't asked (maybe she should have) and Jack hadn't mentioned it, Molly had a feeling that he hadn't been acting in any official capacity, and she felt like crying. It was all her fault. If she hadn't been so mad, Jack probably wouldn't have thought about locking the gates.

'I'm so sorry, it's all my fault,' she began, but Jack didn't let her finish.

'There's nothing to be sorry for. I knew I might be exceeding my authority in locking the gates, and even if I wasn't, I didn't follow the correct process and procedures, so if anyone is to blame, it's me.'

Molly slapped her hand on the worktop. 'No, I refuse to believe that. You were only trying to help. It's the fault of those kids and everyone else who doesn't give a damn about the park. I give up. I'm not prepared to waste any more time on it. Why should I care when no one else does?'

'Reuben does.' Jack's tone was flat.

It stopped Molly in her tracks, just as she was about to have a really good rant. 'Yes, he does,' she said softly. How sad was that? In the whole of Sweet Meadow there were only four people who truly cared about the park – her, Jack, Bill, and Reuben.

'I've got to go,' Jack said. 'Meetings.'

Molly gave him a small smile. 'See you later,' she called after him, but he didn't acknowledge her.

She didn't blame him. Her insistence and bloody-mindedness regarding the park might well have cost him his job.

Sliding to the floor, she wrapped her arms around Jet, who was delighted to find his owner's face on the same level as his, and sobbed into his fur.

She couldn't have made any more of a mess of things if she had tried.

***

Great! Not only was he in love with a woman who was hardly aware of his existence in that regard, Jack also needed to find another place to live sharpish if he wanted any chance of trying to mend his shattered heart. Plus, his job was in jeopardy, he had almost drowned, and now he was at risk of being sued by a chap who was such a brilliant father that he had no idea his kid was out in the middle of the night.

Had he missed anything, he mused sullenly, as he stomped across the council offices' foyer.

Apparently he had, because when he opened his emails he discovered a message from reception saying a caller wanted to complain about people swimming in the pond in Sweet Meadow Park at night and that it should be fenced off. He felt like screaming. He hadn't heard from his phantom message-leaver for a while, and he had begun to think the anonymous caller's complaints had been silenced by all the effort he, Molly, and Reuben were putting in.

Yes, Reuben, too, he admitted, because no matter how much Jack disliked him, he had to admit that the guy was doing a great job.

Oh, and here was Chantelle for good measure, Jack saw when he looked up from the screen.

'I hear you've been making a name for yourself,' she said, coming into his office, her hips wiggling in her tight pencil skirt.

Jack turned his attention back to his emails and ignored her.

'Jack, are you listening to me?'

'Huh?'

'I said, Hayley Crouch wants to meet with you on Monday. Nine a.m. Am I to assume you're free?'

Free? Of course he would be free! The woman was the HR Manager, and not only did he not want to antagonise her, but he was also keen to know why she wanted to see him.

'Er, yes, fine,' he stuttered. 'Any idea what it's about?'

'No, but you can bring a colleague or your union rep with you, if you wish.'

Crap. That didn't sound good. His heart dropping to his boots faster than a block of concrete down a well, Jack could take an educated guess. And for Chantelle to come to his office and tell him in person, meant that she probably knew the reason but wasn't saying.

'I'll be there,' he promised, wondering whether he should ask someone to accompany him. 'What did you mean about me making a name for myself?'

Chantelle raised her eyebrows. 'Don't tell me you haven't seen it?' Then she gave a tinkling laugh. 'Silly me! You don't do social media, do you?' She laughed again and tossed her head, flicking her hair over her shoulder.

He realised she was enjoying this.

'You've created quite a stir in Sweet Meadow. Some people think you're a hero, other people are after your blood.' She paused. 'Not yours, the council's. But you *are* the department head for Parks and Highways, aren't you, so I suppose it's the same thing.' She turned on her heel. 'Don't be late for your meeting on Monday,' she said, as a parting shot, leaving him in no doubt what the meeting was about.

Feeling sick, he waited a sufficient length of time to ensure she had left, then went in search of Pete.

'I've got a meeting with Hayley Crouch on Monday,' he said, walking into his colleague's office.

Pete looked up from his mobile. 'Is it about this?' He held it up so Jack could see the screen.

Jack dropped into a chair, leant forward and peered at it. 'Shit.' There was a whole thread on there about the gates being locked.

'Shit, indeed. You didn't do this through the proper channels, did you?' Pete's expression was sympathetic.

Jack pulled a face.

Pete said, 'Maybe you could argue that you locked the gates because the pond isn't safe. It has already been scheduled to be filled in, so at least the higher-ups will be happy that you are being proactive, rather than reactive. And I'll guess they'll shoot it to the top of their to-do list if that father starts making waves.'

'Hmm, I suppose.' Jack wasn't convinced he could get away with using that argument, but he could try.

'Look on the bright side,' Pete added. 'The kid didn't die.'

'There is that.'

'And neither did you, so that's a bonus.'

'Is it?'

'It'll blow over.' Pete appeared confident.

'But will I have a job at the end of it? This might be the excuse HR needs to get rid of me. It might save them having to make somebody redundant if they go ahead with their plans to amalgamate a couple of departments. I've played straight into their hands.' He buried his head in his palms and said, 'Chantelle couldn't wait to tell me.'

'That's typical of her. Did she say that's what the meeting is about?'

'Not in so many words, but she dropped enough hints.'

'I'm sorry, mate.'

'Yeah, well. I should have known better.' Jack lifted his head. 'I *did* know better, but I saw red. If I'd have left it until the next day, I would have calmed down and gone about it properly. I'd have cited something along the lines of, "gates locked between the hours of eight a.m. and six p.m. for health and safety reasons". Hell, I probably wouldn't have even gone that far. Those damn people don't deserve to have a park, so if they don't care about it, why should I?'

'Because you live smack bang in the middle of it, and you care about Molly.' When Jack glared at him, Pete held his hands up in mock surrender. 'Just saying.'

'Well don't.' Jack got to his feet as his mobile rang, and when he saw who was calling him, he thought he might cry. His mum never phoned him in the middle of the day because she knew he would be at work, and fear shot through him.

'Mum! What's wrong?' he could hear the panic in his voice and he took a deep breath to steady himself.

'You tell me, Jack Henry Feathers,' she said.

'Pardon?'

'You heard. You're all over the internet.'

'How do you know?'

'I've been a member of the Sweet Meadow group since it started. Just because I don't live there anymore, doesn't mean I don't keep abreast of what's going on.'

Jack returned to his office and closed the door, not wanting anyone to realise he was having a telling off from his mother, and he collapsed into his chair and groaned.

'What did you say?' His mum might be in full flow, but she had hearing a bat would be proud of.

'Nothing.'

'Good, because you listen to me, my lovely boy – I'm so proud of you I could burst. You didn't have to dive into that ruddy pond to save that boy, but you did. Not everyone would risk their life for someone else. But if I *ever* hear of you doing anything like that again, you'll have me to answer to. Are you listening?'

'Yes, Mum.'

'Don't you "yes, Mum" me. You're not too old that I can't put you over my knee.'

'You can't do that anymore.'

'Can you not?' Her voice dropped an octave as she growled, 'Watch me.'

'Sorry, Mum.'

'So you should be. Now, get off my phone, I've got a shop to run.'

Jack opened his mouth to say *she* had phoned *him*, not the other way around, when the line went dead.

But when it immediately buzzed with an incoming message from her, he had to smile when he read it, and muttered, 'Love you, too, Mum… love you, too.'

***

Molly spent most of the day worrying, so by the time she arrived home from work she was in a right old stew.

Not normally a fretter, she found that she couldn't keep her mind on her job. And it didn't help that Astrid kept giving her updates – even though Molly had actually asked her to.

It seemed there were two camps: those who argued that the parents should have kept a closer eye on their children and were now calling them out on their parenting skills; and those who blamed the council for locking the gates in the first place and forcing kids to climb over the fence. It was a wonder no one had been impaled, someone had commented, blindly ignoring the fact that those teenagers shouldn't have been climbing over any fences in the first place.

Astrid, bless her, was furious on Molly's behalf. 'He'd sing a different tune if one of those little sods had climbed over *his* fence and was gallivanting about in *his* garden. Stupid man! He'll be one of those idiots who is on the side of a burglar when he injures himself breaking into a house and blames the homeowner.' She rolled her eyes. 'Some people! Huh!'

By the time Friday afternoon drew to a close, Molly was relieved to leave the office and head home. She was desperate to hear what sort of day Jack had had, and prayed he wasn't in any trouble. But when she entered the park (she had decided to leave her car in the street and not risk opening the gates in case anyone challenged her) she was surprised to find the drive empty, which was unusual because Jack normally finished early on a Friday.

However, there was a woman standing on the step, her hands cupped around her face as she tried to peer in through the coloured glass decorating the front door. A slim woman with longish blond hair, who would no doubt be wearing a face full of immaculate makeup.

Chantelle.

Great – that was all she needed!

CHAPTER 25

By three-thirty Jack was ready to call it a day. He'd been at work since before seven this morning (he'd been first in through the doors) and he'd had enough. He was tired, irritable and anxious – not a good combination – and all he wanted was to go out for a long run, then treat himself to a cold beer. Probably more than one. He'd drink them in his bedroom with his earbuds in while he listened to music, because he didn't want to see anyone or speak to anyone, and that included Molly. *Especially* Molly, because she'd probably be doing something conservation-y with Reuben in the park. And neither did he want to listen to the kids whooping it up on the bandstand.

He switched his computer off at the mains, checked his pockets for his car keys and wallet, then hooked his jacket off the back of the chair.

When his office phone rang, he was tempted to ignore it, and he might have done if he'd not had one of those phones that showed the name of who was calling. It only worked for internal numbers, and when he saw who wanted him, he felt like punching the damned thing.

He picked up the receiver. 'Jack Feathers.'

'Hi, Jack, it's Hayley. Have you got a minute?'

'Um, sure.'

'Can you come to my office? I want to bring our meeting forward.'

'Now?'

'Please.'

'Erm, what about bringing a colleague or a union rep with me?'

There was silence for a moment, followed by, 'Do you believe you need representation?'

'I don't know. It depends what it's about.'

'Did you read the email?'

'What email?'

The HR Manager uttered an impatient huff. 'The one in which you were notified of the meeting. I instructed Chantelle to send it on my behalf.'

'There was no email – she notified me in person but she didn't tell me what it was about.'

Silence again, then, 'I see.' A pause. 'Can you come to my office now? I can assure you that you won't need representation.'

'OK, I'll be there in five minutes.' Jack hung up and hurried into the corridor, his thoughts whirling. What the hell was this about? If Hayley was planning on disciplining him, she was going about it the wrong way.

Slowing down when he reached the floor where HR and Payroll were situated, he took a second to catch his breath and straighten his tie, before he walked through the assortment of open-plan desks to Hayley's office. Without making it obvious, he glanced over at Chantelle's desk, but thankfully she wasn't sitting at it, so he took a deep breath and knocked on Hayley's half-open door.

'Come in.' Hayley was a short woman in her early fifties, with cropped greying hair and a no-nonsense attitude. She had worked for the council since the year dot and had been on the panel when he'd been interviewed for his first job. She scared the life out of him.

Her head was bent and she was making notes on a pad, but she looked up when he stepped inside. 'Thanks for coming at such short notice. I've been called away on Monday and I wanted to get this over with, rather than having to rearrange and leave you hanging, so to speak. Take a seat.'

He was right – she was going to discipline him. *Leave him hanging…* her word choice said it all.

She steepled her hands under her chin. 'You're aware the council is looking to streamline some services, and as part of that process some departments will be amalgamated or broken up entirely?'

Jack nodded. He hadn't been expecting her to talk about this, and it took him a second for his brain to catch up with his ears.

'We intend to start with Parks and Highways, because the two don't gel together particularly well. With that in mind, the two service areas will be split, and Parks will be amalgamated with Leisure and Waste, and Highways will incorporate Transportation. I'm aware that Parks will be a bigger department as a result, but there will be a commensurate increase in salary. Now, with Eric Styles from Leisure retiring next month and the vacancy for Waste not yet filled, I will be putting an advert out next week and I want you to apply.'

'Pardon.' He had heard what she'd said, but the words didn't make sense.'

'I want you to apply,' she repeated. 'There isn't anyone else internally who is as qualified and as experienced as you to be Head of Parks, Leisure and Waste, so in effect the job is yours, but I have to be seen to do this the right way. That's so important, don't you think? That the correct procedures are adhered to, even if it is for appearance's sake?' There was a twinkle in her eye, and he knew what she was referring to.

'I'm… er… Gosh! I wasn't expecting that. I'll most definitely apply.'

'I would say "congratulations" but it wouldn't be appropriate.'

'Thanks, I don't know what to say.'

'I'll be in touch as soon as I receive your application. I think it's probably better if you send it directly to me. Have a good weekend.'

Jack stood to leave, a grin spreading across his face. 'You, too.'

He was almost out of the door when she said, 'And Jack… no more wild swimming in Sweet Meadow pond, eh?'

***

'Can I help you?' Molly's hands were on her hips and she knew that her tone was belligerent. It also didn't help her mood that she would probably have to invite Jack's girlfriend in or else she'd appear rude.

The woman whirled around. 'Oh, hi, are you Molly? I was looking for Jack.'

Molly narrowed her eyes and squinted at her. She didn't look the least bit like her photo. In fact, if Molly didn't know better, she would have thought that they were two entirely different people – her hair was shorter, for a start.

Telling herself to get a grip and that the woman had probably changed her hairstyle ten times since the council website photo had been taken, Molly fished her keys out of her bag and walked towards the cottage. She could hear Jet barking and was eager to let him out. Clearly he wasn't enthused by the stranger, either.

Molly knew she was being unreasonable and that the woman was probably lovely, but right now she couldn't care less.

'Is he alright?' the woman asked. 'I can't get hold of him.'

'I don't know. I haven't spoken to him since this morning.' An awful thought occurred to her. 'Has something happened? I know he was worried that he might be in trouble because of the gates…' She wrung her hands. 'He's not been sacked, has he?'

'Gosh, I hope not. He never said. Mind you, *I* didn't speak to him – Mum did. But that was fairly early this morning so anything could have happened since. Do you think he might have been?'

'You should know! You're the one who works in the HR Department, not me.'

The woman frowned. 'I own a guest house. Or I will do when we've cobbled together enough money to buy it. Are you confusing me with someone else?'

Molly blinked. 'You're not Chantelle.'

The woman laughed. 'No, I'm not, thank goodness! I'm Della, Jack's sister.'

'But you're in Alaska!' Molly cried.

'I live there, yes. But I'm in the UK for a visit. Can I come in? I'm dying for a wee.'

'Er, yeah, of course. Let me get the door. And the dog.' Her head whirling, Molly unlocked the cottage and was nearly bowled over by an excited Jet. 'The loo is upstairs,' she said, grabbing Jet's collar to prevent him from bounding after her visitor.

After making a fuss of the dog, she went into the kitchen to put the kettle on. If Della had just flown in from Alaska, she could probably do with a cup of tea.

When Della appeared, Molly asked, 'Tea?'

'Have you got any coffee?'

'Only instant, I'm afraid. Jack's got a fancy gadget—' she pointed to the coffee machine '—but I don't know how to use it.'

'Wow, has he still got this? I'd have thought he'd have bought a new one by now. Has he got any capsules?'

'There are some in the cupboard.' Molly reached up and brought out a box. 'Help yourself.'

While Della made herself a cup of coffee, Molly observed her out of the corner of her eye. Now that she knew who Della was, she could tell she and Jack were brother and sister.

Della told her, 'I'm going back up to York later. I'm not supposed to be in Sweet Meadow at all today, but Mum got in such a tizz when she heard that Jack had nearly drowned, despite her speaking to him this morning and him telling her he was fine, that I offered to drive back down to check he was OK. He is, isn't he?'

'He is,' Molly assured her. 'I've got to admit, I was a bit worried myself, but once he'd caught his breath, he was OK.'

'What happened? I've read some of the posts and comments online, but I don't know how true they are.'

Molly filled her in over a cuppa and a packet of Hobnobs, finishing with, 'Even though not everyone can see it, your brother is a hero.'

'He's always been a hero to me. Did he tell you he used to run marathons?'

'He did mention it.'

'Well, one year he got it into his head to run the Marathon des Sables, which is this ridiculously awful event that takes place in the Sahara Desert. You have to run six marathons in six days, back-to-back. The idiot.'

Molly was incredulous. 'Jack did that?'

'He sure did, and he raised several thousand pounds for charity.'

'He never said.'

Della wrinkled her nose. 'He wouldn't. He's not the type to brag.' Her pride was obvious, and Molly's heart swelled, but before she could delve any further, Jet clambered to his feet from where he'd been lying under the table, and seconds later she heard a car pull up in front of the cottage.

'Your brother is home,' she said. 'I'll leave you to chat in peace. I expect you've got loads to talk about.'

'There's no need. We had a good long chat yesterday.'

'You were here *yesterday?*'

'Not *here*, here. I met him at the old house, then we went for a bite to eat in this lovely Turkish restaurant. I've got to say, your cottage is lovely.'

'Thanks.' Molly's reply was absent-minded. She was still processing the news that it was *Della* who Jack had been with yesterday, *not* Chantelle.

Did it change anything?

She wasn't sure…

***

'Della?' Jack couldn't believe his eyes. Was his sister really sitting at the kitchen table in Molly's house?

'Hello, Jack. I bet you didn't expect to see me again so soon.'

His first thought was that something was wrong, but when he saw his sister's grin, he felt weak with relief. He seemed to have had a day of thinking the worst, only to be proved wrong.

'What are you doing here?' He glanced from his sister to Molly, and back again.

'Mum.'

'Ah.' Della didn't need to say anything more. Jack knew what she meant.

'You didn't drown, I see,' Della observed.

'Clearly not. I can't believe Mum made you drive all this way just for that.'

'She didn't. I offered.'

'She guilted you into it, you mean.'

'It was the lesser of two evils. If it wasn't for the shop, she'd have driven here herself. Hang on, I'd better message her.' Jack watched bemused as Della's thumbs flew across her phone. 'There,' she said. 'That'll put her mind at rest.'

'I spoke to her this morning,' he protested. 'I told her I was OK.'

'She thought you were keeping something from her. Are you?' She said to Molly, 'Mum's got a sixth sense when it comes to me and Jack. It can be quite unnerving. We could never hide anything from her when we were kids.'

Jack sat down and Jet leant against his legs.

'Er, yeah, I was worried about my job,' he confessed. 'I thought I was going to be sacked, or face disciplinary action at the very least. Hayley Crouch, Head of HR, wanted a meeting with me on Monday, and I feared the worst, but...' He paused dramatically. 'I met with her this afternoon instead.'

'And?' Molly demanded. She looked so worried that he wanted to scoop her into his arms and kiss her. Pre-Reuben he might have done.

'She offered me a promotion,' he said. He was still bemused by the whole thing and the news hadn't properly sunk in yet.

'That's brilliant! Well done,' Molly beamed.

'I think we should go out to celebrate,' Della said.

'There's many a slip between cup and lip,' Jack warned, after he'd given them a bit more detail about his meeting, 'so I'm not counting my chickens yet.'

Della sighed. 'You're right. Anyway, I need to go back to York this evening. I won't hear the last of it from Mum if I stay the night.'

'Won't you at least stay for something to eat?' Molly urged.

'It's OK, I'll grab a coffee and a sandwich at the services.' Della got to her feet and picked up her bag. 'It was nice meeting you, Molly.'

'You, too.' Molly's eyes widened as Della gave her a hug, and she met Jack's gaze before quickly looking away.

'I'll walk you to your car,' he offered, after Della had hugged him as well.

'Molly's nice,' his sister said, linking her arm through his as he led her along the path to the gate.

'Yes, she is.'

'She thought I was Chantelle.'

Jack faltered, then resumed walking. 'Please don't mention that woman's name. She's nothing but trouble.' He couldn't believe she had let him think that his meeting with Hayley was going to be a negative one.

'She cares for you. A lot,' Della said, hastily adding, 'Molly, I mean,' when Jack snorted in disbelief.

He snorted again. 'I don't think so.'

'A woman can tell.' Della's smile was enigmatic.

'Don't you think I'd know?'

'Actually, no, I don't.'

'What about Reuben?'

'All I'm saying is, don't give up on her. If you love Molly, you should fight for her.'

Yeah, right, he thought. It was easy for Della to say. She hadn't seen Molly's face light up whenever she mentioned the guy's name. Which she did, frequently.

Nope, Jack thought, He had no intention of making a fool of himself where Molly was concerned. He would bow out gracefully and hope she would never realise that he was in love with her.

CHAPTER 26

Jack and Molly had just finished eating their evening meal, when Jet began to whine. Maybe he was picking up on the awkward and stilted atmosphere between them, but Jack didn't think so.

It had seemed daft to cook separate meals, so when Molly had suggested they eat together, he'd reluctantly agreed. She was trying so hard to be friendly, it seemed churlish not to, so he'd aimed for friendly but distant, because he was too scared to let his guard down in case he gave himself away.

Jet whined again and padded into the hall to stare at the front door.

'Not again,' Molly murmured. 'This is how last night started.'

Was it only last night he had gone for a midnight swim? So much had happened since, that Jack could have sworn it was longer.

'What is it, boy? What can you hear?' Jack followed the dog into the hall, guessing it was probably a bunch of teenagers, come to reclaim the park. Or maybe Mr Fox was out and about already?

'What's that noise?' Molly asked, coming to stand beside him. She was close enough to smell her shampoo and the subtle perfume she wore.

Frowning, Jack slipped his fingers through Jet's collar. 'It sounds like there are people outside. A lot of them. I think we'd better see what's going on.'

Molly nodded.

He didn't know what she was thinking, but he was expecting to see hordes of unruly kids on their way to the bandstand, and probably trampling all over the poor flower beds as they went.

Taking a steadying breath and hoping things weren't about to get nasty, Jack opened the door.

What the—? Who were all these people? And was that *Bill*?

The unmistakable figure of the old man was leading a group of about twenty people, many of them youngsters, towards the cottage.

Jack felt Molly shrink back, and he instinctively put his arm around her.

She shook him off. 'What's going on?' she demanded, stepping outside and walking towards the mob.

Jack hurried after her, his heart in his mouth. After some of the comments online, he was worried this lot might be out for blood, and although locking the gates hadn't been anything to do with Molly, he was concerned that people mightn't see it that way, especially since some of them appeared to be armed with shovels.

He suddenly wished he had his phone about his person and hadn't left it in the kitchen.

'You wanted volunteers,' Bill replied. 'Will this lot do?'

'Liam? Connor?' Molly moved nearer to the mob.

Jack wanted to rush after her and drag her inside to safety, but— He looked closer. The people gathered in front of the cottage were smiling, and one of them had a wheelbarrow – hardly an offensive weapon. Another was carrying a trowel. And one chap seemed to be wearing waders.

'Liam's got something to say, haven't you, Liam?' Bill said.

Liam stumbled forward as the old man gave him a shove. 'Gerroff, you daft old codger,' the boy protested. 'This was my idea, not yours.'

If Jack was expecting an apology from the boy, he was disappointed. However, what Liam said next was apology enough.

'That pond's a menace. We've come to sort it out.'

Molly stiffened. 'What do you mean, *sort it out*?'

'Tidy it up, like. You know, get rid of them shopping trolleys. Connor's dad likes fishing. He knows all about ponds and stuff. He's got all the proper gear.'

The man wearing the waders gave a little bow, and a smattering of applause rippled through the crowd.

Liam repeated. 'It was my idea. This park could do with tidying up. My dad says it's an effing eyesore.'

His dad was also the chap who had been mouthing off about suing the council, Jack recalled.

'He says something should be done about it,' Liam continued, 'and as we're the ones what use it, I thought we should be the ones to sort it out. We want it to look nice, like.' The boy's expression hardened. 'And you can't stop us,' he added.

'I wouldn't dream of it,' Molly replied. 'It's a marvellous idea! You're so clever to think of it.'

Jack was amazed to see Liam glowing from the compliment.

The boy caught his eye and nodded imperceptibly.

Jack wasn't sure whether it was an acknowledgement of his rescue attempt last night or whether it was because this was Liam's way of saving face by pretending it was his idea to tidy up the park. Whatever the reason, it didn't matter. The important thing was that Liam and his little gang of "youffs" had finally realised the park was 'their' space, and they should take responsibility for it. And they had brought along some adults to help.

Jack nodded back.

Delight washed over him. Finally Molly was going to have the park she'd dreamt of. He was so pleased for her!

'Me and Bill are going to oversee everything,' Liam announced grandly. 'And that guy, Reuben, cause he knows about frogs 'n' stuff.'

At the mention of Reuben, Jack deflated. Of course Reuben would be involved. It was only logical he should be.

'That's enough talk,' Bill said. 'We need to see some action. Chop, chop!' He clapped his hands, and the assembled crowd began to shuffle away.

'It's about time, too,' a woman's voice called, and when Jack glanced around he recognised the speaker as Fiona, the lady who had turned up for the first call for volunteers, the one who had thought there was going to be live music in the bandstand.

'I've been on to the council for years to sort this place out, but nothing is ever done. And that woman on reception is a lovely girl, very friendly, but she's ever so nosey. It's none of her business what my name is.'

Jack's mouth dropped open as he realised he had finally found his phantom caller.

'I'd better get changed,' Molly said. 'I can't let them start without me.'

Her eyes were shining with pleasure, and her smile lit up her face. Jack thought he'd never seen her looking so beautiful. It made his heart ache with longing, and he wanted to kiss her so badly that it hurt.

'Good idea,' he said, but he hung back, letting her go ahead of him. He needed a moment to compose himself.

'I reckon your missus is happy,' Liam said.

'She's not my missus,' Jack snapped

'Girlfriend, then. Don't get your knickers in a twist. It's just an expression.'

'She's not my girlfriend, either.'

'Why not?'

'None of your business.'

'I wanna know.'

'Why?' God, this kid was infuriating.

'Cause she's nice,' Liam said.

'She *is* nice,' Jack agreed. 'But that doesn't mean she's my girlfriend.' The boy's logic was beyond him.

'Do you want her to be?'

'That's none of your business, either.' Didn't this kid have any manners? Or any boundaries?

'She wants you to be her boyfriend.'

'Don't be silly! You've got no idea what you're talking about.'

'I do too! She loves you, don't she?'

'She does not!' Jack spluttered. He turned smartly on his heel: he was done with this ridiculous conversation, plus he'd also better get changed into his gardening clothes because no matter how much he didn't want to witness Molly and Reuben making eyes at each other, he couldn't stand by and let other people do all the work.

'She said so,' Liam announced.

'Who said what?'

'Effing hell, you're not the sharpest tool in the box, are you? Her, there—' He pointed at Molly who had come out of the cottage and was walking towards them. 'She said she loved you when you was in the water and she thought you was dead. I reckon you didn't hear her.'

Jack needed to sit down. Liam was spot on: Jack *hadn't* heard her. Could he have misjudged the situation with Reuben, and Molly didn't fancy the guy at all?

He recalled how affectionate they had been with each other before Reuben came on the scene – the meeting of eyes, the long, lingering looks, the touching of hands – and he knew he hadn't imagined it. What he might have imagined, though (if what Liam said was to be believed), was Molly being attracted to Reuben.

'Is anything wrong?' she asked, and he realised his thoughts must be reflected in his face.

'No, I don't think there is,' he replied slowly. Out of the corner of his eye he saw Liam smirking.

'You can thank me later,' the boy said. 'A packet of fags should do.'

Jack snapped out of it. 'What!? *No!* I'm not buying you cigarettes!'

'A bottle of JD then?'

'No alcohol, either.'

'Spoilsport. Wish I hadn't told you now.' Muttering, the lad walked off.

'What was that about?' Molly watched the boy saunter away, a frown on her pretty face.

It was now or never. Jack didn't want to wait a heartbeat longer – he had to know. 'Liam told me you love me. Is it true?'

A blush swept up her neck and into her cheeks. 'I… er…'

'He said he heard you say it last night, when I was in the pond.'

'I said it in the heat of the moment.'

She couldn't look him in the eye, and he didn't know what to think. 'You didn't mean it?'

'I meant it.' Molly's voice was so quiet that Jack thought he had misheard.

'Could you repeat that?' he asked. The pulse in his ears was so loud she must be able to hear it, and his stomach did a nauseating forward roll.

Her eyes flashed and he noticed that her hands were bunched into fists by her side.

'I LOVE YOU!' she yelled, her cheeks crimson, and Jack jumped as her shout bounced off the cottage and the surrounding trees. 'Happy now?' she demanded.

Slowly a grin spread over his face, and his heart began to sing. In wonder, he said, 'You might want to say that again: I didn't hear you.' And he laughed out loud when she glared at him. Fearing for his immediate safety, he said hurriedly, 'I love you, too.'

The fight leeched out of her, and her hands uncurled. He saw a flare of hope in her eyes and her lips parted, and he simply couldn't resist the invitation he saw on her face.

'May I kiss you?'

Molly smiled. 'I thought you'd never ask.'

Gently he put his arms around her, drawing her to him. She melted into his embrace and his lips found hers. They were warm and soft, and her kisses tasted of the future.

And Jack realised that he didn't need to look for another home after all, because he had already found it in the arms of the woman he loved.

***

'What a day,' Molly said. Her back was curled against Jack's chest as he spooned her after their lovemaking.

They were in her bed, with the door firmly closed and Jet on the other side of it. The dog hadn't been happy about being turfed out and he had whined his displeasure for a while, until Molly had promised him he'd be allowed in later.

Much later, as it turned out.

'Mmm,' Jack murmured, nuzzling the soft skin below her ear.

She squirmed. 'Stop that! Unless…?'

'Unless what?' Jack's arm had been draped over her waist, but now it crept south.

Jet barked and Molly pushed Jack away. 'I think someone has had enough of being on the landing. We'd better let him in.'

Jack sighed and Molly giggled at his disappointment. 'We'd also better get some sleep,' he said. 'We've got an early start in the morning. I can't believe Bill has offered to cook sausage sarnies for everyone who turns up. And he's persuaded Fiona to help.'

Molly laughed. 'Did you see her face when he told her she was the best cook in town? She lapped it up.'

'I think she was pleased to be involved,' Jack said, 'and that the park is finally being cleaned up. She's been leaving anonymous messages about Sweet Meadow

Park for the past couple of years. I feel guilty she never got anywhere.'

'She's getting somewhere now,' Molly said, sliding out of Jack's arms and padding naked to the door. She could feel his eyes on her body, and it gave her a warm glow. 'In fact, I think it might have worked out better this way.'

'How do you mean?'

'The park doesn't need the council's help after all, not with everyone working together to bring it back to life. Granny always said that if something is handed to you on a plate, you don't appreciate it as much as if you've had to work for it.'

'She's right,' Jack agreed, as Molly opened the door and Jet bounced in and launched himself at the bed.

'Oof!' Jack rolled over to avoid the dog's heavy paws landing where they shouldn't, and Molly laughed. 'He'd better not think he's sleeping in this bed,' Jack warned. 'I want you all to myself.'

'You've got me,' she promised. 'For now, and forever.' And she meant every single word.

***

'Do you want onions?' Fiona held the bun aloft, her ladle poised to scoop a pile of onions out of the pan.

'No, thanks.'

Fiona handed Molly the sausage bap. 'Help yourself to sauce. Carol is on teas and coffees.' She jerked her head towards a woman standing behind a makeshift table on which sat a couple of kettles, an assortment of mugs, plus tea, coffee and milk. Someone had even brought cupcakes, but Molly had no idea who. To be honest, she had no clue who most of these people were, but she was grateful to see them.

Bill had turned up first, at the impossibly early time of six-thirty, demanding to use her front garden as a "feeding station for the troops". Molly had left him and Jack to set everything up whilst she took Jet for his morning walk, and by the time she'd returned, her kitchen table had been roped into use, along with the folding wallpaper-pasting table and a thick plank of wood balanced on several breeze blocks. An extension cable ran from the house to a couple of kettles (she recognised one of them as hers) and a BBQ was set off to the side and was starting to smoke.

Molly was about to ask what she could do, when Fiona had arrived and hustled her out of the way.

'Leave the cooking to me,' the elderly lady had said. 'You stick to gardening. This lot is going to need to be given some direction, otherwise they'll be digging up the flowers and scaring the wildlife.'

Bill had beamed at Molly, and when Fiona was out of earshot, he'd said, 'She used to own Best Bites in the square. Sold it a couple of years ago and has been bored out of her mind ever since. She's as grumpy as hell, but has a heart of gold.'

Molly didn't say anything, but thought the description was also applicable to Bill.

As she bit into her bun, Molly gazed at all the people who had turned up this morning. She'd half expected no one would bother, thinking that the enthusiasm of yesterday evening may well have waned in the cold light of a Saturday morning, but she had been overwhelmed by the turn-out. Mind you, the lure of a free sausage bap might have had something to do with it…

No matter the reason, she was grateful, nevertheless. And if the majority of them only came this one time, so be it. At least with this many people on hand, they could make a decent dent in all the jobs that still needed doing.

As soon as she had finished her breakfast, Molly organised people into groups, assigning each one a task, and although the bigger jobs, such as addressing the damaged equipment in the children's play area or repairing the bandstand, couldn't be accomplished today, there were a great many other things that could.

Reuben, as usual, was a law unto himself. 'I'm going to tackle the pond,' he said. 'I know it needs to be dredged, but me and this chap here can get rid of some of the rubbish. The shopping trolleys could do with being removed for a start, and the tyres.'

Molly watched him and the man with the waders walk away, pleased she wouldn't have to tackle that job herself. The waders were an inspired idea, though.

'Um…' Jack pulled a face. 'I've got some news that you're not going to like. The pond is definitely going to be filled in. Pete told me yesterday. I should have mentioned it sooner but with everything that was going on, it slipped my mind.'

Molly stared at him in shock. 'Can't you stop it? You *are* the Parks and Highways Officer.'

'I can try, but I'm fairly sure I won't get anywhere, especially if Connor's father decides to sue. They'll insist on it.'

She was stunned. This was bad news for the park's wildlife. Even if they didn't live in its murky waters, many creatures depended on the pond for food, water and shelter in the plants growing around its edge. The park simply wouldn't be the same without it.

Molly had harboured a vision of a path around the pond, and benches dotted at intervals so people could not only enjoy the tranquil view, but watch the wildlife too. It would be a crying shame if it was filled in, and all because of a couple of kids. She had a mind to have a stern word with Connor's father.

Not that it would do any good… If the council had made a decision, then that was it. They weren't going to change it just because she made a fuss. Not even if everyone here protested.

Sadness filled her: the park wouldn't be the same without the pond. It was part of its charm – or would have been once the pond was tidied up.

For Molly, the brightness of the day had dimmed a little, and it was with a heavier heart that she settled to her task of hacking away at the brambles on the edge of the woodland.

A couple of hours later, just when she was thinking it might be a good idea to stop for lunch and a cuppa, shouting from the top end of the park startled her and she whirled around in panic.

It was coming from somewhere near the pond, and her heart sank.

Oh, hell, please don't say someone else has fallen in, she prayed as she hurried across the field, Jack jogging by her side.

She was aware that everyone else had also downed tools and was heading in the same direction, and her only thought was that at least there would be plenty of hands on deck should the worst have happened.

But when she neared the pond, she couldn't see anyone in the water. All she could see was Reuben and the man in the waders crouching on the ground. They seemed to be staring intently at something.

'Don't come any closer.' Reuben held up a hand. 'You'll scare it.'

'Scare what?'

'The newt.'

Molly blinked. Was that what all the fuss was about, a bloody newt?

'I thought something awful had happened,' she said, feeling cross but trying not to let it show.

Reuben was beaming. 'You can have a look, if you like. One at a time, though. As I said, we don't want to scare it.'

'No thanks. I've seen newts before.' She had seen several of the creatures since she'd moved into the cottage in the park – she didn't need to see another one.

'But this one is special.'

There was something in his voice that made her hesitate. Had he found a great crested newt? Is that what he was so excited about?

She moved closer and Reuben beckoned her forward, and lifted up a tyre.

Underneath, eyeing them beadily and looking rather annoyed at the intrusion, sat a black newt. It was wartier than the other newts she had seen, and had white dots on its flanks. It didn't look in the least bit scared.

She said as much to Reuben.

'That's because it hasn't got many predators as its skin exudes a toxic chemical. But only when they reach adulthood. This guy is fully grown.'

'It's not the prettiest newt in the world, is it?'

'No, but it's extremely rare in the UK. They are protected by law and it's illegal to even touch them. You have to have a licence. And it's against the law to do anything that may harm them or damage their habitat.'

Molly's mouth dropped open.

She turned to look at Jack. He must be thinking the same thing, because he looked equally as shocked.

'Reuben, I could kiss you!' she exclaimed. 'Jack, do you know what this means?'

'I think I do. Reuben, shall you report it, or shall I?'

Bill asked. 'Report it to whom?'

'The council!' Molly cried. 'They can't possibly fill in the pond now. It's safe!'

Fiona, who was one of the last to arrive at the scene, huffed. 'Is that all? I was expecting to find buried treasure.'

'It *is* treasure,' Molly insisted, but all Fiona did was wrinkle her nose. She clearly wasn't impressed with Molly's idea of treasure.

As Molly and Jack sauntered away from the pond, Jack slung an arm around her shoulders and pulled her close. She tilted her head up to be kissed and he dutifully obliged.

'I must admit to being jealous of Reuben,' he said, 'but I'm so glad he's here. We never would have discovered the newt on our own. And even if we had spotted it, we would never have realised it was a great crested one.'

Molly giggled. 'You never had anything to worry about where Reuben was concerned,' she said, demanding another kiss. 'I've only ever had eyes for you. I love you, Jack.'

And when he said those three little words back to her, Molly knew she had finally found her Mr Right, and her heart swelled with so much love she thought it might burst.

'If you pair can leave each other alone for five minutes,' Fiona interjected, 'I've made sandwiches for everyone for lunch. Sorry, Molly, I used your kitchen. I hope you don't mind. I've made ham, as well as tuna, plus roasted beetroot and avocado for the vegetarians.'

Molly didn't mind at all. She was just grateful that Fiona was keeping everyone fed and watered. 'It sounds delicious,' she began, then she froze as an idea occurred to her.

It had something to do with a boarded-up cafe and a former cafe owner...

Other books in the series

The Cafe in Sweet Meadow Park
Christmas in Sweet Meadow Park

ABOUT THE AUTHOR

Liz Davies writes feel-good, light-hearted stories with a hefty dose of romance, a smattering of humour, and a great deal of love.

She's married to her best friend, has one grown-up daughter, and when she isn't scribbling away in the notepad she carries with her everywhere (just in case inspiration strikes), you'll find her searching for that perfect pair of shoes. She loves to cook but isn't very good at it, and loves to eat - she's much better at that! Liz also enjoys walking (preferably on the flat), cycling (also on the flat), and lots of sitting around in the garden on warm, sunny days.

She currently lives with her family in Wales, but would ideally love to buy a camper van and travel the world in it.

Printed in Great Britain
by Amazon